Eyes of a Stranger

By
Suzanne Brandyn

Eternal Press
A division of Damnation Books, LLC.
P.O. Box 3931
Santa Rosa, CA 95402-9998
www.eternalpress.biz

Eyes of a Stranger
by Suzanne Brandyn

Digital ISBN: 978-1-61572-666-0
Print ISBN: 978-1-61572-667-7

Cover art by: Amanda Kelsey
Edited by: Pam Slade
Copyedited by: Kim Richards

Printed in the United States of America
Worldwide Electronic & Digital Rights
1st North American, Australian and UK Print Rights

I'd like to acknowledge Romance Writers of Australia. An amazing organization. I have met so many wonderful, supportive people.

Also special thank you to Hunter Romance Writers. Thank you for the brainstorming sessions, the discussions, and interaction over the past years. You are gems.

Chapter One

Tegan Ryan knew there would be trouble the moment her father sold half of the business.

"Ms. Ryan. Do you make a habit of being late?"

There was no delay in recognizing the deep, velvety voice. Her dark lashes blinked with disbelief as her gaze zeroed in on the new partner sitting opposite, at the boardroom table. Six other staff members had taken up nearby seats.

Talk about receiving a good hard whack to her senses. The stranger she'd spoken to earlier that day was—the new boss. She'd shared his umbrella, due to a sudden, tropical downpour.

Embarrassment floored her.

She'd told the stranger that the new boss was probably a grumpy old fart, a man impossible to work for, and so up himself that everyone's life would be sheer misery the day he made a show. Her stomach shriveled with the thought. It made her feel as small as an ant and probably much smaller, if she could remember what else she'd babbled on about. At that moment, dissolving through the plush, carpeted floor would make her feel a whole lot better.

Repeating rumors wasn't in her character, and she couldn't believe she'd actually participated in office gossip. Her body wavered, and filled with warm fluid. Subconsciously her grip over her notebook and loose papers relaxed, and they dropped to the floor. Drawing in a quiet breath, she bent to pick up the paperwork.

"Is everything all right, Ms. Ryan?"

Demanding her weak legs to straighten, she flicked her gaze toward Mathew. "Yes, sorry I'm late...the traffic. I was with a client. And the rain, it's raining." *Oh hell, what a statement. It's raining! He's going to think you're a real genius now, but I guess it's better than saying, 'I've brought a watermelon'.*

"We are aware of the downpour. Can we begin now?"

All morning she'd been so damn edgy, now she knew why. Chatting like a mother hen was one thing, especially to a stranger, but to discover he was her new employer infuriated her to the max. Imagine not announcing he was the new boss of Coleman and Associates, one of Newcastle's top law firms. He'd been so content to let her babble non-stop. The hide of the man! Did he get some type of fix from his encouragement?

As she took the few steps toward the table, under a lowered gaze, she noticed he pulled out a chair beside him and tapped on the edge. Feeling as though her knees were given a great thud with a hockey stick, she ignored his gesture. Instead she slid onto the chair in front of her.

"Wouldn't you be more comfortable over here, after all, you are my personal secretary."

She sucked back a nervous breath, noticing all eyes were on her. Although it could have been her imagination, one thing was for sure, bees were setting up a nice little residence in her stomach. Pushing upwards from the chair and walking around the table, she hesitated behind the high-backed leather chair.

He stood, hand outstretched. "Mathew King."

She glanced upwards, her gaze rested on his rich blueberry eyes. A clock on the wall marked the slow ticking of seconds in rhythm with the heavy beat of her heart.

She always thought her son Robert had the bluest eyes ever, but this stranger presented a serious rival.

Snapping from her reverie, she moved her hand in front of her. The contact of a loose handshake wrapped a silly warm glow around her heart. She snatched her hand from his touch and, with reluctance, slid onto the chair.

It was much too close.

His woody aftershave purposely dispersed over her, prompting a sharp unexpected gasp. The warm dragging sensation circulating in her stomach certainly didn't belong there. What was happening? She'd never reacted to a male like this before, ever.

Reaching down and tugging her skirt back to where it belonged was an ordeal. It had crept up well above her knees revealing more than she had intended. Under lowered lashes, she noticed he was staring at her hand. A confident smirk slid to his strong facial features, irritating Tegan even further.

Drawing in a quiet breath and concentrating on a spot on the table before counting to ten worked. It usually worked when her nervous system was taking her on the ride of a lifetime. Except this time it failed and there was no hope of recovery.

For the next hour, she scribbled her notes with difficulty, considering the atmosphere was so stifling. She shifted in her seat when Mathew stood.

Self-assurance rode over his smooth, sharp features. He held a certain aura about him, a confident ability which mesmerized everyone around him.

"The last few years have been difficult for Mister Coleman. With his mounting health problems, he couldn't continue to run the company—not with thirty employees and climbing, consisting of Solicitors, Secretaries and Receptionists. It was becoming a chore." His strong well-spoken voice echoed throughout the boardroom.

Tegan pretended to listen but knew she, too, experienced the telltale signs of working long hours. Stan her father, decided he was selling half of the company. They'd spoken about it previously, but it seemed to happen overnight. She hadn't known all the details, except the future partner was of high standing. *Huh, high standing my foot.*

When Mathew finished speaking he sat down and a large masculine hand poured two cups of coffee.

"Would anyone else like a cup of coffee?"

A lunch meeting didn't suit her at all. She had to postpone her plans with Sally, one of the receptionists, to sit here and listen to some stranger ramble on about his so-called concern for Coleman Enterprises. He'd never heard of her father or the company until a few weeks ago. Why would he be so interested, so concerned? *Pretentious, pompous man.*

Mathew settled a cup of coffee in front of her.

"I don't drink coffee." Caffeine wasn't something she needed just then. Her jangled nerves were jittery enough, *thank-you-very-much!* She couldn't risk it, not now, not when her nerves were already snaking up her spine and eroding her brain.

With the intention of placing the cup closer to him, she reached out, but his hand moved connecting with hers. The coffee cup toppled, spilling its contents over her navy suit, and splashing onto his dark, designer suit. Trying to turn the cup upright, her hand connected with the coffee pot, spilling its contents as well.

"Oh, hell. I mean sorry. Hell...I..."

Mathew jerked upright to his feet.

Tegan glanced up, straining her neck muscles. His startling height of well over six feet hovered above.

"I think we should close the meeting. We've covered a lot of ground. I'll be happy to answer any questions at a later date."

She grabbed a napkin, and brushed at her skirt trying to soak up the coffee. The remaining staff members began to leave.

"Could you close the door behind you?" Mathew called as the last member left.

Tegan stood and slid a napkin toward him. Burning heat tore up her insides. She grabbed at the edge of the table to steady an unusual wave of giddiness and closed her eyes seeking some self-control before snapping them open.

"Why didn't you tell me you were the new partner earlier today?"

"You didn't ask."

"That's not the point. You let me babble and continue to babble. You even asked me questions."

His dark eyebrows almost joined. "Babble? Questions?" The seemingly intentional glint in his eyes, made her feel like she was standing in front of him naked. Nerves carved up her insides. Talk about feeling tense.

"We can discuss this over afternoon tea."

She glared at him. "That won't happen."

"It won't?"

"I'm busy."

"You didn't say that earlier."

"I forgot," she blurted, focusing on the center of his forehead. "Mister King, I think you should know I'm not too keen on how Stan sold half of the business. You probably think it is none of my concern, but I assure you it is. It was his great-grandfather's business—a family business."

"Call me. I have been advised of your objection to the partnership, but it's your job as a secretary to keep your place."

"To keep my place? I haven't said anything out of place."

"You don't have to. It's written in your eyes. Like an inscription on the side of an aircraft, very bold and bright."

She turned and walked toward the door.

"If you don't mind, would you have the minutes of the meeting typed up as soon as possible?"

Drawing to a standstill, she pivoted on one foot. His unnerving attitude sucked all oxygen from the room. "If that is what you require."

When she stepped into the corridor, her heartbeat thumped like a war drum. She recalled his brief touch on her arm. How could a simple touch create such mayhem—smooth, warm, and so damn tempting? How could she remain in control when he did that to her so readily?

Wiping a shaky hand over her brow, she realized her hands were empty. *The notes!* They remained on the boardroom table. That meant going back in there to face him. Her breath shuddered from her throat, as she turned and pushed the door open.

Mathew sat stretched out in his chair with his hands clasped behind the back of his head. After a few brisk steps, she picked up the notes trying to ignore the tug of sexual attraction. *Hell! I'm not a teenager with a crush. I'm an adult. Control yourself.*

"I thought you wouldn't get far without those." A smirk slid to his face and a devilish sparkle surfaced in his eyes.

She picked up the notes, feeling the burn of his gaze, and condemned the urge to scream obscenities at him. Instead, her lips drew a fine line. She squared her shoulders and walked out.

* * * *

Mathew stretched further back onto the chair, looking at his coffee washed shirt. She sure was a live wire. In all his days he'd never met a woman like Tegan Ryan. Her self-control was intact earlier this morning, but now he wasn't too sure. This morning he met a carefree, happy woman, but her disposition had certainly altered. There was something hovering in those big emerald eyes of hers; something he had no idea how to fathom. He didn't know much about women, but now he wanted to know a hell of a lot more about her.

He found her objection to the partnership odd. Being close to Stan shouldn't make a difference. On the other hand, was it an objection to him? Had she read the articles plastered all over the media about his break-up with Helen—one of Sydney's top models?

A smirk rose to his lips. Tegan was an attractive blonde with a strong mind. A certain aura of intrigue and mystery surrounded her and bewitched him. She stood up to him. He laughed. Not too many women would bite back like she had. She could be one hell of a challenge, given her attitude. She didn't even blink those eyes, knowing he was Mathew King, heir of King Enterprises. He liked the idea of being her boss. A strange inquisitiveness swirled in his mind.

"Goddamn it," he mumbled under his breath. Here he was leaping into a fantasy, and taking much more interest in the woman than as his secretary.

* * * *

Tegan disappeared into her office almost slamming the door, but a voice halted her midway.

"Hold up, Teeg."

"Sally."

"I heard Mister tall, dark, and handsome made it tough for you in there." Sally flicked a dark ponytail from her shoulder.

"Tough. That's not the word. I didn't expect my new boss to look like…"

"I noticed it too. He's definitely 'melt me all over' material," Sally remarked, adding a mischievous grin. "Everyone's been whispering. They say you and Mister King have it in for each other."

"I don't know why. I met him on the street before lunch. I shared his umbrella."

"Shared his umbrella?" Sally's eyes widened and a grin eased to her pink lips.

"Oh, not like that. He may be good looking but I'm not interested…um…it was pouring. Anyhow, I chatted with him and said things I shouldn't. Then I come in here and find out he's the new boss. I could have died."

"Better watch him, Teeg. He's been asking questions since he arrived this morning—questions about you." Sally followed Tegan into the office.

"What about me?"

"He asked about your feelings toward the partnership, what you're like. The answers he received were pretty vague. It annoyed the hell out of him."

"So, he was in earlier this morning. He must have been returning to the office when I arrived. I don't think this will work Sal. It's not the same." Tegan slid onto a chair, arms crossed at chest level.

"Are you sure your father couldn't have taken another avenue?" Sally questioned, propping her petite body on the edge of the desk. "There should have been some other way."

"No. We discussed all avenues. Dad said Mister King was the heir of King Enterprises and experienced in managing companies. King Enterprises owns quite a few companies in Australia. I hear they are raking in millions, and I mean zee millions. It's a family business. You know it's kind of weird. I wonder why King Enterprises would be interested in part ownership of this business? It's a little strange."

"Maybe that's what they do—keep buying companies. I think he has enough power to scrap us all. We could be out of a job just like that." She clicked her fingers in midair. "Poof."

"That's not true. Dad promised no one would lose their jobs.

It's part of the deal."

"But he could try, couldn't he?"

"Yes, but I'm pleased Dad can still step in and have his say."

"I thought about it afterwards—what Mister King did to that Helen woman in Sydney and firing a bunch of people he doesn't know. It wouldn't even make a bleep on his emotional radar."

"What are you talking about?" Tegan's forehead creased.

"Didn't you hear? He was going out with a famous model. They were engaged and everything. Then all of a sudden she's dumped and weeping to the mags. Yet he's calm, cool, and collected—which I think irritated them to the max."

"What a bastard."

"It's true."

"He does seem the type though—all business and no emotion, right down to his spiffy designer shoes."

"Right." Sally noticed Mister King coming to a standstill beside the doorway. She jumped off the edge of the desk.

When Tegan glanced up, the very sight of him sent her nerves into a flurry. She held her breath.

"Ms. Ryan, don't forget to have those notes typed up as soon as possible—if you don't mind."

She nodded and he disappeared.

"I wonder how much he heard," Sally said, pulling a lopsided smirk, before turning her nose upwards and attempting an impersonation. "Oh, and Ms. Ryan, do be quick. I want them done in two seconds flat." A giggle escaped her lips.

"I don't really care."

"Hey, before I go...how's your son doing?"

"Robert. He's fine. He's still on to me about not having a father."

"One day he might."

"I don't think there's any chance of that."

"One never knows."

"Oh, one more thing. I told Dad not to let on to Mister King that I'm his daughter. You're the only person who knows and I'd prefer it stays that way."

"Nothing gets past my lips. I know you don't want your ex to find you. I wouldn't either. From what you've said, he can be damn nasty. Your secret is safe with me."

"Thanks. That's why Mister King doesn't ring any bells for me. He might have the moment I set eyes on him, but I don't need any more destructive relationships." Tegan didn't tell anyone she hadn't filed for a divorce which meant she was still married to

Peter.

"You're a sucker for blue eyes, aren't you?"

A grin edged to Tegan's lips. "I used to be."

"Yeah right...okay, I should get going." Sally walked out of the office, taking long slow strides. She was such a pleasure to work with. She was always joking about something.

Tegan finished typing up her notes and swung around in the chair to gaze through the window. The rain eased. The view of Newcastle Harbor was breathtaking. Blue water bathed in sunlight as tugboats guided a ship laden with coal through the narrow channel. Beyond the channel, the swell of white water formed into tips crashing to the shore.

She turned, stood, and left the office.

Arriving in front of Mathew's closed office door was unusual—her father always left it open. There was never a need to knock. Drawing in a steady breath, her fingers trembled as she reached out and gave it a soft rap. There was no reply.

Turning the knob with uncertainty, she pushed the heavy door open. After taking a step her body froze, and her right-hand gripped the doorknob. A tingling sensation shot through her body as the old tell-tale sign of embarrassment lit up her face like a tugboat chugging through the harbor on a dark night.

Chapter Two

Mathew was slipping on a fresh shirt covering his tanned, muscular chest which destroyed all thought process. His woody aftershave was far too toxic for an office environment. She sucked in a gasp, struggling to find any remaining self-confidence.

"I did knock," she croaked.

"You can let go of the door."

It was as though she had snapped frozen.

"Come in and close the door," he said as he finished buttoning his shirt and tucked it in. "Have a seat."

Struggling to push the crush of raw sexual attraction as far away as possible, she closed the door and took a few uneasy steps before placing the papers on his desk. As soon as she sat, she noticed his lingering gaze. It catapulted her mental and physical state into a frenzy. Trying to block his masculine attempt to squash any existing logic was such a struggle. She slipped a nervous leg over the other and cleared her throat.

"You are different from the woman I met this morning, a little nervous perhaps." He moved to sit on the edge of the desk, much too close for comfort, invoking her body to stiffen.

"I didn't exactly have a good start to the day." How in the hell could one man make her so tongue-tied? She had to say something, but couldn't come out and say he was taking her hormones on the journey of a lifetime.

"That makes two of us."

As his electric gaze devoured her, every nerve she possessed was stripped.

"I'd like to apologize for not letting on earlier. I didn't see it as necessary."

"I shouldn't...have confided in a...stranger. It...was my fault."

"What about this client you said you were with this morning."

Demanding release of the confident woman, who was temporarily locked inside, finally arrived. "I had to drop some papers off at Mister Cartwrights. He didn't understand the forms he was supposed to sign. So, I spent a little time helping him."

"I thought you were hired as the main secretary in this place."

"Yes, I am. At times, I help out with some of the legal issues."

"That's interesting."

The door swung open and a tall, redhead strutted into the office filling the atmosphere with a sweet fragrance that reeked overuse and overpowering. Tegan sniffled and avoided breathing too deeply.

"Hello Mathew. One would think you'd never heard of me. As for not returning my calls..."

"Helen, as I said I've been busy." Mathew stood. Annoyance registered in his eyes. He rubbed his fingers over the back of his neck.

"Are you coming to the Drayton's dinner party? You didn't give me an answer. Everyone will be there and it is such fun."

He stepped forward and turned to Tegan. "Excuse me Ms. Ryan."

It was impossible to focus on anything other than the disturbance now erupting within arm's length. She pushed herself to stand. "I'll be waiting outside." Her legs moved quickly, moving her body toward the door, not stopping until she was in the corridor.

Pacing up and down the corridor filled in minimal time, but Tegan's inquisitiveness wouldn't settle until she took a look. She couldn't help herself. Sneaking toward the door, she peeked through the small gap.

They stood inches apart. He grated, "I told you it was over. How many times do I have to tell you?" He grabbed Helen's elbow and nudged her toward the door before until it swung open.

Startled, Tegan jumped backwards, making sure there was ample space between her and the door.

"But dar...ling," Helen drawled. "You've been under so much pressure lately. Think of it as a break away...away from all this." She waved an aloof hand in the air. "Nothing here is good enough for you—nothing at all."

Tegan's face flushed. *Gee, thank you Miss haughty toughty.* She flicked her gaze down the hallway toward the reception area, pretending to ignore their episode.

"I thought I made it clear six months ago, not to mention this morning. It's over and for good. I'm not interested in going to your dinner parties and never will be," he ground out.

"Don't think Daddy won't hear about this. He'll think you've lost it this time."

"Or that I have a good head on my shoulders. Hell, he's been trying to pawn you off for years."

"I beg your pardon!"

"Do whatever you think Helen, whatever it takes. However, please stop trying to push your way into my life. Our relationship is over."

"How could you be so heartless?"

"I have work to do, so if you don't mind."

"Work? What about me? What about me?"

"I'm sure Daddy will take care of you." Mathew freed his hand. "Goodbye Helen." He waited a few moments until she was in the lift.

"Ms. Ryan, would you come back in to the office please?" He closed the door behind them.

"I must apologize." He gestured with his hand for her to sit, and then resumed his position, but much closer than before.

Tegan tensed, all too aware of his sexual aura. He had it alright, from the tip of his head, over his muscular body to his strong legs. Even the white shirt he wore spoke of what lay beneath, alerting every female within the building of the 'major male attack'.

However, he just displayed how cold and heartless he was, true to office rumors. *How could he be so harsh to that woman?*

"How long have you worked for Coleman Enterprises? I know Stan told me but I can't recall."

Why did a shiver fleet up her spine after such an acceptable question? She drew in a quiet breath. "Five years."

"What did you do before you began your employment here?"

A sudden catch of nervousness ignited at the back of her throat. "Why do you ask?"

"That's all right; I can ask Stan. It's a way to get to know the staff."

Tegan rubbed her lips together.

"Why have you continued working here?"

"I happen to get along with Stan...well, I like my job." Her gaze flicked toward his then back to the wall behind him, lingering on anything but the overpowering knock-me-over that automatically snapped her internal switch to green. At that moment, it was on high beam. For a few seconds she allowed her body to absorb the signals from her brain. She realized what she was doing and stopped. Just because he was drop dead gorgeous didn't mean she was going to fall flat at his feet in a breathless whisper. Her brain was functional and she knew how to use it.

"We need to build a constructive working relationship. There's a lot of ground to go over during the next few days, a lot to take into account. That means we have to get on extremely well. What services did Stan provide?"

Angry color rushed to her cheeks. "I beg your pardon." She sprung upright, but his hand grabbed her wrist. A startled gasp rose from her throat. Her eyes glared with alarm before he released his grasp, dropping his hand to his side.

"What the hell? I didn't mean it like that. I'm sorry. It will never happen again. I promise."

She glanced at the floor. She had to take hold of herself. Take hold of her crazy emotions before something gave way—before something snapped. She drew in a calming breath. After all these years she should have recovered. Her fear should have disappeared by now. Every single day in the passing of six years, she glanced over her shoulder, checked her wake, prayed that she and Robert would remain safe.

"Stan...Stan used to let me bring Robert in if he wasn't well. I kept an eye on him while I worked. And Stan...he always said I could go to Robert whenever necessary."

"You love your husband that much?"

"Robert is my son! I was referring to teacher strikes and the like."

"Well, what about your husband? I suppose he comes in occasionally and keeps you company?"

"My husband?" What was there to say? What would he think of a twenty-eight year old woman who left her husband and took his child from him?

"He's...he's dead. He died six years ago." It was the first thought that popped to mind. He didn't need to know the truth. Didn't need to know that she'd packed up and left Peter, who'd blubbered excuses and platitudes saying it was the drink, the stress, that he'd never hit her again, that he loved her. In the end, his words meant nothing. Escaping to Newcastle and putting distance between them was the better choice.

"I'm sorry. I shouldn't have persisted." He rubbed his chin. "Have you been feeling ill recently?"

"No, I don't get sick." Although this would have been the first with nausea hanging in her stomach all morning.

"It's well past lunch. Perhaps you need something to eat. I noticed you didn't touch anything in the boardroom. What if I take you out for a late lunch?"

"No, thank you. I promised Sally we'd have afternoon tea together." What harm could there be in a small white lie? Spending more time with him wasn't necessary. Sensory overload was enough for one day. She wasn't sure if she had available strength to ward him off for much longer.

"Suit yourself." He moved back to his seat and took a sip of coffee.

His gaze did an intake of her legs as her fingers tugged on a persistent skirt.

"If you didn't wear it like Glad-Wrap wrapped around a pole you wouldn't have to tug all day long."

A rise of irritation swirled in her stomach, making its way to her throat but she swallowed it down and made no comment.

He stood and slipped on his suit jacket. "I'll be back in the office later. I have my mobile with me if anything important crops up." He drew a business card from his top pocket. "Here's the number."

Taking the card, her gaze drifted after him as he walked from the office. She didn't need this attraction, didn't want it. Having a taste of attractive men deterred her from ever starting another relationship. She'd done the right thing by spitting the last one out.

The lingering effects of Mathew's aftershave wafted toward her nostrils. Fighting to avoid drifting into a land where she didn't belong, she allowed herself a few moments to fall into a harmless daydream.

Jolting upright, she realized misleading thoughts like those could get her into hot water—boiling to be precise. Experiencing scalds once in her life was enough.

Her stomach turned sickly with hunger and searching for Sally failed. She stepped into the lift.

* * * *

The sun peeked out from the clouds, trying its best to disperse warmth while she wove a path towards one of the restaurants on the foreshore. After ordering a salad sandwich and coffee, she chose a table beside the water. Her mind was intent on absorbing everything about Mathew King. *What a predicament?*

Even now a tingling sensation remained where Mathew's fingers had touched her. She ran her left hand over her wrist in remembrance. Falling for the boss wasn't a good idea. Why this man? What did he possess other men had failed to match? Tegan pulled a quirky face. She'd only just met the man and already thought of a few answers.

The waitress delivered the order as she wondered how the company would hold up. How much change did Mathew King think the business needed? As far as she was concerned change wasn't necessary. She let out a sigh before taking a sip of coffee and gazed over the water but not taking in the view.

Imagine being popped into an eight by eight meter box with one of Australia's most desirable bachelors and have to work beside him for five days a week, every minute, every hour from nine to five. Witnessing his muscles twitch, witnessing every movement of those strong powerful legs beneath that tailored business suit he wore. Oh, and yes, watching those eyes of his. The eyes which made you want to lose yourself in them, which also had some type of power over women. Her stomach dropped. Most women would wither away with infatuation but she had to be strong to keep safe.

She thought of Robert and wondered how he was, what he was doing. He said so many times how much he liked school. She grinned. Was kindergarten really school? He was too young for school. After paying the bill, she returned to work, but a voice halted her halfway up the corridor.

"Ms. Ryan, be in my office in five minutes." She caught a glimpse of Mathew's back as he disappeared into his office.

After applying a little lipstick and picking up her notebook, she walked into his office.

"Do you make a habit of taking an hour for afternoon tea?"

Was there a time limit for afternoon tea, especially when she hadn't had any lunch? Her heart missed a beat. For long seconds she couldn't get her mind around the fact he was so concerned about the length of time she'd taken, especially over something so minor.

She dreaded this day for one whole week, now she knew why! Taking a moment, her eyes fluttered closed. He purposely choked up all her breathing space, and scattered her brain cells to Venus and back. This wasn't going to work. She felt it, saw it. How would she survive?

* * * *

"Mum. Why can't I come with you?"

"No sweetie, not today. We'll have breakfast soon."

"It's not fair."

"What's not fair?"

"I don't like school. I don't have a close friend. The other boys have Dads. Dads who play with them."

"Come on, don't start that now. I play with you...I won't be long." Tegan dashed upstairs and returned carrying her briefcase.

"Robert, come on. Are you ready for breakfast?"

"Yeah, Mum."

After they'd had breakfast and were organized, Robert ran out through the front door and Tegan locked it behind them. He bounced into the car.

"Seat belt on. I do play with you, sweetie."

"Yeah Mum, but you're a girl."

"That doesn't mean I can't do boy things."

"Do you fish? You don't even know how to put bait on a hook."

"I know you love fishing ever since Grandpa took you, but I could learn." She pulled a quirky face while thinking of putting a live worm on a hook.

After dropping Robert off at school, she noticed a few fathers also dropping off their children. Knowing there wasn't a male figure around for her son, she went on a guilt trip blaming herself for everything that had happened. But hell, there were hundreds of single mums out there doing a wonderful job—more than wonderful, just perfect. She hoped she would be able to do the same. The truth was she had to leave Robert's father. She didn't have a choice. The scenario went over and over in her mind.

* * * *

The drive into Newcastle was a reasonable distance. That's what everyone thought. It was a pleasure to get out of the city at the end of each working day and slide into the tranquility nature provided. However, she wanted to stay away from the crowds, be hidden. It was for the best.

She pulled her white Laser into the parking space near Coleman Enterprises. After settling in, she attended her usual morning routine: checking messages and double-checking what the day had in store.

Hearing a noise by the door, she swung around. "Stan, no one told me you were coming in today."

He walked through the door and gave her a kiss on the cheek. "Is everything all right?"

His grey eyes appeared as though they had sunken further into his face.

"Yes, Dad," she whispered. "I'm worried about you. You don't look well."

"Perhaps a little tired, that's all."

"I know you wanted to retire, but something doesn't seem right—especially selling half of the company like that. Did you really need a business partner?"

"You know I did. We've gone over and over it. You know it was a wise decision. Don't worry. Besides, I did offer to sign half of the company over to you."

"I know. But I want to spend more time with Robert not less."

"I realize that. Robert is important. I accepted that fact which is why I chose to find a business partner."

"But it's not what you truly wanted. It's not what Grandpa would have wanted either."

"As the old saying goes, it's called change. Nothing stays the same. The staff will continue with their present employment. You have nothing to worry about."

Tegan shot him a disbelieving look.

"Don't look at me like that. We have to get moving. They'll be waiting for us in the boardroom to finalize the last details."

"We spoke about maybe finding a manager."

"Selling has already lessened the burden. Having a manager, well, I'd be always looking over their shoulder and checking up on them."

A sorrowful feeling hit Tegan's stomach as he gave her another kiss on the cheek, along with a hug.

"It'll be fine, don't you worry. I hope Mister King appreciates your finer qualities. You're an excellent secretary, not to mention the best Personal Relations Manager we've had. The be—"

"I hope I get that much admiration." A voice called from behind startling Tegan.

"You have to earn it first." Stan shot Mathew a wink.

Tegan gave Mathew an irritated glance, then picked up the papers. "Well gentleman, I believe we only have a matter of minutes. We should be heading down." She walked briskly through the door and down the long wide corridor toward the boardroom.

* * * *

After the formalities were over Tegan felt the change happening. She secured her world for six years and it had worked. Now, it was as though she expected her secret to explode in her face. Didn't they say things happen in threes? This was number one, and she was scared to death of the other two. Her breathing became shallow and she dipped her gaze.

"It is decided that Coleman Enterprises will keep its name. King Enterprises now has the pleasure of being in a partnership with one of the most prestigious law firms in Newcastle."

Tegan glanced over at Stan. The expression on his face was drained. At least the name would remain the same, but hell Stan was losing half of his company—a business he'd worked so hard to build. Mathew obviously influenced his decision. For a moment, she forgot her notes and scrambled to catch up. Mathew didn't have the company's interest in mind at all as he went on to speak about so-called future changes.

The more Mathew rattled on, the higher her scale of annoyance grew—especially after witnessing such a defeated look upon Stan's face. Unable to stand it much longer, something snapped inside, pushing her upright to her feet.

Bemusement crossed Mathew's face. Lines etched over his forehead as he noted the sour flash of hostility ready to combust over such a delicate face.

"Mister. King, I see you delight in such a triumph. But don't expect Mister Coleman to agree into selling the other half of the business. It's not for sale. I can also assure you, Stan wants no changes." She jerked her head high, pointing her petite nose toward the ceiling before she walked briskly to the door, hesitated, and turned back.

"I do hope you have the staff's interest at the forefront of your mind. They are our main concern."

Stan stood, interrupting her. "Tegan, there's no need for this."

Tegan's gaze reverted to Stan then back to Mathew. "Do you realize Stan isn't a well man. Take a look at him for once. Or are you only concerned for your own well-being?"

She swung around and walked from the room, feeling so much better. She'd expressed her opinion twice in a span of only a few short days, regardless of the repercussions. Witnessing her father's defeated expression wasn't an option. The failure she saw in his eyes resembled the same rejection she'd seen the day her mother walked out on them. She wasn't about to let someone come in and walk all over him, not again, and she wasn't about to allow anyone else to take over. It would shatter him beyond repair. He might be old but his mind was intact and he still owned half of his company.

* * * *

"Are you still sure you want to take this on?" Stan questioned. "I'm sorry about Tegan. She's so protective and she's had a pretty tough life, go easy on her."

"Go easy. I think someone should tell her to go easy on me. I was a little surprised at first, but I realize now it's going to be a challenge." He grinned. "I'll do my best Stan. My father regards you in high esteem. I won't let you down."

"Thank you. I don't want Tegan fired. I don't usually fire people around here. I like to give the staff a few chances. They're a good bunch of people and great workers. You'll find out once you get to know them. I'm sure you'll get the hang of everything. I won't be around to meddle in whatever you undertake, but as I said, run the bigger decisions by me."

"I'm sure I will. With the figures here everything looks to be running with greater profits than I originally anticipated."

"Tegan has been helping out quite a bit. She's been gaining new customers for the firm for a while now. Business is flourishing." Stan leaned back in his chair.

Mathew's lips formed a tight line. "How have you put up with a secretary like that for so long, especially one that's so stubborn?" He clasped his hands behind the back of his head.

Stan grinned. "It's never happened before. I It shouldn't happen again. As soon as I leave, she'll settle down. You know when a man has one child, a daughter, well...you'd understand. I guess you can say it was a natural reaction."

Mathew jerked forward. "Tegan's your daughter," he blurted.

"I thought I told you about her."

"No...I must apologize. I had no idea."

"There is no apology necessary. I know what she can be like at times, and as I said, it's a natural reaction. She's set her sights on my concerns, for my well being. I want to thank you for taking part in this. It has removed a large burden from my shoulders. Oh yes, there is something else. Tegan and I prefer not to let anyone know she's my daughter. She mentioned to me about making sure you didn't know. But at this point and considering what has happened I thought you should know. It's a long story and well...she feels safer having it this way."

"That's fine, no qualms on my side. Knowing Tegan is your daughter does explain a lot, given her attitude. I'll bring her around. There will probably be a few sparks around the place, but

I won't let that deter me. Your company will be safe, there's no need to worry. After-all I've been running businesses all my life."

He stood and shook Stan's hand with the word, 'safer' impregnated in his mind.

Safer from what, from whom?

* * * *

Tegan closed the door and walked to the window trying to steady her jangling nerves. Her blank gaze rested in the distance through the pane of glass. Why did her insides feel like a tsunami was about to hit? Her stomach wouldn't settle no matter how hard she tried.

Taking refuge in a chair nearby, elbows propped on the desk, regret overtook her. She'd let her emotions sway her usual professional attitude. That was something she'd promised herself never to let loose again. Would her job be in jeopardy? What was Stan thinking? Surely he knew she was only trying to help him, trying to stand up for him.

Perhaps coming to an agreement to help run the business as he'd suggested, would have been the better option. Only it meant less time with Robert, and Robert didn't have a father. She'd wanted him to have a normal life, well as normal as possible. A sigh shuddered from her lips.

The buzzer rang on the intercom. Reaching out she snapped it down with her index finger. "Yes."

"Well, if it isn't my secretary. Have you burnt off all your steam yet? I have a funny intuition you haven't."

"I'm not going to apologize, Mister King."

"I didn't ask you to Ms. Ryan. I would like you in my office in two minutes."

The arrogant click in her ear boiled her blood. *Nope, not going in there, what, so he can rant and rave then fire me. You damn well know you have to face him.* She blew out a frustrated breath.

It was a short, brisk walk across the corridor to his office door. Swinging it opened she walked in. "You asked for me?"

The bite in her voice didn't deter him from reading a letter he held in his hand. His cool, somewhat confident manner infuriated her.

"Have a seat." He continued to read.

The annoying strain of silence was too much to take. Folding onto the chair didn't help the battlefield of emotions coursing through her body.

He looked up. "That was a wonderful display. You should be pleased with yourself. It's not often a woman lets her hormones run wild in front of me." A dark, almost wicked look textured his face.

Bull! I bet scores of women have let their hormones run wild in front of you and not with words alone.

"Do you realize you could lose your position right at this very moment?"

Tegan felt sick to the stomach. Her nerves screamed for release. If he honestly wanted to sack her, whether he had the right to or not, she'd go. Trying to breathe in the same office would be life threatening, especially if he didn't want her there. That thought sent a chill up her backbone. She crossed her arms over her chest.

"Stan came to your rescue. He assured me it doesn't happen often." He made direct eye contact, sat forward in his chair, then clasped his hands over the files in front of him. He studied her as though he were a chess player debating his next move.

"Ms. Ryan while I'm here, it will never happen again! Do you hear me?" His voice was a slow, deep drawl.

She released an indrawn breath. "I hear you. But I happen to know you cannot fire anyone without Stan's approval."

He shook his head and the sides of his lips twitched. "That's all." He looked back at the papers in front of him.

That's all. His words repeated in her mind. She stood and couldn't get out of theirs fast enough. Oxygen punched from her lungs.

* * * *

Tegan rushed to work the following day. It was the second time in two weeks she was late. Life was changing right before her eyes. She drew in a breath before stepping from the lift and headed toward the office.

Sally grabbed her by the arm. "I wouldn't go in there if I were you," she whispered, rolling her eyes upwards.

"Why not? It is my office." She broke from Sally's grasp and took quick steps toward the office. Sally followed.

Tegan stopped, dropped the briefcase, and stood in the open doorway of the office. Empty! Everything was gone. She sucked in a slow, disbelieving breath, glaring at what was once her office. What the hell was going on? Her right hand rested over the swirl of nausea clawing at her stomach. The desk, the computer, filing cabinets—everything was gone. But where? Even the photograph of her son hanging on the wall had disappeared. She swung back to face Sally.

"Does this mean I no longer have a job?" Nerves snaked up her spine. "It can't be true; it can't. Stan wouldn't allow it."

Tegan stared at Sally in shock unable to digest what was taking place. Sally appeared as though she was about to cry. "He truly doesn't want me here," she shrieked.

"I'm sorry. I just arrived. I haven't any answers."

"It's all right. He wouldn't dare, would he? The hide of the man! What does he think he's doing?" She slumped back on the edge of the doorway. "I knew having a new partner would turn the whole bloody world upside down. This is ridiculous. I wonder if Stan knows about this."

"I think I'd better go. My boss will be here soon and I should be in my office before he arrives. Good luck."

Tegan watched Sally disappear down the corridor. Someone had to know what was going on. Glancing down to the opposite end of the corridor, Bridget on reception was answering a busy switchboard, apparently unaware of her dilemma.

She flicked her gaze to Mathew's closed door. For some moments, staring at the door was all she could manage. Naturally, Mathew chose that very moment to walk out, coming to a standstill barely centimeters away.

"Tegan, it's about time. Could we speak in my office?"

His gaze roamed over her teal suit, coming to rest on the opening of the jacket, then flicked up to her eyes.

"Mister. King..."

"My office would be more appropriate." His voice held a demanding tone—one he probably thought she'd obey.

To hell with obeying him. She wouldn't lower herself.

"I'm not following you anywhere. Not now; not ever." Tegan's hands balled into fists by her sides. "Mister King, if this is your way of saying my employment is terminated I don't think it's a wise decision. I've worked for this firm for five...five long years." She thrust her hands onto her hips. "I don't deserve to be treated in this manner. Does Stan know of your rash decision?"

A small gathering of office workers congregated at the end of the corridor.

"Do you really think snaking your way into a law firm and then getting rid of employees one at a time will do the firm any justice?

You have no idea how the company operates. It has fifteen solicitors. I thought..."

"Can you slow down for a moment?" His eyes grew darker as he leaned closer. "Apparently everyone is aware of your small tantrum," he whispered. "Will you just be quiet and accompany me into my office?"

His breath fell over her ear, instigating a shiver to race over her skin but she wasn't about to step foot in his office ever again. Taking a step backward, she propped one hand on her hip.

"It's obvious you think my employment is to be terminated. I don't have to take orders from you ever again. Stan needs to be informed of this at once."

"Stan doesn't need to be worried at present."

"Mister. King. I don't..."

His right hand lashed forward, grabbing her around the wrist, pulling her across the corridor. She tugged with all her might but soon realized the firm grasp and the strength in his hand was overpowering.

He released his grasp just inside the office door. Gazing around with disbelief, she closed her eyes before snapping them open. The entire contents of her office sat on the left side of his desk. What did this mean? Did he expect them to work together, so closely, in the same office?

"We have a large amount of work to be entered into the computer and several letters to be dispatched. I know the intercom and the office network does a great job, but I feel it would be best if we communicate face to face. It will save valuable time if you are in here with me." He crossed his arms.

She gazed at the side of his face—it was chiseled like a superior Roman solider. Taking hold of a swallow, she tried to push it down. Her throat tightened with every passing moment. She spluttered, "It would have been nice if you'd confided in me first, don't you think?"

Under raised eyebrows, he gazed at her. "I didn't think you would put up such an objection. I assure you, any future changes you'll certainly be the first person I'll notify, believe me."

It all seemed so straight down the line, so professional. So, what was eating at her? What made her feel as though there were something much deeper she should be concerned about?

Chapter Three

Tegan's desk sat about a meter to the left of Mathew's, but placed a little forward. Was this so he could check up without her knowing? It was going to be difficult working in the same office with someone who choked up all her brain cells.

"Are you happy with the arrangements?"

She felt like saying 'no'; one big fat 'no' but chewed on the inner side of her lip to stop herself from spitting back objections. She'd move the desk the moment he left the building.

"Wherever did you get the idea that I'd dismiss employees? You're completely mistaken if you think that is my intention."

"I'm sorry. I thought that..."

"Yes. Everyone knows what you thought. Please sit down. We need to discuss our working arrangements."

The irritation she'd seen in his eyes earlier disappeared. She slipped onto a chair opposite his desk.

"I think we should try our best not to get on each other's nerves. Ranting and raging at each other is not healthy. Let's set a good example, shall we? I know you disliked me buying half of the business but I purchased it with good intention. I have not forced Stan into any decisions he didn't want to make. If anything out of the usual crops up, naturally Stan will be required to comment." He moved to sit on the edge of his desk.

"I'm sorry for going off. I thought because of the scene the other day Mister King..."

"What's this Mister King business. Call me Mathew."

She nodded a 'yes' in acknowledgement.

"Now, if we're all settled, let's get to work."

A twinge of stupidity wound through her, making her feel like a school kid. She didn't tell him how much she needed this job, needed this income. It wasn't any of his business.

Typing constantly and realizing the grumbling in her stomach signaled she hadn't eaten all day, she decided to take a lunch break. Mathew continued to read the many letters in front of him and barely looked up. She still thought his idea of combining both offices ludicrous. Knowing half of the company was his and learning to keep her trap shut from time to time seemed a good idea.

"Enough." She stood and tugged her skirt downwards. "Don't you ever take a break?"

"When the work is finished."

"Well, I'm off to have some lunch. A lunch break I somehow missed. I'm starving." Grabbing her bag, she walked through the door and saw Sally stepping into the lift.

"Sally, wait up."

"How's it going?"

"Our offices are combined."

"Combined. What's he up to?" A curious light flickered in her eyes.

"He said there is a lot of work to get through and it would be more appropriate, time efficient, blah, blah, blah."

Sally smirked. "Hmm, doesn't sound like a logical idea to me, not from an employer. I think the man has eyes for you." Her hand cupped a rising giggle.

"Don't be silly." Heat rushed to Tegan's cheeks. "He's...he's my boss, that's all." The lift floated to the bottom floor and a burning sign of anxiety crept into her stomach.

What if that's the only reason I'm in his office?

* * * *

Tegan didn't have to turn to know Mathew's gaze lingered. Every nerve sizzled. The tiny hairs on the back of her neck stood up and prickled against her skin. It was all the proof she needed.

She gazed at the pile of work in her tray. So much work to be entered into the computer. Business letters and invitations to meetings he'd organized for the following week. Meetings to discuss the future of Coleman Enterprises and the clients they had in progress, plus future clients. Sensing a movement behind her, she turned.

Mathew slipped on his jacket. "I'm off now. I have a meeting with Wayne Bates. I don't know what time I'll be back."

Tegan didn't reply, couldn't reply. A slight shake of her head was all she could manage. Her gaze didn't leave him until he disappeared. A few hours didn't leave much time to finish typing up the letters. She slumped back onto the chair, wishing she had more time to rearrange the furniture, to set it out in a position which would make her feel a whole lot more comfortable. That'd be the day. She'd never feel comfortable around Mathew King.

For the following two and a half hours, aching fingers danced over the keyboard. At five-thirty, her limp arms dropped to her side. She'd organized Clare, her baby sitter to keep an eye on Robert until seven, which should be plenty of time to complete every letter.

Streetlights filtered through the panes of glass. Time flew by fast and everyone left. A creepy silence hovered throughout the office. Pushing herself to her feet, she switched on more lights, hoping it would disperse the unease crawling in her stomach.

A draft skittered around her ankles. She glanced around the office and held an indrawn breath. A ghostly eeriness of cool air enclosed around her. Her gaze ping-ponged the office then settled on Mathew's filing cabinet. It was as though something pushed her toward it. Her steps were uneasy as she crossed around behind his desk and spotted a photograph. Tucked behind a document frame, she stared at two small boys, a man, and a lady. Her stomach tightened and she drew in a slow deep breath.

Her trembling fingers picked up the gold framed photograph drawing it closer, hoping something would convince her it was a mistake, and that her highly active imagination was responsible. However, the boys resembled her son too much to disregard the matter.

Her breathing intensified, her gaze not leaving the photograph. *No...it couldn't be. It just couldn't. The same photograph! Is it the same photograph I saw when I lived with Peter? He told me his mother, father, and brother died in a car accident.*

Although her memories of that time were a little rusty, something didn't sit quite right. The uncanny resemblance couldn't be ignored. Could the children in the photograph be Robert's cousins? Her eyes rounded and she stared closer. Chills crept over her clammy skin. A line tugged between her eyebrows as her heavy lashes closed. Was there a reasonable explanation for the similarity? Was there a connection at all? Nausea swam in her stomach.

"Great photo," a voice called from behind, splintering the silence.

A startled jolt pelted through her. Her eyes snapped opened, and the photograph slipped from her hands disintegrating into shards as it hit the floor. A cold fist clawed around her heart.

"Are you all right?" Mathew asked. She looked like a caged animal desperate for escape.

"Tegan, it's Mathew." Within seconds he closed the space between them. A horrid gurgling sound passed her throat. "I didn't mean to scare you."

Tegan didn't move or say a word. The fear embedded in her eyes horrified the hell out of him. He steadied her with his hands, resting them on her small waist, before his right hand moved to her back, rubbing it gently.

"Hey, it's okay. I'm here now. It's all okay," he murmured.

Hearing his reassuring words, her body went limp. His firm hand moving over her back soothed the previous shock and she began to settle. Their eyes leveled and the sincerity she saw softened the core of her heart. His lips moved closer, distorting her vision before tenderness and warmth melted over her lips. Her body molded against his and she felt as light as a feather. His affection swamped her. It was something she'd thought never existed—that is, not within her world anyway.

Warmth travelled in waves, highlighting a flood of desire. In automatic reaction her arms slid around his neck, her breasts firmly up against his solid chest. Abandoning the kiss, their gaze remained steady.

"You're trembling. Are you sure you're all right?"

"Yes."

"You seem pretty shaken by a mere photograph. Am I the cause of your fright, or was it the photograph?"

"I'm sorry. No. It's…I guess I'm tired, that's all. The photograph is ruined. I'm sorry." Her voice struggled for clarity.

"Not to worry." He bent and picked up the pieces of glass.

The residual of shock coursed through her body. Bending her legs in an attempt not to fall in a heap, she grabbed hold of the corner of the filing cabinet. Using her free hand she began to pick up splinters of glass. "I'm sorry."

What he saw was heartache, but he couldn't decipher what he thought was pain, hanging like jagged pieces of ice in those beautiful pools of green.

She stood and dropped the glass into the bin.

"At least the photograph is still intact. Did it interest you?"

"Yes, are they your children?"

His head jerked up, his forehead creased. "No, they are not my children. I'm not married and I don't have any illegitimate children hanging around—if that's what you think. The photograph is of myself, my brother, Mum, and Dad."

At least they aren't, Robert's cousins. She let out a sigh. "Um… you've never been married?"

"No. I know what you're thinking. Why someone advancing on mid-life isn't married."

"Advancing on mid-life. What, thirty-five at the most."

"More like thirty-nine."

"Why haven't you married?"

"I guess you can say I haven't found the right woman as yet. Women want kids and I'm not in the position to consent to a lifetime contract such as that."

Tegan was horrified. "You don't want children. How could anyone not want a child?" Fear tried its hardest to override anything related to sounding normal. She had to find out more, had to be certain that what she thought was just a misleading notion.

"Look." He stood, holding the photograph in one hand, the other clinging to the splinters of glass. "I haven't had much to do with children and I'm not in a position to say anything on the subject."

Knowing she'd gotten this far, she wasn't about to stop with the questions. "Surely you've had the desire to have a son—someone to carry on your name?"

"No!" Long angry strides stalked to the bin, and the sound of shattering glass echoing through the silence reminded her she was stepping way past the boundaries of boss-employee relationship.

"Don't get me wrong, I think children are important. They are the bloodline of a family which is imperative. It's just with the lifestyle I lead, it wouldn't be fair on a child."

"Which one is you?"

"The one on the right side of Dad."

"Your brother and you are so alike."

"Yeah. Dad is pleased at least one of us turned out like him. Pete isn't with us anymore. Pete's dead now."

Tegan's throat plummeted to her stomach sucking all oxygen from her lungs. "Oh...I'm...sorry." Her hand rested over her chest.

"That's okay. What drew you to the photograph?"

"I happen...I happen to like family photographs." Tegan tried to calm the rising panic surging inside. She recalled her father stating her highly active imagination would get her into trouble one day. Yes, that's what it was, her silly imagination.

So, why did she think the photographs were alike? The similarities were there. If his brother were dead that meant Robert's father was also dead, which was preposterous! A sigh escaped her lips. She was mistaken. Peter's last name is Knight, not King. Once again, her foolish imagination led her astray.

The pleasurable after-effects of Mathew's kiss lingered and she toyed with her bottom lip. However, that first kiss with Peter

folded. "Let's forget it."

"As I said, a woman alone."

"I'm not alone now am I? You're here. Noone will hit...I have one more letter to finish." She tried to drown her words with a much louder statement hoping he hadn't heard. However, she knew words spoken couldn't be retrieved.

"What do you mean noone will hit...what? Hit you. Is that what you were about to say?"

Her body iced. How could she get out of this one? She wasn't one to tell lies, well maybe a small white lie, but that was occasionally when necessary.

"It was a long-time ago and I guess it's taken some time to deal with."

Mathew moved over to the desk. "I had no idea. I shouldn't have kept pestering you. If you need someone to talk to, I'm here."

"I don't like talking about the subject but thanks anyway." She blew air from her lips. "It was a relationship which turned sour. To put it simply, he hit me—I left."

I'm not about to tell you of my scars. Indelible reminders of what can happen when a relationship changes, when love curdles into one of the darkest nightmares a woman can experience. The fluttering of thick eyelashes wiped her tear-filled gaze. "I'm sorry," she whispered.

"You have nothing to be sorry about. He should be the one feeling sorry. At least you've spoken about it. They say talking about problems makes one feel a whole lot better. Have you ever spoken about it before?"

"Only to a girlfriend."

He walked to her desk, his hand prompted her chin upwards and she stood, her gaze leveling with his. A deep purr stirred in her stomach before his smooth, warm lips blocked out the entire world. They overrode any ability to put a stop to the sudden cascade of emotions now flowering through her.

The kiss intensified before he drew back. She'd been through a lot. He knew he'd have to take it very steady now, well as steady as his male testosterone would let him.

"I have to finish the last letter," she spluttered before breaking contact and sitting in front of the computer again.

"Leave it. It's not important."

"I want to finish what I started."

Mathew idly walked to his desk, aware of the football match taking place in his stomach.

Tegan finished typing the letter, turned off the computer and tidied the desk.

"Oh, I almost forgot. I haven't briefed you as yet." He moved and sat on the edge of the desk.

"I have to make a business trip to Port Macquarie and your services are required."

"My services—what do you mean?"

"I have a meeting with two Japanese clients. They requested I meet them in Port Macquarie as apparently they have other business dealings to take care of while there. We're discussing the prospects of Coleman Enterprises. They are requesting us to represent them and their company with any legal formalities and future proceedings. I feel this would be an excellent step, a great opportunity."

Tegan bit on her lip. "I just can't up and leave my son."

He rubbed his chin with his finger. "Hell...I forgot about your son. The company will consider paying for child-care if that's the problem."

"No, it's not the problem. You don't have any understanding of children do you, or about a child's needs?"

"No...I'll be the first to admit to that. Listen...it'll be for a few days. We'll be leaving this Friday morning and returning Sunday, late in the afternoon."

"But...but that's the whole weekend. I couldn't possibly."

"As I said, your services are required. Couldn't you see some way around it just for this weekend? Naturally we will have different suites. All expenses paid."

Not only was she expected to leave Robert, one entire weekend in Mathew's company would be asking for trouble. "I don't think so."

"If that's the case I'll have to find a replacement for the weekend."

"That won't be necessary. I'll make the arrangements," she stammered, never having to leave Robert overnight ever. How would he react?

"Are you ready to leave?"

"Yes."

"I'll escort you down, safely."

Safely, hell, what makes him so sure I'm safe with him especially after a kiss like that?

His presence was so close behind her, the lingering after affects of his kiss played havoc with her nervous system. She fumbled for the keys in her handbag before taking several attempts to put the key in the lock. The damn thing wouldn't cooperate.

"Would you like me to try?"

"No. I can manage to open a car door," she stammered. When the key slid into the lock, it brought a bucket full of relief.

She turned. "Good night."

"Night. Drive safely."

Tires screeched as she left the car park. The thought of spending a weekend with the man, which meant nights and days, scared the hell out of her. Finally, deciding if she stuck to business nothing would go wrong.

There was no remembrance of driving the long-distance home and it came as a shock, knowing her mind was so preoccupied.

Clare opened the front door.

"I heard your car sweetie. How'd it go?"

After giving Clare a kiss on the cheek, she dropped her briefcase. "It's all finished but I've been asked to go away on a business trip. Would you mind looking after Robert this weekend?"

"That's fine, sweetie."

"Thank you so much."

After saying goodbye to Clare, Tegan tiptoed up the stairs and walked into Robert's bedroom. His bedside light was still on and a little snore echoed from a tiny body in a pair of his favorite cartoon pajamas.

Bending over and giving him a soft kiss on the forehead, she whispered, "You're such a precious child, sweetheart. I'll never let anything bad happen to you. I love you with all my heart." She moved a lock of dark hair from his eyes and switched off the bedside light.

Trying not to make a sound, she closed the door and prepared for bed. Mathew's intentions came to mind. Was she going mad? He seemed genuine, but still...something told her to back off. His brother is dead and Robert's father is alive. There is no relationship whatsoever, besides Peter always said he had no living relatives.

Snuggling under the soft quilt, she reinvented every emotion, every soft movement of Mathew's lips. There was no mistaking that she was attracted to him and had enjoyed his kiss. She tried to fool herself with the statement, 'Hundreds of men can kiss like that'. She wasn't too convincing.

Her stomach knotted as she thought of the coming weekend. How would she last? How could she control her hormones? The

Suzanne Brandyn

more she thought about it the more her nerves high-jacked her heart. She damn well knew Mathew wasn't just any man. He was the type of man who always got his own way.

Lordy, she wasn't and hadn't been a good swimmer. She needed a life raft, a buoy—something to keep her head above the oncoming rocky seas.

Chapter Four

Tegan tossed a little black dress into a suitcase and then tugged it out again. Strictly business entered her mind. That meant the usual business suits. She neatly folded each suit before adding a couple of casual summer dresses. Somehow the little black dress, along with a teal one, popped right back into the suitcase.

"Hey Mum," Robert called as he leaned on the edge of the door.

"Yes sweetheart?"

"When you're gone, Clare said we could go to the beach."

"That's fine sweetie, after school of course. Are you sure you're...well...are you okay with me leaving?"

"I'm...not...a ba...by."

Indeed he was a baby, her baby. At six years of age, what else could he be? However, he was an intelligent, sensible baby.

"Clare will look after you. She has the number of the motel. I think it's called Rydges in Port Macquarie. I'll ring as soon as we arrive. It only takes about a three hour drive from Newcastle."

"Do you think your new boss likes you?"

Tegan tucked a stray strand of hair behind one ear. "Well, I hope he does. I do work for him."

"No. I mean loves you."

"No sweetie. I work for him and this is part of my job. I expect I'll be sitting, feeling bored, and taking notes all weekend—boring notes. Not as exciting as your weekend."

"Oh." Robert looked deep thought.

It's amazing. Children seem to know more than they let on.

"Will...I meet him?"

"I expect you will one day."

"Robert." Clare called from the kitchen.

"You should go and see what she wants. My taxi will be here soon."

He spun around and disappeared through the doorway.

Carrying one suitcase, a vanity case, and a handbag, Tegan arrived by the front door. Turning to Robert, her eyes welled with tears.

"I hate leaving you, sweetie."

"Err, it's okay Mum. I'll be okay."

After a cuddle and kiss, she turned to Clare. She always looked happy. Her hazel eyes sparkled. Being a retired preschool teacher and adoring children was a bonus when she'd hired her five years ago.

"I don't know what I'd ever do without you."

"Now don't worry, we'll be fine. You just do what you gotta do and we'll be having fun, won't we Robert?"

"I'll ring you each morning, lunchtime, and at night just to be sure."

Clare chuckled. "Okay love. We might be out but leave a message and I'll ring you right back as soon as we get in."

After kissing Clare on the cheek, she heard the taxi toot its horn. "It sounds like he's in a hurry. Bye, take care, and you be good Robert."

"Bye Mum."

They stood on the veranda waving as the taxi drove away.

* * * *

Mathew was waiting on the pavement when Tegan arrived at Coleman Enterprises. He approached the taxi as soon as it came to a standstill. A clamping device locked around her heart. Her mind meandered to a place it certainly wasn't supposed to go and definitely not at that moment.

He wore cream tailored pants with a deep, blue polo shirt. It was almost too good to be true, being fussed over by one of the wealthiest men in Australia, especially one that was so damn handsome. A nervous excitement brewed in her belly.

Mathew opened the door and his gaze lingered over long, silky legs.

"Morning."

"Morning." She kicked her legs out from the taxi and stepped onto the pavement. He walked to the boot, pulled out the luggage, and placed it on the pavement. Then he spoke to the driver.

When he stepped back, and the driver pulled away Tegan heart's missed a beat. "I didn't pay him."

"As I said, all expenses this coming weekend are not your responsibility."

He noticed her healthy glow, noticed the way the colorful dress clung to her curves, and the extra height added by a pair of slinky black sandals. All polished to perfection. He also admired the light pink toe nail polish, which matched the color of those creamy succulent lips. *Hell, I couldn't get you out my mind last night. If only you knew what you do to me every time I lay eyes upon you.*

"Are you finished?" The snappy tone in her voice had his gaze skidding back to her eyes.

"Sorry, it's...nothing."

A black limousine pulled up beside them and the driver stepped out.

"Ready Mister King?"

"Yes. Just this luggage and then we're off."

Tegan's legs slipped into jelly mode. Coping with feebleness, she adjusted her feet—trying to keep her balance while Mathew opened the car door.

The coolness of the beige leather seat was comforting until Mathew walked to the other side of the limousine and slipped onto the seat barely inches away. Her heartbeat sped up and palms perspired.

"Sean, I'd like you to meet my secretary, Tegan Ryan. Tegan this is Sean, my driver. He's been with me for a number of years."

"It's nice to meet you."

"Good to meet you too. So, are you ready for your flight?"

"Flight, what flight?" She shot an alarmed gaze at Mathew. "You didn't tell me we were flying! I presumed we would be driving to Port Macquarie."

"Flying is quicker, more practical. We're driving to Williamtown, Newcastle Airport. From there, we fly to Port Macquarie."

"Oh."

Tegan's nerves high-jumped and grated on bare bones making her feel utterly sick. She'd never flown anywhere. Suffering from claustrophobia had put a stop to that, not to mention the fear of being high, up there, hanging limply in open space. A plane could drop from the sky within seconds, just like that, although she did attempt to step into an aircraft some years ago. The outcome was disastrous. Even thinking about being in a plane built pressure over her chest, forcing her lungs to struggle for oxygen.

Mathew settled two glasses on a tray in front of him. "Wine?"

"Yes, please." She needed a good fix of alcohol, something to stop the cascading of warmth trying to break through the barrier she'd tried to set in place earlier that morning. She prayed it would also dampen her rising anxiety. Crossing one leg over the other in an attempt to camouflage the jitters hopefully worked but nothing could disguise the trembling of her hands.

As she was about to pick up the glass, he put out his hand, wrapping it around her wrist to ensure there were no more accidents.

The torturous currents of his touch speared heat to circle her heart and forced her breath to catch in her throat. Trying to control the burning desire splintering her anatomy hadn't been successful.

"Thank you," she spluttered. When he broke contact, her fingers tightened around the glass. The glass tilted, spilling some of its contents onto the seat.

"Oh...I'm sorry."

"Here." He grabbed a tissue from a box nearby and patted the dampness on the seat beside her. Her body stiffened as she watched his masculine hand. This was supposed to be a business trip, why so romantic, so perfect? Taking refuge in the wine, she ensured both hands clung firmly to the glass.

"I was going to offer you a cup of coffee but thought better of it." His mouth slid into a devilish grin.

She had to count to ten to put a stop to the smile that was on the verge of erupting but there was no preventing a nervous giggle escaping her throat.

"Something is obviously funny?" His eyes narrowed.

"Recalling the coffee in the boardroom," she said softly before turning to glance through the window as they travelled north crossing the Hexham Bridge, which spanned the Hunter River.

"It would have been better if we'd been alone," he replied.

Then I would have chucked the whole damn pot at you.

"I hope you're looking forward to a break?" he murmured.

She turned. "A break, certainly not. That is impossible."

"Why's that?"

"This is strictly business. I'm here because I'm your secretary. Nothing more, nothing less."

"Have it your way but sometimes business and pleasure balance out and leaves one feeling very fulfilled."

Oh, nice. Very nice, she thought and wondered how many times he'd mixed pleasure with business.

* * * *

Stepping from the limousine, she gazed around and recalled the previous attempt to set foot in an aircraft. Her stomach flipped with nerves. She rested a hand over the unpleasant sensation gaining momentum in her stomach.

"What are you looking for?"

"Nothing in particular."

Spinning around to face him, a gust of wind caught her dress and sent it flying much higher than she would call decent. Hell, didn't he melt when he caught a glimpse of a black g-string with the tiniest straps he could ever have imagined. Something glittered at him. His heart went into overkill.

Tegan's hands struggled against her thighs, trying to smooth her dress back into place. She turned to obstruct his view but the wind stirred once again, flipping up the back of her dress and leaving Mathew pleading with his mind for sanity.

The sight of a beautiful, shapely bottom registered its full impact. So perfect, so creamy. He was melting and knew control was required. He turned, trying to block the tantalizing sight from view only to notice Sean standing behind him with a huge grin plastered over his face.

"Get your mind out of the gutter. Let's get this luggage to the aircraft," he snapped, feeling an unusual stab of annoyance—quite aware he wasn't the only one to partake in the enjoyable view.

Guilt hurtled around inside him and he couldn't decipher exactly what it was. *Jealous...no, how could I be?* He was never envious of anything or anyone, so why now?

"Sure thing Mister King." Sean was still smiling when the last of the luggage was set under the aircraft.

Tegan continued to feel the burn inside, continued to feel the warmth tingling in her cheeks until they arrived beside the aircraft.

"Here we are."

Drawing to a standstill, she glared at the strange aircraft. "What...what is it? What do you call that?" Her body dived into a tumble dryer of nervousness. The rotation of anxiety almost made her feel as though she'd vomit there and then. Inhaling a slow steady breath, she continued to stare with unease.

"A Cessna Caravan."

"Hmm, looks like a van. It's a strange shape. Where's the pilot?"

"You're looking at him."

A lump lodged in her throat. "I...I" She glared at him, then back to the aircraft. "I...I couldn't possibly get into that thing." Panic rushed through her veins as fear crawled over her skin.

"Why not?"

"Well...for a start, I...I don't like the looks of it. They're confined and stuffy."

"This aircraft is far from confined. It's spacious. You'll love it."

"No, I can't!"

"Why don't you have a look inside? You might change your mind."

"Well, maybe one quick look around but I can assure you, I will not change my mind."

"We have to have some means of transport to travel to Port Macquarie."

"What's so wrong with a lovely seaside drive?"

He mumbled something under his breath but Tegan was unable to hear.

When she stepped into the aircraft, her gaze circled the vast expanse. It wasn't an aircraft, it was a flying motel with a six star rating. Her fingers ran over the plush beige leather seats. She wandered slowly, counting at least eight until arriving at the cockpit.

She glared at the fancy instrument panel which looked like a space ship's control station. *He thinks he's going to fly this thing. Who in the hell does he think he is? The Flying damn Doctor?*

She shook her head and turned noticing a mahogany table, above it timber ledges where one would place drinks. Small screens were anchored on each side of the aircraft, which pivoted with a single turn for comfort viewing of the television.

It certainly didn't feel like she was in an aircraft.

"What do you think? Are you going to take the plunge or do we have to unpack and limo it up to Port Macquarie."

"I...I don't know."

"What's that supposed to mean? Listen, I am an excellent pilot. Nothing will happen to you."

"Yes...but...I feel so uptight, I really don't think I can manage this."

"Why didn't you tell me earlier? You are my secretary and if you aren't going to travel with me in the style I'm used to, then perhaps I'll reconsider and find someone who will appreciate flying in an aircraft as luxurious as this one." He rubbed his fingers over the back of his neck.

Long moments passed. Indecision wasn't a normal part of her character and how she hated herself or hated Mathew. It was his fault she was in a predicament such as this. She twisted one side of her mouth.

"We haven't got all day you know."

Rubbing her dry lips together in thought she finally blurted,

"Yes...okay...seeing you have put it so bluntly. Where do I sit?"

"You can sit beside me in the cockpit if you like. Anywhere. I don't care. You do have a choice."

Flying backwards certainly wouldn't be a good feeling, so she slid onto one of the back seats which faced the front of the aircraft.

"I have to do a pre-flight then I'll be back."

Pre-flight, what in the hell was that? Little butterflies were having a party in her stomach despite the lavish comfort of her surrounds. She rested back in the seat, feeling the soft leather underneath. Her hands slid over the armrests. *So, is this what it feels like to have money and bags of it?*

It wasn't long before Mathew was back in the aircraft, locking the hatch behind him. "Settled in I see."

A quirky smile slid over her face. "I guess you could say that."

"Would you like a drink? Help yourself. There's wine, champagne, spirits, or coffee."

She was fascinated as she watched Mathew at the controls. Although he blocked partial view, she listened to the radio calls he made.

"Are you sure you're okay up there?" He glanced over his shoulder.

"Yes, I'm fine."

"Seat belt on."

Trying to clip the belt into place was an ordeal. It was only a standard looking seat belt but it refused to click into position no matter how hard she tried to buckle it together.

"Need a hand."

"Um...maybe."

His few paces ate up the distance between them before he knelt. "This thing is relatively new and this has to happen."

A sudden rush of his aftershave with the scent of fresh pine hit her senses. Inhaling much too quickly gave her a double dose, spinning her mind into luxurious meltdown. Even when he clipped the seat belt into position, the scent of his hair targeted her heart. She closed her eyes.

"There." His cheek brushed lightly against hers before his lips connected in a sensual, hypnotic kiss of wet passion. Tegan's eyes sprung open while the kiss continued. Struggling against objection from her mind, her heart secretly begged for more. His mouth coaxed hers and she eagerly anticipated following his instruction. Automatically her arms coiled around his neck, clinging to him. Her fingers slipped through his hair, urging him closer before she realized that meltdown had gone too far.

"No more," she pleaded.

Pushing him back a little, she tried to maintain some self-control. "What was that for?"

"In case we crash. Now I won't have any regrets about not experiencing that last kiss." His smile was wicked and his eyes channeled passionate evil. The perilous depth of blue made her conscious of what could really happen if she wasn't careful.

He stood, leaving her to deal with the lingering cascade of deliriousness his touch had triggered. It felt like minutes passed before she responded to his words.

"Crash. Oh, come off it."

He hesitated before the cockpit. "Are you all right to take-off now? I do have a flight plan to follow."

"No."

"What is it now?"

What is it? Just you and your damn sexual ability. She felt like saying but didn't. His lips were so intoxicating she had a job to control the 'strictly business' relationship she'd tried to cement in her mind. "How long have you been flying?"

A dark wicked grin textured his face. "You don't have to worry about that."

"I asked you a question. I want an answer. Listen." She unclasped the belt and pounced to her feet.

"If you expect me to accompany you in this darn thing, I'm entitled to answers. I'm concerned about my safety. In case you didn't realize, I have not only my own life to consider but I have my son's as well. It would be nice if his mother returns from this stupid trip." His grin infuriated her. "Oh come on what's so funny?" Her hands clenched.

"Mathew, knock, knock. Where's your mind?" It certainly wasn't on the job of flying.

"Sorry. I've been flying since I was seventeen. I am a good pilot. I fly practically everywhere."

"Oh." He made it sound so casual, like having sex...*oh, hell*. She swallowed and slumped back onto the seat before he took the few paces toward her and knelt to buckle up the seat belt once again. As he finished clipping the belt into position, his lips made contact with her forehead, leaving a warm twinge penetrating the spot before he strolled away.

Half way toward the cockpit he turned. "Did I ever tell you that you're very sexy when you're mad?" He then resumed his short walk to the cockpit.

Sexy? She drew in a startled breath. *What have I gotten myself into? Thanks for abandoning me to deal with this heap of emotional mess. That's one more thing you're accountable for Mathew King.*

As the aircraft roared and moved forward, her spine stiffened. She glared through the window. Mathew spoke into a mouthpiece and for a second, thoughts of sitting in the cockpit beside him might have been the better choice. However, the thought was quickly whacked off as plain stupid in many ways.

First, he would be only centimeters away and then there was all that open space, the almost direct contact with the sky, the clouds, and she certainly wasn't born with wings. She wished at times like this she did have wings. Her fear of flying soared and claustrophobia deepened. Not daring to look through any window, she grappled for the blind close by and brought it down with a sudden snap.

With clenched eyes, head down, the space underneath the aircraft grew. Tegan stayed like that for some time before she straightened her spine and opened her eyes.

She drew in a sudden gasp and inhaled more oxygen than needed, only to hold her breath.

Chapter Five

"Would you like a cup of coffee or something to eat?" Mathew began to make a coffee.

A clash between brain and body continued. She propelled herself upright. Her chest tightened.

"Are you okay?" he asked, noticing the sudden change in her complexion.

A few silent, panicking moments passed and she whooshed out a breath between pursed lips. "Does it really look like it?"

"What's the problem now?" He couldn't understand what was making her react in such a way. Then he noticed the pallor on her face increasing.

"I want to know one damn thing. Who the hell is flying this bloody giant?" The sound of a low chuckle certainly wasn't appreciated, especially after having to deal with so many challenging emotions.

"It's on autopilot. Really, one would think you have never flown in an aircraft."

Her nails dug into the leather on either side of the seat.

"If you don't ease up, those nails could do some aerating."

Loosening the tension in her fingers and feeling oddly embarrassed, she flipped up the blind. Gazing through the window, she noticed the aircraft was actually flying smoothly. The clouds, like little white puffs, sailed by.

"Here, I think you need a glass of wine. It might settle your nerves."

One glass? She needed more than one glass, almost snatching it from him.

"Autopilot—do you use it often?" She took a gulp of wine then another, and finished the whole glass within seconds.

"I use it now and again, especially when I need something... mostly when I fly alone."

Overcome that such a large aircraft could fly by itself, she felt like a complete idiot and slowly began to defrost.

He slipped into the seat directly opposite. Their knees brushed lightly.

"More wine?"

"Yes, please. I'm sorry to be such a fuss. It's...well, I haven't flown anywhere. I prefer the good old fashion method—by car. Oh..." She took the wine from him. "I attempted. I climbed into a small plane once. Then after I took a quick look around, my feet were back on the tarmac immediately. I vomited before I made it to the rest room."

His lips slid into an understanding grin. "If I'd known you were afraid to fly, I would have offered to help you be more prepared. Aircraft these days are quite safe. That isn't to say they don't have problems but a good pilot always double-checks everything before takeoff. With regular maintenance, they are as reliable as most cars. Why didn't you tell me?"

"I didn't want to cause a scene." Their gaze locked and she pressed her lips together.

"You amaze me; you really do. It's safe. You'll be okay." He smiled one of those smiles which made her go gooey on the insides.

Before drowning any further in his seductive attributes, she quickly added, "What would something like this cost?"

"Over one and a half million dollars."

Mister Money bags.

"King Enterprises leases it out. It works out better for tax purposes."

"Oh." It was only a whisper as she pressed her back into the seat.

"Another wine?"

Twirling the long stem of the glass in her fingertips she noticed it was empty, having no recollection of it ever sliding down her throat.

"Yes, thank you." At this rate, she wouldn't be able to feel any-thing—let alone see anything. She concluded that it was appropri-ate just this once, considering her flying fears made her feel like such a fool.

"You might feel better up front with me. Sometimes it helps to know a little about the operational side of things, not to mention the view."

Tegan finished the glass of wine and pushed herself upright to follow Mathew toward the cockpit. She noticed on the way it wasn't as difficult to stand as she'd imagined. Through the large windscreen, a cotton wool wonderland floated silently below.

"It's so beautiful." Mesmerized, her words barely escaped her lips. She slid onto the seat beside him.

He leaned over to buckle up the seat belt. When his hand

brushed her hip lightly, she jerked in reaction feeling a hammering over her heart.

"I don't bite."

"Um...sorry."

"It's all advanced technology. Quite simple. This is the autopilot, a flight directory system." He pointed to the panel in front of them.

"Looks more like a jumble of metal. How could you possibly understand all that?"

"With a lot of study and practice. If one does it long enough, it falls into place."

He popped his headphones on before turning. "These are for you. You can hear everything going on."

Her body stiffened. "I'm not sure I want to know."

He slipped the headphones over her ears.

The marvel of moving through space near the vault of heaven, flying high above the golden Earth and glorifying in those little white puffs sweeping by, helped in small measures to conquer her fear of flying.

"So, what do you think?"

"Um...yes...it's so...glorious. It's another world." She continued to absorb the adornment until the aircraft shuddered. It instantly halted any desire to go further. She jerked upright.

"What was that?"

An uncontrollable chuckle passed his lips. "It's only a little turbulence. It's nothing to be afraid of—it'll settle soon."

As soon as he finished his sentence, the aircraft was once again on a smooth flight.

"What's below the clouds?" She peered at the white fairy floss.

"The Pacific Ocean. Do you want to go down and take a closer look?"

Before she had time to answer, the aircraft dipped through the clouds taking her stomach with it.

"But you can't see."

"The instruments—it's all right, don't worry. I can tell by the instruments if we are upside down or not."

"Oh, upside down. Hmm." She let out a squeak.

The aircraft carved through the clouds, giving way to a view of the ocean as it glistened under the morning sun. To her left a green escarpment of rolling hills and deep valleys stretched as far as the eye could see.

"Is this close enough—five hundred feet?"

"Hmmm."

"We'll be arriving in Port Macquarie soon."

Tegan peered below, noticing the curling, white tips of the waves. Then the aircraft gradually ascended.

"All Stations, Port Macquarie. This is Sierra, Quebec, Sierra. Two zero miles inbound from south, tracking coastal, maintaining one thousand five hundred feet."

Well, it all sounded quite professional, although gibberish was the first word that popped into her mind. As they approached land, her nerves served up gigantic waves of unpleasantness.

He moved the microphone. "Landing soon. How do you feel?"

"Um, okay." She lied.

"All stations, Port Macquarie. This is Sierra, Quebec, Sierra, joining circuit downwind for runway zero three for a full stop."

She marveled at his ease and ability. *So, my new boss is a pilot and a damn good one at that.*

The aircraft approached the runway and her body slid into freeze mode. They descended closer toward the trees, moments before touchdown. Something warm enclosed over her hand.

"It's okay, smooth sailing."

She glanced down at his large hand covering hers. It was amazing how the warmth of a human touch could give her that extra bit of reassurance she needed—until the ground loomed up and she held her last intake of oxygen.

It was surprisingly only a small skip before they skimmed down the runway. Tegan expelled the lungful of air and relief surged through every shaking part of her anatomy.

"There...told you...a piece of cake."

They taxied away from the runway toward hangars in the distance.

"Sierra, Quebec, Sierra. All stations, Port Macquarie is now clear of runway zero three."

The aircraft slowed and came to a standstill. Her heart fluttered non-stop until the firmness of the tarmac was securely underfoot. While she waited for Mathew to fill in some little book, a black limousine crawled toward them. The driver of the limousine opened the door.

"Did you enjoy your flight?" Mathew asked, as he slid into the back seat beside her.

"Yes, I did. It was wonderful."

"Did you conquer your fears?" He smiled a wide, white smile sending a delightfully oozy feeling to purr in her belly.

* * * *

They pulled up in front of a large, cement rendered beige building. Tegan stepped out into warm humid air and looked around. Port Macquarie had changed, with its modern buildings and new restaurants. It wasn't the town she remembered.

People walked lazily on the footpath. Families sat in a park, feeding sea gulls or watching the tide of the river making its journey through the channel toward the ocean.

Mathew placed his hand in the small of her back as they walked to the car. The sensation was electrifying. She tried hard to rein in any objection.

"You do look incredibly beautiful."

There was no answer. Although it was a complement, she'd have to make it clearer this trip wasn't for personal pleasure—his or hers. She'd made enough scenes for one day and didn't want him to think she was a complete fruitcake.

* * * *

The driver retrieved their luggage and followed them through large, glass sliding doors. Enormous black pots sat displaying greenery on cream slate tiles.

Feeling out of depth, a sturdy 'no' to his request to accompany him on this trip would have been wiser. Then she remembered the awkwardness she'd felt when he said he'd hire a temp for the weekend.

As they approached the sweeping reception desk, his hand slid from her back allowing her to breathe normally. She glanced around and the restaurant came into view.

On the far side of the restaurant, through glass sliding doors, the river sparkled summer blue. Her gaze darted in all directions, enthralled by the lavish, elegant décor.

"Sir, one of the porters will take your luggage to your rooms," the receptionist stated.

"Don't bother. We haven't much. I'll take them up with us."

When they arrived at their separate suites, Mathew unlocked her door with a small plastic card.

"My room is this one." He walked toward the next door, dropped his suitcase, and then returned propping the door open. Following with the luggage, he placed it on the end of a queen size bed.

"If you need anything, don't hesitate to give me a call."

"Before you go, I would like you to know this happens to be a business trip like you stipulated. It isn't for pleasure."

"If you insist. We have a meeting at five this afternoon, then dinner. Be ready at four." With that, he turned, leaving Tegan feeling completely wound up.

"Blah, blah, blah." She hissed in the air. *Be ready at four. He didn't even blink an eyelid, twitch a muscle, not anything. Men, huh, they have the fine ability to restrain from any emotion whenever it suited them.*

What about lunch? It was almost twelve. After a quick shower and change, food was the only thing on her mind.

Walking toward a coffee shop on the corner, the river came in to view. The exotic atmosphere washed away the previous tension, which had mounted on such a strange and difficult day. She could finally feel her limbs relaxing.

After ordering a coffee and a toasted Turkish sandwich, she made her way outdoors toward the chairs and tables lining the balcony. The scent of salt air drifted on a breeze. It was a perfect, cloudless day. Resting back in the chair, she crossed one ankle over the other moments before the waiter delivered the order.

"Excuse me, could you tell me the way to the main street?" A man in his twenties stood before her.

"Horton Street—just up around the block and you're there."

"Thank you. Do you mind if I take a rest on the spare seat beside you?"

"No, not at all." Her brain sung. If only I was twenty again. His Italian accent was divine, as well as his striking olive complexion and alluring dark-set eyes.

"You're lucky to live in such a wonderful place. It is so...what would one say, so exotic."

"Oh no, you're mistaken. I don't live here. We're staying at the Ridges. I'm from Newcastle, although I used to live here for many years."

"You gave this up for the city?"

"I guess you could say that." But she hadn't given it up. She'd run and as fast as she could.

"My name is Martino."

"Mine's Tegan."

Mathew's voice from behind jolted her upright in her seat.

"I have combed the entire shopping area of Port Macquarie

looking for you."

When she turned, the concern she heard softened and he shot her a smile. He wore a pair of fawn shorts and a blue open collar shirt. He did look the picture of sex on legs, very muscular ones at that. It didn't change the fact they all ended up as damn loony cases, as far as she was concerned. She sucked back a breath. *Hell, who was she trying to kid?* "Mathew, I would like you to meet Martino. He wanted directions."

Mathew produced his hand and Martino stood, exchanging a firm handshake.

"I'm so sorry to intrude on you and your wife."

"Martino, he isn't my..."

"Nice to meet you Martino. Are you on a holiday?"

"No, no, business. I'm a little lost but your wife was very helpful in providing directions. It's good to find someone who lives here." He smiled. "Or used to live here. What is it that they say, once a local always a local? I should be going. Have a nice time."

"Nice to meet you too." She watched him walk away while Mathew took a seat beside her.

"He seems a nice person."

"I don't need you to look out for me. I can take care of myself."

He shot her a quizzical look. "Hang on a minute. I was concerned and wondered where you'd got to." He drew the chair closer.

"So, you thought if I wasn't on call the very minute you summoned me, you'd come looking and make certain I was."

"Tegan," his voice lowered as his gaze narrowed.

"You said four o'clock. It's only three." She pointed her petite nose upwards.

He propped an elbow on the table and leaned forward. "I thought you were a stranger to this town and maybe lost. I had no idea you used to live up this way."

"I used to live here for some time. I moved to Newcastle around six and a half years ago."

He rubbed his chin. "That's a coincidence. Pete used to live up this way."

Her heart pounded as she thought of the brother he'd lost.

"You say you left six and a half years ago. Pete died six years ago." His gaze was despondent as though he was recalling a painful past. Guilt shadowed his eyes.

"I'm sorry. It's obvious you and Peter were very close. Was he the youngest?"

"Yes, two years younger. We had so much fun as kids—doing boy stuff, climbing trees, cubby houses. My parents weren't around much and I sort of looked after him. He also looked up to me, his big brother. You could almost say we were twins.

"I didn't look after him as much as my parents expected. He climbed a tree once and broke his arm. They blamed it on me and said I'd failed him. I guess you can say I failed them as well."

"Heavens. I don't think it would have been your fault. You were young yourself. How old was he when it happened?"

"I think he was six—the same age as your son."

Tegan tossed a laugh into the air. "I don't think an eight-year-old should have been given the responsibility of looking after a six-year-old child. I wouldn't blame you. Accidents do happen."

"Yeah. An accident I could have prevented. I could never look after him properly. It's been a hell of a time during the last six years since his death. Even when he moved from Sydney, I believe he led a quiet life. He never spoke about his personal affairs and I never asked. We didn't keep in contact that much."

Her ex-husband Peter, would be thirty-seven—the same age as his brother. That is, if his brother were still alive.

"I don't know what to say. You seem to have dealt with your grief and you've gotten on with your life remarkably well."

"I'm not sure I have." He looked away, his jaw line squared. "I suppose you realize I was engaged for the last two years?"

"Um, yes. I heard a little."

Turning back, he continued. "Helen wasn't the right woman for me. In the beginning I thought there might be a spark, something to hold us together. As I got to know her, well...everything changed. I like a woman to be a little natural. She was fake from the inside out. Helen was hurt but I couldn't continue in a loveless relationship. Her only concerns were marrying into money—anyone's money if she could get her hands on it. Sorry, I didn't mean to burden you."

"It's okay. I'm sorry you had to go through so much before you found out what she was really like."

"I should have seen it coming. Anyhow...can you recall meeting Pete, or perhaps you've heard of him?"

"No. I don't ever recall meeting your brother. There are so many Peters in this world." She drew in a breath. "I think I should get ready...are you sure you're okay?"

"Yes, thanks for listening."

"That's okay. What time did you say dinner was?"

had been amazing as well and look how that turned out! Painful and disastrous. First kisses were never an indication of how a relationship could change, how a man could change. Mathew may be a good kisser but she wasn't interested in journeying down that path again. Not now, not ever.

"That shouldn't have happened."

"What? The kiss or the photograph?"

"I meant the kiss. Why did you kiss me?" She coughed to clear her throat.

"I guess I acted out of line, for that I'm sorry. I thought you wanted me to kiss you. You could have said 'no'."

Tegan grated her teeth together, knowing he was right. She hadn't refused his touch, couldn't refuse.

"Let's forget it."

Mathew's brows rose. "Why are you here so late?"

"I had to finish a few letters."

"You shouldn't have stayed back. Anyone could have walked into the building. I noticed it wasn't locked. Don't you realize that it's dangerous, too dangerous for a woman to be alone in the heart of Newcastle at night."

He found himself wanting to kiss those cute bow lips again, wanting to take away the pain he saw hanging like a damn nightmare in those eyes. But it wasn't only pain he witnessed. A haunting curtain draped behind that pain, hiding so much. He couldn't figure out what. Then again, he couldn't figure out any woman for that matter.

"I'm sorry. It's just I—"

"Don't be; it's not your fault. I should be more careful."

"I'm concerned."

"Concerned...concerned about what?"

"Every time I look into your eyes, shadows of your past stand out as though you've been through so much heartache, so much pain. It's not concealed as well as you imagine."

Tegan's eyes misted. "It's none of your business, none at all." She knew he was much too close to the truth—too close for her liking. "Mathew, Mister King, whatever. You're stepping where you don't belong." Her gaze flicked with uncertainty around the office before taking the few awkward steps to her desk and sitting on the chair.

"I'm concerned. Is there any harm in being concerned for someone, for you? It's a natural trait one would say."

Tegan looked at the desk, her legs crossed at the knees, arms

"Five o'clock. We're having drinks in the bar at four."

"In that case I'll meet you in the bar."

"No. That isn't how I do things. I'll be waiting for you beside your door at exactly four."

"See you shortly then." She gave him a quirky smile before walking away.

He watched the way she moved. Too damn elegant, too damn sexy and the way her butt twitched, *hell*. The essence of his manhood couldn't take it much longer.

Chapter Six

Tegan swung the door open. Her gaze drifted over dark, satiny eyebrows that hooded deep blue eyes. A smile curved his mouth.

"Ready?"

Doing a brief intake of his blue suit, light blue shirt, and sapphire tie against his olive complexion—he was stunning. But she wasn't going to let him think for one moment she thought so. Her brain cells were slowly sifting through sand, dissolving any reasonable judgment she held.

"You look lovely," he murmured.

"I don't see a black business suit any lovelier than what I wear to work each day."

"What you wear to work each day is...well..." His sentence trailed.

Surprise washed over her, knowing he actually remembered what she wore to work.

"Shall we?" He put out his hand.

Without thinking she placed her hand in his. The feel of his fingers trickling over her skin forced her breath to catch in her throat. Heat not only saturated the space between them, his touch burnt. A pooling of warmth seeped to her belly.

He glanced down to meet a delirious gaze before a lopsided grin rode over his face.

"What's so funny?"

"Nothing. I was thinking what a lucky man I am."

Moments lapsed. "What do you mean, lucky?"

"To have you as my secretary."

"Oh."

Talk about feeling spoiled. Is this what she'd been missing? Going to one of the finest restaurants in town, wining and dining- to actually have a life.

Hang on a minute, it wasn't a date. There wasn't going to be any wining and dining as far as she was concerned. She took another glance at his face and realized what type of man he was. A very nervous belly filled with flutters. Was this the first sign of falling in love?

"Well?"

The feel and texture of his masculine fingers stroking the back of her hand, instigated a wave of dizziness to ribbon through her. Sucking in a calming breath, but finding it hard to ignore the burning intensity, she found concentrating on anything else impossible.

"Let's go."

They walked to the door and took the lift downstairs.

The restaurant was lit up with the remaining frayed edges of sunlight as it filtered through the glass doors.

Mathew's aftershave drowned her with succulent persimmons and lush green notes, forcing a wave of delight to scamper through her sending her off balance. Secretly the moment was very enjoyable.

They approached two Japanese men sitting at the bar. His hand broke contact.

At least being in the company of others was a temporary floatation device. How long would she be able to keep her head above water? She didn't believe in office romances, didn't believe in dating coworkers...*hell*, her chest tightened. Mathew was her boss and accepting his kisses might have instigated the beginnings of something she wasn't prepared to take on.

Fear escalated. If only she could get past the fear of being with someone, of falling head over heels for a male, of being trapped and not having a way out. She bit on her lip and swallowed, remembering how crazy love was. Remembering what love allowed in a relationship, how it blinds a person, and how it can totally obliterate a woman's soul. Her father and Sally told her repeatedly not all relationships ended up like the one she had with Peter. But it didn't discard the terrifying feelings that were so vivid in her mind every single day.

She focused on the man in front of her. She sucked in a composing breath and stiffened her spine. Business, yes, this is only business. The way she was going to keep it and the way it would remain.

"Good to see you." Mathew shook hands with the men. "This is my secretary, Tegan Ryan. Tegan, this is Yasashika."

"Good evening, *Hajimemashite*."

"*Komban-wa*," Tegan smiled at the older man, noticing he had gentle eyes and was very polite.

Mathew jerked his head up in stunned surprise.

"*Ogenki Deska*." Tegan exchanged handshakes.

"You know the language of Japan," Yasashika inquired.

"Yes, just a little. It was one of the subjects I undertook at university. I do remember some of what I learned but not all." A polite smile eased to her lips.

"This is Yakia, his son. We met a few years ago in Sydney. Yakia and his father are well-acquainted with my father. How about a round of drinks? What would you like Tegan?"

"A white wine. Thank you."

While Mathew ordered the drinks, Tegan popped herself on a bar stool next to Yakia.

"Are you here visiting Australia or do you live in Japan?"

"We spend most of our time travelling lately." Yakia replied. "Although in my early years, Dad and Mum lived in Sydney. I was born here. I'm an Australian Japanese. Dad insisted I spend my time at Sydney University." He let out a chuckle.

"I've never left Australia. I have a fear of flying." A warm rush filled her cheeks.

"You must conquer your fears."

"I'm trying to, believe me." A curve rose to her lips thinking of the plane flight. With Mathew's help, she was beginning to conquer the fear of flying. She hoped it would be as easy with the rest of her fears. *Please make them go away. Please.*

"How long have you been working for Mathew?" Yakia asked.

Mathew turned to notice the relaxed attitude Tegan portrayed as laughter erupted from her sensual mouth. He ground his teeth noticing Yakia was being more than just polite. Yakia's hand swept to Tegan's face, capturing a stray piece of hair and moving it from her eye.

"Here you go, one white wine. Yakia your beer and Yasashika, your scotch."

"Arigatou."

"Yakia was telling me about your episode in Sydney when they first meet you and a lady who stormed into your office."

"That was a big misunderstanding and she certainly was not a lady!" Mathew's voice was graveled.

"I remember when she sat on Dad's lap. It scared the hell out of him." Yakia laughed. "What was her name? It was like the lady of Troy. What was it, that's right Helen? Was that her name?" Yakia jested.

Tegan was intrigued. Was it the same woman who'd stormed into the office on Mathew's first day at Coleman Enterprises?

"I can't remember too much. It was a few years ago. How about we find our table, time's getting on?"

Tegan carried her glass of wine to a white linen draped table. Mathew made certain she sat beside him, opposite Yakia and Yasashika.

* * * *

"What do you think of the details I sent you?"

"It is all very promising. After some consideration, we've agreed to use Coleman Enterprises. It has an extremely good reputation."

"All settled. Thank you, Yasashika. Cheers and a long life." Mathew raised his glass to toast the deal.

Tegan glanced at her watch once more. They'd been in deep conversation for almost an hour and she'd said very little. They spoke mainly about King Enterprises. She finished the meal of seafood and the last of the herb bread. As she was about to stand, Yakia looked her way.

"Would you care for a walk to get some fresh air? It must be boring for you?"

"Yes, thank you." *Hallelujah. Someone finally noticed.* But not Mathew, he was too engrossed. All he spoke about was King Enterprises and the many smaller companies they'd bought at a cutthroat price.

"We're taking a short walk, the night is so beautiful." Yakia announced placing his hand around Tegan's waist.

Mathew caught the action out of the corner of his eye and the reflection on his heart surprised him. He studied them closely until they disappeared.

* * * *

Tegan drew in the sultry air. "It's a lovely night."

"I want to tell you something," Yakia said.

"Yes?"

"I am very attracted to you."

Surprise jolted her. "That's nice. I'm very flattered. I'm not really interested in a relationship at this time."

"Why not? You are very beautiful."

"I've just met you and..."

"Sorry, I knew it was silly of me to mention the subject. I see Mathew has eyes for you. He hasn't claimed you as yet, which I think is sad."

She giggled and swung a petite nose into the air. "You have that wrong. We're business associates."

"No, no, I see you too. You have eyes for him. The green sparkles like a special jewel, coated with passion."

Tegan shook her head. "No, I don't think so. You have it wrong."

"I see you two are getting to know each other."

Tegan heard Mathew's voice from behind and swung around. "Yes, we are."

"Your father said to say good night to both of you. He's worn out."

"I think I should be leaving too." Yakia shook hands with Mathew and turned toward Tegan. He brought her hand to his lips.

"Arigatou, komban-wa." Holding her hand for a time, he kissed it softly.

"Komban-wa, gomen." Tegan watched him walk away feeling touched by his words.

"What was that all about?"

"Your attitude isn't called for."

"Hey, you're the one who took a fancy to the man."

"I beg your pardon. You hardly included me in the conversation. As soon as Coleman Enterprises was dealt with you launched into everything about King Enterprises."

"There was no need to. We sealed the deal earlier in the night. When I spoke to Yakia and Yasashika on the phone, they hadn't made up their mind. I gathered a lot of persuading was to come but it wasn't necessary."

Her hand swiped the side of her skirt as she took one-step aside and started to walk off.

Mathew's hand reached out. "Where are you going?"

"To get another drink. I think I need one."

"Let me get it for you."

The sudden contact of his hand was a pleasant surprise as frissons of warmth hurtled up her arm, spearing right to her heart.

"Let me guess, another wine."

"No, an orgasm."

His gaze flicked in astonishment. "A what?"

"You heard me, I said an orgasm. The drink, a cocktail."

"In that case we'd better have two."

The grin sliding over Tegan's' face wasn't supposed to be there. Matthew ordering an orgasm?

Sitting at the bar, a smirk rose to his lips when he placed the order.

"Did you honestly think I was interested in Yakia? I only wanted a little fresh air and he did also."

The waiter placed two cocktails on the bar.

"I'm sorry...well, I hope they're good. Fancy little things aren't they?"

She shot him a glance. He stirred his drink with the straw and discarded it before taking a swallow.

"Not bad. Not bad at all." The real thing would be much better. However, he knew he was definitely a long way from that.

She stirred her drink with the straw in an anti-clockwise direction. "I'm glad you like me...I mean it."

Her words faltered and he remembered she'd consumed one entire bottle of white wine at the table, and a glass beforehand, now this. His brows knitted.

"Something wrong?" She took a sip, her lips lingered over the straw.

"I was recalling the alcohol you've devoured. You've had quite a bit you know."

"What's called quite a bit, your calculations or mine? When someone drinks too much, I figure it's by the way sex...I mean love...hell, forget it."

His dark brows rose and a playful grin eased to his lips.

"Don't you think I can walk straight? Just wait and see."

"Yes let's." He continued to drink his cocktail until the glass was empty. Spinning around on the bar stool, he noticed the restaurant was much quieter now. Only a few couples occupied chairs in a far corner.

"Would you like to take a walk?"

"Why not."

As she drew in the fresh air, it was like a drug. Her head spun, she stumbled and fell into strong, accommodating arms. Mathew steadied his balance.

A warm wave of dizziness hit her at full blast. Her legs, were they still anchored to her torso?

"I think we should give the fresh air a miss tonight. Come on, let's head back."

When he took her by the hand, his warmth penetrated and it didn't stop until they arrived by his door.

She floated into his suite, realizing rules could be broken. The sparking of sensations, alive and vibrant overrode all possible objections. Even the alluring tone of his voice cornered her heart with a compelling attraction she couldn't push aside. This man had the ability to change her mind in a second and change her thought process by instigating what she didn't want.

She stopped and pivoted on one foot only to stumble once again. His hand flew out grabbing her arm, and before she had time to adjust her balance, his lips met hers swamping her with fevered passion. Her heartbeat accelerated and she molded against him.

A murmur escaped her lips. His hand curled around her palm and he broke the kiss before moving back a little. Her gaze didn't leave the liquid blue in his eyes. What she saw captivated every cell she possessed. It was then she felt drugged beyond return. It was a delirious possession with no way out and she didn't mind one bit.

"Are you sure you want to continue?" his husky voice prompted.

His words induced a small flicker of fear. But as her need grew, the fear lessened. After such a long time of never experiencing a male's touch, of not having warmth curling around her body at night, she gave in to what was natural—to a craving. That craving was Mathew King.

"Yes!"

Their lips joined in a desperate, hot passion. When he broke free she realized she stood naked in front of him. His hands explored the concave of her back before he guided her toward the bed, easing her down and propping himself beside her.

Large hands tripped over bare flesh, wandering with a tenderness she hadn't expected. They tumbled over sheets, twisting and turning in unison.

Nothing mattered anymore except what was happening at that very moment. Her eyes closed, shutting off the outside world as their bodies entwined and joined with intense need, delivering what they both craved, what they both deserved—each other.

He let out a groan. She felt his desire intensify, matching her own, until they lay coiled in each other's arms, exhausted, satisfied, and uncertain. Her fingers crept over his chest as she languished in his deadly poison, in the warmth of his body, only now to realize she'd become just as fatal.

They drifted to sleep.

* * * *

Consciousness trickled through a fog of dreams, of murmurs, moans, a recollection of bodies entwined. Was his passion really a deadly poison? She'd not only slept with her boss, she'd fallen asleep in his arms.

"Oh, no." It wasn't meant to escape her lips.

"What is it? Are you okay?" He turned, propping himself up on his elbow, noticing the strange way she clutched to the sheet in an attempt to conceal her nakedness, or so he thought.

She scrambled to a sitting position dragging the sheet as she went. Guilt tore to the surface. *I had sex with my boss.* All lingering thoughts of passion, of hanging in limbo, disappeared leaving mounting questions. Was this the real reason he'd asked her to accompany him to Port Macquarie?

Grappling in the soft light for her clothing, she dressed in haste.

Mathew sat upright. Through the dim light he studied every move she made. "Are you leaving?"

"Yes." She turned. "You said we had an early start, breakfast at six."

"Slow down. There's more to it than that."

"No. Not really." She scrambled from the bed pulling her skirt down.

"It's well past midnight and I really do need some sleep."

"What was wrong with the bed you were already sleeping in?"

She took a quick glance at the crumpled sheets beside him. "I...well, I like to sleep alone." She lied and drew in a deep breath, hoping to squash any unease.

She didn't want him to see her scars—scars which haunted her every day. A vivid reminder of how abusive Peter had been. In the morning the room would be a lot lighter and he'd surely notice them. That was something she didn't want to risk.

"See you in the morning." Picking up her bag, she vanished.

For a moment, he could have sworn he was dreaming, but he wasn't. She'd definitely gone. He lay awake for hours, thinking of reason after reason why she'd left. He recalled their lovemaking almost every minute. Everything about Tegan tightened his heart. Had he finally found the right woman?

Deep in his gut, he knew they'd made love, and he wanted to repeat it for the rest of his life. He desperately wanted that love returned. It was more than desperation—it was a driving need that arose from somewhere inside. A need he wasn't aware of earlier. He hadn't wanted anyone so bad in his life and he wasn't about to stop until he claimed her as his own.

He recalled picking her up earlier in the morning. She was

different. Jittery, anxious, and hell he couldn't get a handle on what she was thinking, or hiding. *Damn it.* He was sure there was more to it than the fear of flying that caused such strange actions. He cursed once more under his breath, remembering her statement of not mixing pleasure with business. The truth was she already had. A contented grin edged to his lips.

When the buzzer hooted its morning wake up call, he had no recollection of being asleep at all. He forced his eyes to open.

Lying motionless, he thought of the many ways to win Tegan's love. Then he remembered breakfast at six. He sprang from his bed and into the shower in no time.

* * * *

Tegan was wandering around the restaurant when Mathew approached the entrance. He rested silently on the edge of the architrave, infatuated. She certainly was a woman with a strong will. He loved everything about her. She was the perfect package. However, he'd have to get to the bottom of whatever it was that sent her into orbit every so often. Find out what was going on inside her mind. Why she acted so fearful. He wanted to help her, look after her, and make sure she was safe. He'd fallen in love. Reality bit him and surprise washed over him. He grinned.

She turned, facing him with a smile that could crush anyone's logic. His heart rate went up. Closing the space, an uncomfortable quietness hovered between them. Their gaze locked.

"Morning." His voice was a husky purr.

"Morning."

"Sleep well?"

"Yes." She lied.

"You?"

"Yes." He lied.

"Breakfast," he inquired, continuing in a husky purr. "Follow me." He placed his hand around her palm.

* * * *

The haziness of the night before and the early morning wake-up call gradually cleared Tegan's mind after her second cup of coffee. "I spoke to my son again this morning. He seems to be doing well."

"So early. Is he usually up this early?"

"Yes, always. I ring him morning, midday and night."

Mathew raised his eyebrows. "How old did you say he was?"

"Six. He's generally a good child."

"He must take after his father."

"I wish I could say 'yes', but the answer is 'no'. He may have his father's eyes but that's about all. Thankfully not his temperament either. He's a very intelligent child."

"Sorry, I didn't mean to intrude into bad memories."

"That's okay. I guess there were good memories...once." She smiled, filling him with so much warmth he nearly choked on his bacon.

"Does a relative look after him when you're not around?"

"No a baby sitter. Robert only has me and his grandfather." Unease dug deep, reminding her of the possibilities. She needed to find answers.

He wondered why she'd changed her name and why there was never mention about Stan being her father. At least he had both parents but one day they'd be gone. He decided to play along with it. As he promised Stan, he wouldn't say a word.

Whatever she hid was obviously something upsetting and very important to have remained that way.

"No relatives except for your father. That must be tough."

"Yes, at times it has been but we get by. Ever since Mum left when I was eight, Dad tried his best. Also I wasn't aware I was pregnant when I left Robert's father. Dad insisted I contact him, saying it was the right thing to do. I only wanted him to know he was a father. Nothing more...there was relief though when I found out his mobile was disconnected. And...well, he had no living relatives." She was about to add, 'that's what he told me anyhow'...but swallowed it down before it had a chance to escape.

"I'm sorry, Tegan."

"It's not your fault that Peter was a son of a bitch." She cupped her mouth in the hope of concealing her words but wasn't successful. "That didn't mean to pop out."

His eyebrows coolly arched, and his forehead rippled in lines. "What is it you're hiding?"

"I'm not hiding anything...well." She drew in a much-needed breath. "Peter Knight...was a man with no relatives and a bad temper, especially worse when he was intoxicated."

"I recall you saying a bit about the relationship."

"Yes...I had the bruised cheeks to prove it. I was out of there so fast no one could stop me. That was before I had Robert."

Telling him about the ugly scars would be far more humiliating than letting him know about Peter. Finding them unbearable herself, how could she expect someone else to stand even a glimpse? What would he think of such a horrid disfigurement? It was shameful enough letting him know about Peter. He may even think she was to blame. That's what Peter had said. It was always her fault.

Not knowing what she'd done wrong was frustrating enough but not knowing much about relationships or men, she'd accepted the blame for her predicament.

"He hit you...while...you were pregnant?"

"I didn't know I was pregnant at the time, but yes."

Mathew's stomach churned and anger rose. "No one would ever call him a man then...hell Tegan, I'm so sorry."

"Don't be. It was a long time ago."

"So, you had your child alone?"

"One could say that. I had the doctor and a lovely nurse."

Regret rolled around in Mathew's gut. Regret that he hadn't known her earlier as he may have been able to prevent what she'd suffered. "Does he live here, in Port Macquarie?"

"Yes, as far as I know."

He felt like taking the man out. Felt like finding the woman beater and giving him a taste of what it was like. His fists clenched, his heart pounded against metal or so he thought. The muscles in his face tightened and red heat dispersed, filling him with anger.

"It's okay. Robert and I are fine. It's been more than six years. Time heals." She lied of course. During the last six and a half years, nothing had healed. The scars felt so fresh. That was something which would always remain with her. They'd never go away. They were always a reminder of how life can suddenly change.

"You're a very remarkable woman."

"Thank you." She placed one leg over the other before flicking her gaze to his which prompted memories of the previous night.

"Tegan Ryan."

She turned and noticed a tanned, sandy-headed man strut toward them. "Dave, Dave McMahon."

"I thought it was you...don't you look gorgeous? I knew you wouldn't last too long in the big smog."

"I'm here on business. How have you been?"

"Good, real good. Thanks...you?"

"Well, thanks. Are you still into diving?"

"Yeah. Donna and I are always sneaking off on some adventure here or there...what have you been up to, Teeg?"

"Besides having a six-year-old child, not a great deal. You do know Peter and I broke up a long time ago, don't you?"

"Yes...I did hear."

"Oh, sorry. Dave, this is Mathew King."

Dave turned and shook Mathew's hand. "Good to meet you."

"Would you like to join us?" Mathew said.

"Yeah, thanks." Dave slipped into the vacant chair beside Tegan.

"You remind me of someone. Dave rubbed his chin. "Hang on, I know. Peter Knight."

Tegan's stomach fell through a trap door, snagging on the wooden splinters on the way. Apparently she wasn't the only one to notice the uncanny resemblance. She held an indrawn breath.

"Don't you think so, Teeg? I could have sworn Mathew and Peter were brothers."

"That's strange," she said, as she let go of her breath. "I was telling Mathew, that Peter's name is Knight, not King. So, any relationship is completely out of the question. Peter has no living relatives." A nervous giggle struggled up her throat.

Mathew jerked upright in his seat. "I said my brother lived up this way before he died. Could it be possible?"

Strange waves of fear mounted inside of her. "I don't think so. It'd be a miracle if he were. Besides having no living relatives... well, that speaks for itself doesn't it?"

"I suppose you're right." Mathew rubbed his chin.

"I should get going." Dave said. "Nice meeting you Mathew. Look after Tegan. She's one hell of a special lady." He stood bending over the table to shake Mathew's hand.

After kissing Tegan on the cheek, he left.

"It does seem strange though doesn't it? He thought I looked like your ex-husband."

"He...he only met Peter once. It's unlikely he remembers him that well." Anxiety fed her words. "I...really don't think you look that much alike. Besides, many people look similar and aren't related. Eye color does not belong specifically to a handful of people."

Mathew took a mouthful of coffee. "It's a family characteristic. My father's eyes are the deepest blue ever, as was his father's." He shrugged. "I guess you're right; it isn't possible. We have different last names and you did say Peter Knight has no living relatives."

Tegan's nervous system ignited with fear. It took sometime

before they settled.

"I got a call this morning. Yakia and his father Yasashika had to leave unexpectedly."

"I hope it's nothing too serious."

"Yakia's mother took ill. They sent their apologies and will be returning to Newcastle later on in the year."

"She is all right isn't she?"

"It was a stroke but she's stable. The Cessna is having a service today, so here we are stranded together in paradise."

Tegan rubbed her lips together. "Para...dise."

"Don't you think we should make the most of it?"

"I guess so."

"We can leave early tomorrow morning. Today, I was thinking of something along the lines of spending it together."

She shook her head acknowledging 'yes'.

* * * *

Warm, humid air filled the atmosphere as they took a stroll up along the Hastings River, past tall date palms, and along the break wall toward the ocean. On one side, vibrant color consisting of inscriptions and local artwork decorated large boulders. By the time they reached the end of the break wall, they chatted with strangers and watched surfers riding waves meters away.

Tegan sat and dangled her legs over the edge of a boulder. Mathew copied her movement and edged closer.

"You'd like my parents."

Her curious gaze locked with his.

Slipping an arm around her waist, his fingers tightened. His touch transmitted an overwhelming comfort. She wished their meeting could have been in some other way, some other lifetime, another situation.

Loving a male again would be difficult and learning to trust would be almost impossible.

Chapter Seven

Bodies tangled, heated passion, the contact of Mathew's touch swirled in Tegan's mind as she drove to work. It was the first time a male had stepped in on her personal space in years. Well, she might have instigated it a little but now it left a craving like no other.

Was she falling in love? If so, there was no cut-off switch. She'd gone along, thinking she could switch off whenever it suited. Trying to find that switch was completely out of the question. It had suddenly vanished.

She couldn't afford to fall in love, wouldn't allow a feeling like that in her life—not with the pestering thoughts her mind fabricated. They weren't rational. Sleep was constantly disturbed with dreams. Naturally, Mathew stood in the very center of each one. Even her appetite had diminished. She'd skipped tea late last night and this morning breakfast wouldn't sit comfortable in her stomach. She was falling apart.

Sally helped move the desk and they placed it a little further back from Mathew's, giving her some satisfaction. The filing cabinet, made of heavy metal would be difficult to move. She'd have to leave it to a strong male. Surely the office had a few hanging around.

"You're very quiet about the weekend. How did it go Teeg? Don't keep me in suspense."

"All right I suppose, except the clients had to leave on the Saturday. There was an emergency."

Sally's eyebrows shot up after placing some files on the desk. "So, did Mister Plumb in De mouth keep you occupied?"

Tegan grinned. "We sort of fell into bed."

"You what? Tegan you slept with the boss." A giggle escaped her lips.

"Hmm, I guess you could say that but not for the entire night. I did leave early in the morning."

"Told you he had eyes for you."

"It happened so fast, I didn't exactly plan it. The entire weekend wasn't what I thought it'd be."

"Have you ever thought he planned it?"

"No...I really don't think he did...at least I don't want to believe he did. I feel bad enough as it is."

"Face up to it, you haven't been with a man for such a long time and you're a grown woman. Why feel guilty?"

"I know. Let's not talk about it, not just now, okay?"

"All right, but it's nothing to be ashamed of. You know where I am if you need me," she called, just before passing through the doorway.

Tegan reconnected the computer and printer and organized her desk. Mathew hadn't been in that morning so she'd whisked down the corridor into Sally's office.

Filling in quite a few hours and sitting with Sally over lunch, she returned to the office, trying to keep occupied.

"Didn't you like the way I had it?"

The voice startled her and she glanced up. Mathew leaned on the architrave, his gaze piercing.

"No, I prefer it this way. That is, if you don't mind."

He walked toward his desk, slipped his suit jacket off, loosened his tie, and slid into his chair.

"I can't see what you're up to from here."

"I can always tell you," she stated primly, pretending to organize her desk.

"Mathew, the weekend...I didn't... It was a mistake. I'm not..."

"So, now you're apologizing to me because you feel guilty for jumping in my bed."

"I did not jump, thank you!"

"You leapt then. I didn't force you. It was your decision, entirely yours."

"You took advantage of me while intoxicated." Her defenses were up, knowing damn well she wasn't intoxicated.

"Advantage? You weren't drunk. You managed to tempt me somewhat. I even asked you to reconsider. There was no denial at all. Now if that isn't an invitation, hell, what is?"

Crimson heat rode to her cheeks, not knowing or remembering anything about him asking to reconsider. There were gaps in her memory and she couldn't come out and ask him what exactly happened. Talk about feeling mortified and knowing the subject wasn't getting anywhere. Her unsteady gaze rested on his.

"Let's forget it, okay? It's something that shouldn't have happened and that's it."

"Why are you doing this? Why are you being so stubborn in refusing to believe that you care about me, about us?"

"I shouldn't have slept with you. It shouldn't have happened."

"But it did happen, Tegan. We can't pretend otherwise."

"Change the subject."

"Have it your way. How's Robert?"

At the mere mention of Robert's name, a fine splinter of caution shot through her heart.

"Fine." Tegan gazed at a blank screen. "Fine thanks."

"You are a woman of little words this morning."

"I don't indulge in idle conversation, especially during working hours," she stammered.

"When we're finished here, how about a nice relaxing meal tonight?"

"I...I can't. I promised Robert I would spend the night with him making popcorn." For long seconds she imagined sitting with him over a soft candle-lit dinner, looking into each other's eyes, experiencing his touch, and feeling his toned body under her fingertips.

"Popcorn sounds interesting, perhaps some other time then. You must love your son a great deal. Don't you find him time consuming?"

"Time consuming. That really takes the cake." She shot him a heated glare. "Robert is my responsibility. I chose to have him and I choose to do whatever it takes to be a good mother." Her words were caustic. She couldn't understand someone not having or knowing, the slightest bit about children or the depth of a mother's love.

His eyebrows rose. Her fascinating personality was electrifying. If he didn't watch himself he'd be strung out, almost electrocuted. Then again, he'd already taken many sparks, what did it matter? Anything from Tegan Ryan he'd be grateful for, after all, he was in love.

There was one thing he learned. Robert was her pride and joy, her life was this child. A twinge of guilt twisted in his gut. He'd failed his brother; how could he possibly succeed in fatherhood? His father had drilled into him for years how important the bloodline in a family was and to carry on the King name. He'd never met the right woman to have a child, anyway he was it. The only person who could carry on the bloodline of the King generation and that seemed very unlikely. He'd failed his parents as well. Knowing Tegan loved kids, it was likely she wanted more, and that was something he couldn't deliver. He wasn't about to risk failing again.

He looked up. "Before I forget, I'd like to change the letter to Mister Abrahams, the one about the meeting next week."

Tegan nodded. She turned toward her computer and switched it on.

Nothing.

After checking all the leads, everything was in place. What had she done? Pressing the button once more registered a blank screen. There were no lights, nothing. It was dead.

"Is everything all right?"

"I think so."

Mathew's brows drew closer together. "Are you sure?" he questioned, only to watch her disappear underneath the desk.

Standing, he walked toward her noticing she was tangled in a jumble of wires.

"Tegan."

"I...well...it isn't working," she stammered.

"Let me have a look. It's too dangerous for you to be messing around down there."

"Too dangerous. You've got to be kidding. Maybe for you perhaps, not me."

As he crouched, his shoulder brushed against hers transmitting an even deeper dilemma.

His eyes narrowed. "You're shaking."

"It's...it's cold in here." What else could she say, tell him he was responsible for sending zaps the full length of her body, tell him he was responsible for her out-of-character attitude that really sucked sometimes? One moment control was in place, the next her emotions were so extreme she wondered what he really thought about her. However, she could guess and she didn't want to hear how much of a fruitcake she'd been lately, especially coming from him.

"Get them to turn down the air conditioner. Now what did you do?"

"Nothing. I hooked it up."

"Great, that's all we need. We have so much work to get through and now this. Don't you realize you can't pull out all the cords if you don't know a damn thing about it."

Beads of dampness trickled over his brow. She scrambled out from under the desk.

Mathew checked to see if all the cords were plugged in securely before standing, only to stare at Tegan. He felt like a real heel. "I'm sorry. I didn't mean to sound so annoyed. Could you call a technician please? We have to have this up and running as soon as possible."

It took three hours to get the computer working efficiently. She had to stay back and catch up with her work. Mathew decided to stay back with the excuse he hadn't read the latest letters.

By the time she left the office, her nerves were hijacked, seized beyond repair. What sanity she had left was dissolving. Remaining sane seemed so far off. She slid into her car and glared through the windscreen.

Darkness was well on its way and she thought of Robert. Being lucky to have Clare picking him up from school each day was a blessing. Sometimes she'd prepare an evening meal for them and at least three times a week Clare would stay to enjoy the meal. Tonight, the thought of relaxing with Robert in front of the television and becoming a lounge lizard, eating popcorn made her smile.

When she approached the front door, the television blared from the lounge room.

"Well, how's it going with the new boss?" Clare questioned, opening the door.

"Not too well. Everything has gone wrong since the day he arrived. I can't believe the chaos he's caused."

"Sounds like you've had a bad week. Robert is fine. Robert, come and say hello to your Mother. He's in the lounge-room."

Tegan kicked off her shoes and left the briefcase beside the door. This weekend she would cast all thoughts of the office, of Mathew, completely aside and enjoy herself.

That was a statement and a half. As soon as her head hit the pillow, all thoughts and dreams were of Mathew. She tossed and turned until finally, in the early hours of the morning sleep came easy.

After spending the best part of the weekend at the beach with Robert, collecting shells, swimming and building the biggest sand castles ever, it left her exhausted. A six-year-old could drain a lot of energy. Either that or the lack of sleep was responsible.

* * * *

Reaching over to turn off the annoying alarm, a stir of nausea crept to her stomach. Dragging herself from the bed then making it to the shower was difficult. Her muscles ached. Her body ached. She ached all over.

After drying herself, which wasn't the best of attempts, she slipped on a fresh nightie and covered it with a jade bathrobe. Knowing she couldn't very well turn up to work in this state, let alone drive, she rang Clare to take Robert to school.

A clammy feeling swept over her, even slipping off the robe in an attempt to cool down failed. Realizing there was little strength to attempt anything she clutched the furniture struggling to get to the sofa.

She was burning up.

The room spun.

Making an earnest attempt to reach for the telephone only to drop against the cushions was pitiful. Moments later, grappling for the cordless phone was a success and she rang the office.

"Sally Wentworth please."

"Hi Sal, Tegan. I have a small problem. I don't feel very well. Nothing serious, just a bug I suppose. Yes Sally, I'll be fine, I just need to rest."

"Tell him I up and died." She breathed. "Tell him I'm not well and I'll be off for a day, maybe two."

It was an exhausting effort. Retreating against the cushions, she closed her eyes with the cordless phone hanging limply in one hand.

* * * *

"A few days!"

"Yes Mister King. Tegan's not well." Sally stood by his office door.

"I need that woman here beside me. She knows everything about this business. Doesn't she realize that I need a hand?" Mathew slumped back in his chair, running his fingers harshly through his hair.

"I only have a mobile number. Could you get me her home number Miss Wentworth and right now?"

Sally mumbled something but he couldn't hear.

Tegan always insisted if she was needed day or night, to give her a ring.

The shrill of the telephone disturbed Tegan's mind.

"Hello, Tegan speaking."

"Tegan."

"Mathew, what can I do for you?"

"If you put it that way I'll be over in a jiffy."

His words unsettled her nerves. "I meant as your secretary. It takes much longer than a jiffy to drive down here."

"I was only joking. Sally told me you were ill and you won't be in today. I need you beside me. I have two rather large meetings today and tomorrow that have to be finalized."

In for the kill she thought, closing her eyes. "Surely someone else can cover for me for a few days."

"That's the problem. Apparently no one can. I have asked around and you're it. It seems everyone concerned values you and your position. I need you here beside me, today."

"If I were well enough, don't you think I'd be at work? I'm entitled to sick leave and honestly, I'm not really up to it." Tegan hadn't realized she'd pushed the button to end the conversation. The room was in constant motion.

* * * *

Mathew gripped the steering wheel of his black Maserati. He tried to determine his exact whereabouts, cursing under his breath for not getting the satellite navigation system repaired.

He was sure he'd missed the turn off as he pulled off the highway. He crunched the gears, came to a sudden halt, then jammed on the handbrake. He rang Sally and spoke for a few moments.

He'd driven south as Sally instructed, passed a large round about then straight down the highway. There was only one turn off, without a sign, leading to nowhere. He figured he was already nowhere and decided to do a U-turn to see what he could find at the other end.

When Sally had told him that morning Tegan would be off sick, it aroused his suspicions. He was sure she was fit and healthy and probably trying to avoid him. She'd looked fine last time he'd seen her. He needed to see her. All weekend his mind tormented him, and God, he loved her like no other. His jaw line squared. She may not be well after all. This thought forced him to jam the accelerator much closer to the floor.When he had to slam to a sudden halt, he cursed under his breath.

Dead end.

Damn. He loosened his tie and slipped off his jacket, then pressed the button to lower the window. He glanced at his watch. He'd been on the road for an hour, Sally had said forty-five minutes at the most. Moments later, he veered the car back on the track, grinding the gears as he went.

In sheer frustration he spun his car back up the track. When he made it to the highway, he swung north, heading towards Newcastle.

"Damn it!"

After driving a few kilometers, he noticed a sign to his right, clearly stating Catherine Hill Bay. Now where had that come from? He was certain it wasn't there earlier. He veered off the highway and took a turn onto a smoothly tarred road that curved through a small, but beautiful rainforest. Tropical palms were anchored on either side of the road, soothing his nerves.

The road opened after a five-minute drive and, scattered on either side, small properties nestled into the valley.

He continued up the winding road until he came to the top of the hill. Jerking his neck around, he couldn't see a house up here at all. Then he saw a driveway to his left, shadowed by tall Cocos palms. Large shrubs came into view. *This had to be it.* He turned into the driveway taking it slow until a heritage style cottage came into view, behind tall, wrought iron gates.

He opened the gates and edged his car toward the house. He couldn't see a car anywhere.

Stepping from his car he walked toward a veranda, which enclosed three sides of the home. A brass doorknocker of a lion's head, stood out prominently in the center of the door. He reached up and rapped at least seven times, waiting for a reply.

* * * *

Tegan woke to the echo of bashing. She tried to yell.

"Come in, it's open."

"Tegan, it's Mathew."

The sound of a masculine voice echoing through the house startled her senses, bringing her back to reality with a swift jolt.

"Holy hell. What is he doing here?"

Turning to the side, the sight of Mathew doubled the crippling wave of nausea swirling in her stomach. She managed to grapple for two cushions and stuff them around the front of her upper arms.

He'd taken the few steps into the lounge-room only to stop suddenly. His gaze rested on her creamy white complexion sprawled out on a sofa. It swept the entire length of her body and then he retraced his steps. His jaw line squared, noticing her pale face surrounded by tousled hair.

"Mathew," she whispered. "What are you doing here?" Her gaze locked with his for a split second. She quickly moved a hand over her nightie, trying to adjust any gaping holes.

"Tegan, I never thought you were this ill. Why didn't you call me personally and inform me?" he questioned, as he knelt beside the sofa.

Perspiration ran over her forehead. Her face looked as pale as fine, white talc.

"You called me back, remember?"

He placed a hand over her forehead. "Hell, you're burning up."

Tegan squirmed.

"This isn't a time to play games. You need a doctor."

"No, no doctor. No."

"Well, at least tell me where the bathroom is so I can get a cool cloth for your forehead"

"Upstairs." It was a faint reply. Her weak gaze watched as he disappeared into the hallway.

Listening to the sound of his footsteps taking the small flight of stairs, it suddenly dawned. It hit with a rush of adrenalin, slamming into her like a ton of bricks. She had to get all the photographs of Robert from view and that included the ones upstairs in the bedroom.

Summoning stored energy, she moved around the room managing to slip six photographs into a cupboard below the entertainment unit.

He could never see the photographs. What if he recognized the resemblance? What if there was a connection? She wasn't going to risk it. Taking a frantic gaze around the room, making sure she hadn't missed a single photograph and progressing with difficulty, her hand clung to the stair rail, as she pulled herself upwards.

Using the wall for support, she closed the bedroom doors then took refuge against the wall to prevent her weak knees from giving way underneath. It worked momentarily.

Heat rose to her face. A circle of stars passed through her mind—exploding in a flash of white, before a faint call registered. Preventing herself from falling was impossible.

Mathew appeared at the end of the hallway. With urgency, his giant strides ate up the distance between them. He caught her with one hand, moments before she fell.

The powerful surge snatched her feet from the floor. She heard his heartbeat pounding in his chest, his breath barely centimeters away.

"No, no, please don't."

"Tegan, I'm going to carry you downstairs. Do you want to go back downstairs?"

"Put me down," she insisted, trying hard to raise her voice but it was only a whimper.

"Tegan, it's Mathew. We're going down to the sofa, maybe bed would be a better place," he stated, glancing at the closed doors beside him.

"Which one's yours?"

"No, I don't want to go to bed."

"Will you shut up and listen to somebody for once! Damn it woman." With the help of the wall beside him, he balanced her on one knee and opened the door closest to him. After a brief inspection of the room, he noted a large brass four-poster bed scattered with cushions, in the middle of the room.

"Well, that looks a lot more comfortable than the sofa," he announced, kicking the door wide open with one foot and then carrying her to the bed. He withdrew the covers and eased her against large, white pillows.

Relief oozed through her the moment his contact disconnected. He didn't seem to notice the two photographs sitting on the bedside chest. She swallowed against a dry raspy throat, knowing the photographs had to go.

"I'll get you a glass of water and then we'll discuss the options."

What options? She thought, as he walked from the room.

He was in no position to talk about options. Reaching for the photographs in an attempt to slip them in the drawer below, his voice echoed much too soon.

"Here."

He approached the bed and she fumbled with one of the photographs until it slipped from her hands and settled on the carpet.

Mathew recognized that panic-stricken look, the one he'd witnessed many times. "You have a habit of dropping things lately, especially photographs." He picked up the discarded photograph and settled the water on the bedside table. He turned the photograph face up. His brows knitted. It was a picture of Tegan and Robert taken at the front of the house.

Tegan's nerves expanded along an emotional current. She gazed in astonishment at his sudden chuckle.

"You know, people could almost mistake him for my son. He has the same eyes, hair and skin coloring. Good looking boy but I can't see any resemblance." He shot her a questioning gaze.

Paralyzed, palms sweating, she watched with disbelief as he placed the photograph back on the bedside table, then he gestured with one hand for the second photograph, positioning them together.

She was so sure he would link the two of them together. But apparently he hadn't. So, what was giving her the heebie jeebies? Why was her mind taking her on a roller coaster ride?

When he took no further interest in the photographs, she finally gave in to the demands of her body and sank back onto the soft cushions.

"Here drink this."

The coolness dampened the fire in her throat, although the annoyance of his hand on the back of her neck incited an even hotter wave to sweep to her belly.

"You need a doctor."

"I'm okay; I'm a bit nauseous and weak. It'll pass."

Without a word, he left. After an in-depth search of the house he finally discovered a telephone anchored on the kitchen wall and punched in the digits.

Mumbling sounds came up the stairs. She couldn't decipher what he was saying. She summoned enough energy to drag her aching body into a sitting position and slid her legs over the edge of the bed.

The white haze drifted into focus when he was only a few meters away. Gone were the furrows in his forehead and the rigid tightening of his facial features. Now a look of concern spread over his face.

Tegan felt the tug of his persistent attraction. Any closer, her body would be in defeat, and the sickness wouldn't be entirely responsible. Wrapping her arms around a trembling body, she dazedly looked upwards.

"You shouldn't be sitting." The tone of his voice softened. "Come on, lie down." The touch of his arm on her skin almost took the breath from her lungs.

"I've called a doctor; he's on his way." He glanced around, saw a cream wicker chair and dragged it beside the bed.

The pull of heavy eyelids eventually won over and sleep came easy.

Mathew rolled the sleeves up on his shirt, ran his fingers through his hair as his gaze traced over an angel's face. *Hell baby, don't get sick on me now. I need you. Don't you realize how much I really need you.* His vision flowed over beautiful, delicate cheeks coming to rest on her cute, bow lips.

The clang of the lion's head disturbed his thoughts.

Chapter Eight

Tegan opened her eyes and gazed around the room until the blur of her focus cleared. Mathew drifted into view. He was gazing through the window.

He sensed her awakening and turned. "Welcome back."

Pushing upwards to a sitting position, she tucked the sheet around the upper part of her arms.

"The doctor has already left."

There was no recollection of anyone else being in the room. "A doctor? I told you I didn't need a doctor," she blurted sleepily.

"He thought it was a good idea. I told him about your raspy voice, your temperature and dizziness, not to mention the nausea. He left antibiotics for you. He said you were run-down and probably had a touch of sunstroke. Another possibility is you've contracted a virus." He walked toward the bed and settled on the edge.

"Rundown, Tegan. Was it because of all the work?"

"What are you talking about?"

"You know what I mean. You stay back, working long hours and then come home to take care of your son. Plus all the housework and whatever else it is you do. The doctor said you needed rest for the entire week."

"How absurd! I don't need that long. Why, after today I'll be on my feet again."

"No you will not!"

A sob caught in her throat. Tears ran down hot cheeks.

"I apologize for being abrupt with you." He knew the sound of his voice had triggered a flow of emotion. "I have a habit of snapping, especially if it has anything to do with someone I care about."

Tegan continued to sob. It wasn't him—well, not really, not just now. Everything was getting the better of her, the partnership, and the fear of losing Robert.

Maybe Peter was his brother. But she couldn't come out and ask, 'are you my husband's brother'? No, she wasn't going to let on about anything, not now. Not until she'd found out more. But perhaps hinting around the subject might give answers.

"I'm sorry to upset you."

A cool cloth glided across her forehead, then over hot cheeks. "You're not well. Crying will only make matters worse."

"I'm sorry, but I have to tell you something. It may not be..."

"Another time, you're not well enough."

* * * *

She stirred, feeling cool sheets against her skin. Her eyelashes fluttered and opened to a darkened room. Apparently Mathew had drawn the blinds. Reaching up to turn on the bedside lamp she glared at the clock—it was two in the afternoon.

Feeling a little better she rolled onto her side, and saw Mathew was asleep in the wicker chair. As she attempted to climb from the bed, his words stopped her midway.

"Oh, no you don't." He rose to his feet. "Doctors orders. You're quite a persistent little woman, aren't you?"

She gasped and slipped back in-between the sheets.

"You look much better," he remarked.

"I feel better, thank you." Her anxious gaze flickered around the room.

"I made you lunch." He turned and withdrew a throw over covered sandwiches and a glass of orange juice. "They've just been made. It's only something light as I didn't think you'd be up to eating much." He passed the plate toward her.

"Thanks." They looked too inviting to refuse. The first bite said it all. He could actually make a decent sandwich.

"When you finish lunch you have to take an antibiotic."

Tegan noticed a bottle of tablets and a glass of water sitting beside the photographs.

"It's an unusual place you have here, Tegan."

"I like it. I'm not particularly fond of the city. It's great to get out at the end of the day and the ocean is close by."

"Did you do all this renovating?"

"Yes, six months after I moved in. What happened to your meetings?"

"I cancelled them." His lips curled upwards.

"You can't just cancel them at the last moment!"

"They're set for next week. Apparently Moss and Vale weren't prepared anyway."

"You mean to say you cancelled them to come all the way down here."

"I came all this way to look after the only person who knows what is going on in the damn business."

"You don't need to look after me. How absurd. I'm capable of looking after myself." She shoved the last bit of the sandwich into her mouth.

"Capable of looking after yourself. You've shown me all morning just how capable you really are and I don't think you passed—you didn't even come close. In fact you failed. I said I care for you and I intend to show you just how much. Anyone with a mind can see you need someone to look after you. Is there anyone who is able?"

"I don't need anyone, and if I did, I have my baby-sitter. She picks Robert up from school and sits with him. Clare helps me out quite a bit." Tegan toyed with the folds on the sheet.

"There's something you're not being completely honest with me about. I feel it Tegan. Am I that bad you can't stand me, or is it the fact that I'm running Coleman Enterprises which upsets you so much? That I'm the new partner. Tell me, why have you concluded you don't want anything more to do with me? What infuriates you so much?"

"I know my behavior has been a little up and down and..." She shook her head. "I'm not sure what got into me. I realize I wasn't prepared for Stan to sell half of the business. I'm sorry. I know I came across as a little bit forward."

She drew in a weary breath. "Our relationship was something flared by alcohol and fueled with wildness. It wasn't something I'd normally do. I don't have any intention of repeating it, even if we do continue to work together."

From what she'd heard and seen, relationships at work ended as disasters as well, not that she was willing to go down that path. She shouldn't have to explain the reason her experience with men, had put her off from ever falling into that trap. Even if she did hint on the subject, she'd have to explain what she'd suffered at the hands of Peter. Mathew already knew too much, knew she'd been beaten. He didn't have to know anymore. She wasn't about to put herself in jeopardy again and that was that.

"So, it all boils down to Stan. He got a very good deal. What I'm doing for Stan I have never done for anyone else! He was a little worried at first but not anymore." Irritation hovered in his voice.

"Really," she looked up, leveling her eyes with his.

"Why can't you let go of whatever it is and give us a chance? You know, it might make you happy."

"I'm already happy."

"No, you're not. I see it in your eyes. You have eyes which send me a gold invitation. Those eyes are what drew me to you in the first place, so open one moment then so mysterious the next. There is something hidden there, something you camouflage, something which hints at fear and secrets. I can understand the secrets. We all have them. But the fear? What do you fear? Are you afraid of making a commitment to a male or is it just me?"

"That's absurd and you know it." Tegan's nerves grated up her spine.

He moved closer. Just as he was about to add his touch to her lips, she jerked back.

"No, no...I."

"You want me as much as I want you. You want me as bad as that first night in Port Macquarie."

The slow husky drawl of his words didn't make matters any easier. She struggled against a call from deep within, rising, pushing all logic aside.

"That's not true. You have it wrong."

"Why deny it? It's electrifying. I feel it; you feel it."

Suddenly his lips moved over hers. The warmth of his touch drew her into a world where there was no hope of returning.

He continued to drown out any verbal objection and she gave in to his demanding lips. When he broke free, his right hand traced a line down the side of her face.

"I care about you. I did the first moment I laid eyes on you. I couldn't get over the way I yearned to be with you."

"Was that the reason you combined our offices?"

A hint of wickedness flickered in his eyes. "Yes basically, but time consideration did play a major role."

Tegan managed a wavering smile. The ridiculous virus was intolerable. Her eyelids were heavy and she forced them to remain opened.

"Is it Stan you're worried about? I feel it's much deeper than that."

A zigzag of thoughts scampered through her brain. What if he already knew about Robert? What if he'd tracked her down on Peter's behalf? He had the money, the power. Those thoughts put a halt to any statements relating to Robert.

"No, no, as you said, maybe I've been fighting this bug for some time and it's finally taken its course."

"Good to see you agree. When will Clare be here?"

"Twenty past three." She glanced at the clock. It was two-forty-five. He couldn't be there when Robert returned. He just couldn't.

"I have to leave now. I have one meeting I didn't cancel. Don't forget to take those tablets, otherwise you'll never recover."

She watched him pick up the tray and disappear through the door. Then she opened the bottle of antibiotics and swallowed two with a little water before settling back.

A clanging sound rose from the kitchen and after some moments he returned. He stood in the doorway. Uneasiness worked though her. What in the hell was he thinking?

"I'll call you later to see how you're recovering." He walked to the bed, bent over, and kissed her on the forehead. "Take care, if not for you, for me, please."

She cocooned herself into a ball as the door closed and squeezed her eyes shut to the sound of his car drifting away.

* * * *

Despite the lingering dizziness, the aches disappeared, and her temperature dropped. Not long after Mathew left, Robert bounced through the door with Clare and bolted upstairs.

"Mum." He raced toward the bed and gave her a hug.

Clare stood beside the doorway before moving toward the bed and sat down. "How are you feeling, love?"

"I'm a lot better than I was this morning. Thank you Clare. Thanks for picking up Robert."

"That's all right love. I don't mind."

The shrill of the telephone interrupted their conversation.

"I'll get it." Clare stood and walked down the stairs. She picked up the telephone just inside the kitchen door.

"Tegan Ryan's, residence."

"Hello, Clare. It's Mister King, Tegan's new employer."

"Yes."

"I was wondering if you could look after her. She needs around the clock care, meals etcetera, say until Saturday. I'll give you adequate payment to compensate you for your time. I know it's a lot to ask, but Tegan does need a hand."

"Yes. Thank you, that'll be fine."

"Thank you. I would appreciate if Tegan doesn't know about the dollar side of it. Could I speak to her please?"

Clare went in search of the cordless telephone, and then went back upstairs to Tegan.

"Mister King is on the phone." She passed the phone to Tegan. "I'll put the jug on."

Tegan gathered her senses. "Yes."

"Feeling better?"

"It's only been half an hour since you left. I told you I'd be fine."

"Yes, you did but I asked Clare to take care of you for a while anyway."

"I don't need anyone to take care of me. That's ridiculous. I can take care of myself."

"Your demonstration today didn't indicate anything remotely associated with your ability to take care of yourself."

She was silent.

"Is it a sin to be concerned for your well-being? I have to go; take care. I'll ring later." He clicked off.

Clare returned to the room. "He asked me to keep an eye on you, love."

"Yes, I know. Mathew told me...I really can manage."

"I don't mind, love. It gets awfully lonely at home."

"Are you sure?"

"Yes, I'm sure. Don't worry so much. I really don't mind. How are you feeling?"

"Much better."

"I'll put a lovely casserole on for tonight. I suppose you haven't had any lunch."

What could she say? That Mathew stayed almost the entire day and made lunch, waited on her hand and foot. "That'd be great. How's school, Robert?"

He ripped off his school shoes as he sat on the floor, his school bag next to him.

"Good, I have a new friend now, and his name is John. He doesn't have a Dad either."

"Oh." Guilt hammered home every time Robert mentioned the word 'father'. How much more guilt would she suffer if she'd stayed with Peter?

"Don't forget to put your shoes and bag away before you go out to play. And don't forget to ask Clare to pour you some milk and have something to eat."

"Yeah, Mum."

Tegan gazed at Robert, only to study him much closer. He and Mathew really weren't that alike after all. The only true resemblance was eye color. Robert's eyes had a darker blue hue, surrounding the already deep blue. Something Mathew didn't have.

She feared the impossible. Good heavens, how many children have blue eyes?

"Mister King must care for you a great deal especially to ask me to keep an eye on you. Not many bosses do that."

"He's only interested in his own welfare. He said it was part of his business to look after valued employees. Right from his lips, so don't go getting any ideas."

* * * *

Tegan slipped one leg over the other as she sat in a wicker chair on the side veranda. In one hand, she held a small china teacup filled with lemon tea. It soothed her throat all week and now she was acquiring a taste for it.

After taking the rest of the week off, like the doctor had stated, she'd realized she was run-down. She knew good health was important. But something else was niggling at her mind. She'd missed her monthly period.

"Come on Robert. Do you want to take a drive to the shops?"

"Yeah, Mum."

She buckled him securely into the car and they drove through the winding bends filled with shading palms.

"What are we getting? Can I have an ice-cream?"

"Mummy has to go to the pharmacy. And yes, you can have an ice-cream."

When Tegan arrived home, she went straight to the bathroom and drew the contents of the pregnancy test kit from the box. Leaving the bathroom for a few minutes to check on Robert would allow enough time to confirm her suspicion.

Upon returning, she walked slowly up to the little strip. A cupped hand covered the squeal that shot up her throat. Two stripes edged their way across the white strip. She closed her eyes. In one passing moment, a pleasing tug pulled on her lips as she thought about a brother or sister for Robert. It soon disappeared.

She was going to have a child.

Mathew's child.

Her stomach knotted.

She drew in a slow, deep breath trying to contain a surge of emotion as she packed the contents out of sight. Pulling her mind back into some type of sanity, she decided to make the second test the following morning just to be certain it wasn't a mistake.

Mathew had rung several times in the last few days. He'd been so kind, so understanding. Was she too harsh saying he was only interested in her well-being because she was a valuable business commodity? He did say he cared. Could she trust him?

* * * *

"Robert, time for lunch." She watched him chase a butterfly.

"Aw, Mum. I nearly caught it."

Tegan smiled. "He's probably off to have some lunch as well, come on."

Robert pulled a face and turned to walk toward his mother.

A tooting car horn sounded from the gate. Taking Robert's hand, they walked to the other side of the house.

"Who owns that, Mum?"

"I don't know." In the back of her mind, an idea was floating around. She squinted for a better view and raised her arm to block the sun's rays, trying to distinguish if it was Mathew sitting behind the steering wheel of an expensive black car.

When the car door opened, a mass of dark hair sent her heart into a double hopscotch.

"Go inside, Robert." Her peaceful mood dissolved, her body tensed. "Do as I say."

Reluctantly, Robert turned and disappeared through the open door behind them.

She felt awkward dressed in a little pair of white shorts, frayed at the bottom. A red shirt clung centimeters above the shorts. She tugged on the top trying to cover any exposed flesh of her stomach.

"What brings you all the way down here?" She walked down the steps.

He recognized the bite in her voice. She was ready for battle. He smirked, and admitted that her feistiness was such a challenge. God she was beautiful.

"I was on my way back from Sydney and thought I'd drop these files in so you can look them over. Stan said you have a fine ability to pick out any problems. If you don't mind, see what you think."

"No...I don't mind."

"Great. Oh, one more thing. Yakia and Yasashika asked if we could join them in Sydney in September."

"Oh," she whispered, feeling a bubble form in her throat. She felt a little disheartened knowing his visit was strictly business. But the fact remained he'd told her he cared, not loved her.

"Did you drive to Sydney? What happened to your wings?"

He stopped at arm's length. "I decided to find out why you thought a sea-side drive was so relaxing."

"After being in your airplane it's a draw but from here to Sydney isn't exactly a sea-side drive."

"I can't say I really enjoy driving alone."

The agonizing penetration of his gaze started at her ankles, riding over long slender legs, the feminine curves of hips, and then settled on her face only to retrace his steps. Biting on the inside of her lip, she knew he did it on purpose, knew he was trying to get some sort of reaction from her. Knowing circumstances could suddenly change, she put her energy into Robert and prayed he would do as he was told and stay indoors.

Mathew's expression suddenly changed as he drew closer. He leaned over and gave her a peck on the cheek. She jerked back, on full alert.

"What's the matter? Are you all right?"

"Nothing is wrong," she replied vaguely. Her gaze darted in all directions, knowing he probably thought she was off in la la land once again. She scampered up the three timber steps and swung back to face him.

The corners of his mouth curled, his eyebrows rose and a mischievous grin slid over his face. His masculine scent floated through the air, and no doubt, he did it on purpose.

"I see you have recovered."

"Yes, thank you."

"Has Clare left?" His gaze scanned the area.

"She left a few days ago." Tegan grabbed hold of the railing to steady herself. He looked great but she didn't need him here, didn't need him to pry any deeper.

"I saw someone standing with you. Was that your son?"

My son, oh no...why does he want to know? Her body trembled, her throat immediately dried up.

"We're quite busy at the moment."

He slipped off his dark suit jacket and rolled up his sleeves. He completely ignored her words as he went about making himself quite at home. At that moment, Robert bounced out to greet the stranger.

Chapter Nine

Tegan swung around sending her off balance. In automatic reaction, Mathew took one giant stride and shot up the three steps, grabbing her before she fell.

"This is becoming very repetitious," he purred, his breath teasing her face.

Her heart pounded as his strength wrapped around her. She jerked from his electrifying touch and slid one arm around Robert's shoulder. "Didn't I ask you to stay inside?" she scorned weakly, before taking a glimpse at Mathew.

He was analyzing them with a significant lack of expression. Something he was good at—hiding-his feelings. You could never tell what he was thinking. Sometimes she wished she were a psychic.

"Robert, this is Mister King. He's my boss."

Robert strained his neck upwards.

"Call me." He put out his hand.

Robert took the few steps around his mother and mimicked Mathew's hand motion.

At that moment, a string of memories flooded Mathew's mind. He felt a tremendous buzz flow through his body the very moment his hand made contact with Robert's. The startling blue in Robert's eyes overwhelmed him and he noticed familiar expressions. Disturbing thoughts rocked him.

"Hello. Do you want to have lunch? We were just going to make some."

"I'm sure Mathew has many things to attend to." Tegan flustered.

"Well, if your mother doesn't mind." He made direct eye contact with Tegan.

"Not at all."

'Never, ever', she felt like saying. How could she avoid his persistent sexual appeal? She didn't want this, didn't want him sitting at her table having lunch with them and blurted, "That's if Mathew doesn't mind a salad sandwich."

The bite in her voice didn't go unnoticed. "My favorite," he replied with a grin.

Robert looked at him. "It's my favorite too."

"Robert, seeing Mathew is your guest, you'd better show him where to wash up."

"My guest. All right, follow me."

Tegan eyed them cautiously. Had he noticed? She tried to look for an expression of concerned shock but the only thing she saw in his eyes was humorous delight which infuriated her even more. He had a way of getting under her skin and he damn well knew it.

Robert took hold of Mathew's hand and pulled him along. As he tugged him toward the door, Mathew turned his head.

"Kids; aren't they adorable?" His dark eyebrows shot up and his lips moved into a mischievous, sexy grin.

Tegan held her teeth firmly as she watched them disappear. Then she moved quietly, hoping to hear anything out of the ordinary. There was nothing.

Apparently he hadn't noticed the resemblance. Maybe he never would. Maybe she'd overreacted. Giving up on the ridiculous idea was something she should do for the sake of sanity. She blew out an exasperated breath, re-assured herself a salad sandwich wouldn't be a threat whatsoever, and walked into the kitchen.

As she prepared the sandwiches, the bubbling chatter coming from upstairs was hard to ignore. She stood on tiptoes and leaned over the breakfast bar, trying her hardest to eavesdrop.

The idea of having a man around enthralled Robert.

She took the platter of sandwiches out through double glass sliding doors to the back veranda, set them down on a cast iron table, and returned for the orange juice.

Mathew swooped into the room as she tried to balance three glasses and a bottle of juice between two hands.

"Let me give you a hand." He grabbed the orange juice and followed with Robert bobbing along behind them.

"Nice place," he stated.

The view to the ocean through the tall gum trees was spectacular, giving a peaceful and relaxing atmosphere. He pulled up a chair next to Robert.

Tegan eyed him suspiciously from the opposite side of the table.

"What class are you in at school?"

It was the beginning of a long drawn out conversation. Robert told him practically everything about school down to what colored toilet paper they used. When he added that his mother didn't even have a boyfriend and never had one, she could have died.

"Robert," she snapped. "That's enough!" The coral in her cheeks flushed to red, bright red. She could feel it. "I'm sure Mathew doesn't want to hear about me." Her fingers curled into the palms of her hands.

"He's not harming anyone."

Mathew studied Tegan's reactions and she knew he was questioning the raw ice picks in her voice.

"That's not the point. How about you talk about something else."

By the time four o'clock arrived, the two males found they were interested in fishing and Mathew promised to take Robert sometime.

"Did you hear that, Mum?" His eyes sparkled. "Now I can catch some fish for tea."

"That would be lovely." She stroked his hair and glared at Mathew.

"Can we Mum, can we?"

"I suppose so." Holding her teeth firmly, she seethed. What could she say to a child whose eyes danced with an excitement she had never seen before?

Looking up, Mathew smiled. A cheeky boyish smile, which was enough to knock her senseless, and at that moment she was thankful she was sitting.

She also noticed something that others wouldn't. He pulled the crust off the edge of his sandwiches, just like Robert...just like Peter. It wasn't only the sandwich thing. The occasional expressions on Mathew's face and around his eyes were similar to Peter's.

It was as though a ghost was haunting her, ensuring she remembered her painful past. She forced herself to remain calm, not wanting Mathew to notice she'd been on tender hooks, and practically holding her breath since he'd arrived.

* * * *

Anxiety seeped from Tegan's body when they finally stood on the front steps watching Mathew's car veer down the driveway. Robert waved until he was out of sight.

"I asked him to come to the beach tomorrow so we can fish."

"You what? Tomorrow?"

"Awe, Mum, you said we could fish."

"Hmm, yes I did."

* * * *

After she tucked Robert in bed for the night, her hand traced over the smooth, timber railing as she headed downstairs before crossing over into the lounge to turn on the radio.

A strange emptiness engulfed the room, engulfed her heart. A loneliness she thought she'd conquered after leaving Peter. Although the first time she' set eyes on Mathew, certain disturbances gave her a hell of a jolt. She realized he filled an empty space that wasn't apparent before he arrived on the scene. Still she couldn't dismiss his resemblance to Robert.

Dangerous ground was all she could expect if she let her feelings for Mathew loose. She couldn't face the abusiveness and the mind games. No...putting herself or Robert through something as disastrous as that would not, and could not, be allowed. She'd have to lock her heart away. There wasn't any sense in pretending she didn't have feelings for him. How to take the next step, without picturing some type of disaster instilled in her mind.

Feeling completely overwrought, she drew in a heavy breath. How could life become so difficult in such a short span of time?

* * * *

She rose earlier than usual the following morning to perform the second pregnancy test and must have glared at the strip for ages.

Negative.

Studying acutely, she picked up the strip. It definitely didn't have two stripes running across the center. She blew out an indrawn breath, not sure whether to laugh or to cry. Surely she hadn't undertaken the first step in a wrong manner? Surely? Now it stood out as negative, plain and simple.

Deep down the feeling of having a brother or sister for Robert seemed thrilling. He wouldn't be a lonely child anymore. He would have someone to play with, to hang out with. Although relief welled as she didn't want to have another child to a different father, especially out of wedlock. Tegan believed a child needed both a father and a mother. She ran a hand over her stomach before packing away the remains of the kit.

It would be a dream, a big dream to marry Mathew and have his child. That thought triggered her maternal clock forcing her eyes to fill with tears. She'd buy another kit to make sure. After all there was a chance she could be pregnant. It would give her the reason for being so tearful all the time and perhaps the reason for being so edgy. All the emotion she remembered having when she was pregnant with Robert.

She turned, walked down the hall, and opened Robert's bedroom door. He was awake, sitting in bed. "Come on sweetie; come and have some breakfast."

He didn't answer.

"Robert."

"Coming Mum."

"Aren't we waiting for Mathew?"

They waited for half an hour and Tegan didn't want to wait any longer. "He knows where we'll be sweetie. Come on."

After breakfast, she packed a picnic lunch and headed off to the white sand below. With a picnic basket in one hand, a colorful beach umbrella tucked securely under one arm, and the other hand clinging firmly to Robert's, they began their trek down toward the beach.

She chose a spot not too far from the water's edge to set up Robert's sand bucket and spade, along with plastic toys, which he began to fight in the small sand dunes.

She stripped off her shorts and top revealing a tiny black bikini and then slid on a black cap.

"Sunscreen, Robert."

"Aw, Mum."

"Don't aw me. That sun is too hot today. I can feel it eating my skin already. Remember slip, slop, slap. Your hat and sunscreen will protect you." She started to rub the sunscreen over his back and arms, then slipped on a rash vest, which had a built in fifteen plus sun protection.

"Going a bit overboard aren't you?" The voice startled her. She swung around.

"Mathew," Robert called. "Can we go fishing?" he asked, noticing a beach rod and bucket in his hands.

Tegan made a hasty dash and slipped on her T-shirt. Mathew's puzzled gaze disturbed her, filling her with embarrassment.

It wasn't as though he hadn't seen her naked before, although it had been in a dim light. Then he recalled she'd covered herself the following morning. She'd covered herself as though something was wrong, as though hiding something, and for the life of him he didn't understand. Thinking he knew women, he now doubted his intuition.

"In a while—if it's all right with your mother—after all I did promise."

"I don't think saying 'no' would go down very well with Robert." Her gaze tripped over a muscular chest. So solid, so masculine, and she wondered how he ever managed to keep so fit.

He wore a pair of dark blue board shorts with a white stripe down each side. Not the long kind or the short kind, the type that was just right. She quickly dipped her gaze and forced herself to concentrate on putting more sunscreen on Robert.

"He'll never get any sun if you continue to put that over him."

"The Australian sun is far too harsh, especially on a six-year-old's skin. I don't want him getting skin cancers when he's older."

Mathew raised his eyebrows as a steady glint beamed from his eyes. "I suppose your mother has a point there." He watched closely as she continued to put sunscreen on his legs. His gaze wandered. She suited the black slinky thing she wore. He couldn't take his eyes off those slender long legs. Although a T-shirt now concealed the top half of her body, he'd taken a good look before he approached.

He dropped his belongings, turned, and walked toward the ocean.

Recalling their night together swamped her with pleasing thoughts—the way he held her, the way his touch took her breath. His dark image disappeared under a wave and then reappeared, swimming with large competent strokes away from the shore.

With irritated motions, she propped up the colorful beach umbrella. She hadn't been one for sunbathing and started to apply sunscreen as Robert ran toward the edge of the ocean to greet his newfound friend.

"Want to come in, Robert?"

Alarm bells clanged loudly in her head. Mathew took Robert's hand and moved into the water. She yelled with motherly concern, "He's a weak swimmer."

Mathew took him on the edge, jumping over the waves, and chatting about boy things, or so she thought. Despite knowing nothing about children, he was a natural. Robert wasn't his child and she wondered how much difference it would make if he were.

Their resemblance standing side by side was something she couldn't ignore. They appeared related, as father and son. Both had the same olive skin coloring and the same dark hair. It drove her nuts. Their ability to chat about nothing was also surprising. She soon snapped from her silly thoughts when they returned begging her to swim.

"No, I don't feel up to it." It wasn't until after a long drawn out plea she found she was losing. "As long as you don't splash."

Cool water ran over her feet. She hesitated.

"Go on, Mum," Robert pressed. "They're only little waves."

Wading further into the water until knee deep, she gasped at the sudden change in temperature.

"What about your shirt Mum?" Robert called.

Swinging to face Mathew and before saying a word, Robert piped up. "She's trying to cover up her ugly scars."

"That's enough" she scolded, noticing they were bending down in an attempt to splash her and nearly succeeded. If she hadn't taken quick strides and dived under the next wave.

"There, does that satisfy you?"

"No." Mathew's tone was playful.

She splashed Robert.

"Who said 'no splashing' Mum?"

They started splashing. Tegan couldn't believe she'd laughed so much and by the apparent grin on Mathew's face, he was enjoying himself as well. For some time, they wandered idly on the shore, picking up anything that caught their attention.

"Hungry?" She spun around on the damp sand and began to walk backwards. Mathew had brought happiness, if only for a short passing moment. For a time, life felt so perfect.

They sat under the shade of the umbrella and she set out sandwiches, cake, and a cold drink each. They chatted for a long time. She smiled, laughed and the previous tension previously constant in his presence began to fade.

After lunch, Tegan wandered to the water's edge and sat down on the moist sand. She drew idly in the sand until Mathew suddenly plonked himself right beside her.

"Having a nice day?"

She turned to him. "Yes I am, are you?"

"Very nice," he replied.

Tiny shudders ran up her body when he moved closer. Just as his lips were about to explore hers, a little voice stopped him.

"Mum."

She snapped upright and swung around. "Yes, Robert."

"Can Mathew and me go fishing?"

"Mathew and I," Tegan corrected him.

"No, Mathew and me. I didn't know you liked fishing."

Tegan giggled.

"Sounds like a great idea. We'll try beach fishing first, then next time we might try Lake Macquarie. I've heard it has some great fishing spots."

Tegan left them to fish and explained to Mathew that Robert knew the track back but warned him to be careful.

Robert had said ugly scars. He'd never noticed any scars before. When she went swimming, he couldn't keep his eyes off such a slender, graceful image. Her body pierced the water with ease moving with sleek, slow movements.

Now he watched her from the corner of his eye. The way she slid a little pair of denim shorts over her smooth, silky buttocks made him think of doing the opposite. She did it so slowly, so seductively. After a short lapse in time, he spoke to Robert suspecting she might catch him drooling.

"Now, this is the way to bait the hook." He took another glance and found her walking away.

"Be careful and not too long," she called over her shoulder, knowing Mathew would take good care of him.

Arriving back at the house, she took a shower. After towel drying her hair, she slipped into a white dress, and applied a little lip-gloss, then walked barefoot down the stairs.

She picked up a book and made herself comfortable on the lounge. It wasn't a bad story, a romance story where fantasy and dreams did come true. She wondered if there was a place in her life for dreams and fantasies ever becoming a reality.

Glancing at the clock and realizing it'd been two hours since she'd left the beach, worry clawed at her chest until the mutter of voices drew closer. Robert was chattering without drawing a single breath. She bit on her lip. The sound of his voice, joyful and bubbly, she wished the circumstances with Peter had been different.

"Mum, Mum." He ran in through the door carrying a blue bucket.

"Look." He passed the bucket right before her face with, a twinkle in his eyes that jerked on her heartstrings.

"Yuck." The fishy smell was repulsive. She turned her head but then took another peek at the three large fish, cleaned and gutted.

"Can Mathew stay for tea? He helped me catch them."

His enthusiasm forced a grin to her face before she drew upright. "Mathew is a very busy man; he might have other..."

"I can't say that I do. The rest of my day is free."

Tegan chewed on the inner side of her mouth, gazing at

Mathew leaning on the architrave in the doorway. A mischievous grin surfaced over his face, delight shone from his eyes, and she knew he'd done it on purpose. Forced the issue. What choice did she have? They hadn't anything planned for the rest of the day but she intended to give Robert a very good talking to about inviting dinner guests without consulting her first.

"All right then, the same rule applies."

"You're my guest Mathew," Robert explained.

"Put them on the sink. I'll do them shortly. You can have a bath young man."

"Do you mind if I use the shower, Tegan?"

She glanced up. "No...not at all." She tried to put a stop to the images of Mathew showering upstairs naked but failed.

"I could help Robert with his bath."

"Thank you. Robert, show Mathew the way."

He was becoming quite a habit. He was showering and having supper. The other day he made lunch, ordered a doctor, and saw to it she had someone to take care of her. Although his previous words hovered in the back of her mind, words too precise not to ignore.

"I have to look after a valued employee."

Was that all she was to him, an employee? He did say he cared, but now that wasn't enough. Hell, what was she thinking? She didn't need him, didn't need his love. She sucked in a nervous breath, knowing the feelings she had for him had deepened. It was then she wondered if those feelings were blurring her judgment.

She jumped up and headed to the kitchen to place the fish in foil with a little lemon juice, olive oil then into a hot oven. Afterwards she prepared a salad, with buttered herb buns, white wine for Mathew and orange juice for Robert and herself.

Half an hour later, Robert and Mathew appeared in the family room.

Mathew looked deliciously freshened wearing a sea-green T-shirt which softened his previous stiff image. He looked nothing like the business tycoon she saw in the office and his face had a tinge of color from the Australian sun. He was one big hunk of tempting manly flesh, right before her eyes and in her home. *Oh, stop it girl*, she scolded.

Robert bounced ahead of him, dressed in the latest craze of printed pajamas. Following them into the family room, Mathew sat on the edge of the lounge. She passed him a glass of wine and sat opposite. Robert turned on the television.

"Tegan, do you know the reason I took on the partnership of Coleman Enterprises?"

"Not really."

"I'm not the big bad wolf you make me out to be."

"Why's that?"

"I have only undertaken the partnership as a favor for my father and for Stan. Not for material gain."

"I didn't know your father knew Stan." She took two sips of juice.

"It's strange Stan didn't mention it. King Enterprises purchase companies that are in financial difficulties. Most of the time those companies do not have a choice. We pay them precisely what their businesses are worth. We don't deceive anyone. With Coleman Enterprises we bought into the partnership as a one-off business deal."

Tegan knew parts were missing to her puzzle, big parts. "You seem to like children. I know I've asked you before but why haven't you had any of your own?"

"I don't mind other people's children. As I said, they are important for families, very important. But with the kind of lifestyle I lead, I have never considered having children of my own."

Tegan's heart skipped a beat. "Oh, I see." She murmured, retreating to her juice. Deep down in her inner realm she wished Robert was his and he wanted them both, really wanted them, and loved them. She knew that was impossible, a silly dream. A sickening wave of terror welled, forcing her to doubt if she would ever get past the fear factor, the fear of knowing any relationship could turn sour. So, why did Mathew turn her insides into a purring kitten, into a weak kneed adolescence?

"I don't have the time to raise a child. It wouldn't be fair on the child. Running companies and travelling. It certainly wouldn't give me much time to spend with them."

"I'll check supper."

A man that hadn't considered having children. What man doesn't want a son, or a daughter? No time? You make time for your children, like she had with Robert. Maybe she wasn't there in the afternoons but she always tucked him in at night and they had great weekends together.

Most of their conversation was directed at Robert over the meal, and Mathew commented on the fish. Fresh fish was a delight to cook, you could be sure it tasted just right. She spent some time picking out the bones for Robert. In the end, Mathew took over.

When he and Robert insisted they wash up, she didn't argue, and decided to settle in front of the television.

Apparently, he didn't notice any resemblance. If he had, he would have questioned her, would have said something. He didn't which made it obvious there wasn't any. She'd been worrying over nothing.

When it was time for Robert to go to bed Tegan accompanied him upstairs and tucked him in.

"Robert I don't think it is a good idea to ask Mathew to tea and to take you fishing. I really don't want him around."

"I like Mathew. Why can't he come here? I like...him," he protested.

"Well, he's a stranger." Tegan tried to console him.

"He's not a stranger...he can come here. He's your boss...he's my friend."

Tegan recognized the despair in his voice and knew how much she upset him. What was she thinking; trying to break her son's heart wasn't good? Even though she didn't want Mathew there, she knew how much Robert loved his company. Feeling stuck, wanting to please her son, and wanting to put distance between herself and Mathew, she had no option. There was none.

"All right. As long as you ask me before inviting him to supper again."

"I will, Mum, thanks. You do like him a little bit don't you?"

"Yes, I do like him a little bit." Her lips thinned." Now, off to sleep young man." She kissed him on the forehead, then tucked the sheet around him.

"Night, Mum."

"Night, Robert."

Tegan returned to Mathew. An underlying truth arose. She enjoyed his company too much and the symptoms of falling into a pit of quicksand intensified. Also there was Robert's fascination and she certainly didn't want to upset him. Sub-consciously she ran her index finger over her bottom lip. The constant ache for his kiss was with her each day and night.

Mathew had poured another glass of wine and was sitting comfortably in front of the television. Tegan sat next to him, making sure the distance between them was adequate. It wasn't too long before he lessened that space.

"I was thinking about the meeting tomorrow night."

Tegan's forehead scrunched. "Oh...yes."

"Don't forget; it's at the Apollo."

Tegan didn't say a word. She wasn't going to let on that she'd completely forgotten about the following night.

"Did you enjoy supper?"

She turned to face him only to be confronted with glistening midnight eyes jump-starting her heart.

"Yes, Robert loved it." She cleared her throat. "He was so proud that he caught a fish. He couldn't stop chatting."

"I meant did *you* enjoy it?"

"Yes. I did."

"I'm so pleased. Come here."

His strong powerful arms slid to her waist and he forced the space between them to close. His kiss was full of passion, impelling desire to flood her belly. Need escalated. Accepting that she could no longer suppress the desire within, her hands snaked around his neck.

"Hmmm...now, that's what I call a kiss," he murmured huskily from under the kiss. She leaned into him, drawn to the muscles of his sturdy physique. His hands moved with ease over her body as his lips continued their journey.

Mathew was a drug-induced poison. His touch so deadly, she didn't want him to see her so needy, so out of control, not again. The first time in Port Macquarie was enough embarrassment to suffer. For the past six and a half years she'd been independent, with a predicable life style just the way she wanted.

Now, giving into his touch, letting her heart seek its own path, and knowing the risk involved, she couldn't help herself. Letting go of all the frustrations, of all the disasters that could happen, she succumbed to his instruction as though following hypnotic musical notes on a harp. His hands explored her back, the nape of her neck, circled her breasts. His lips continued to roam with hungry enthusiasm before he stood dragging her into his arms.

"Do you want to go somewhere a little private, perhaps your bedroom?" The electric seduction in his voice withered her body into a state of no return.

"Yes..." she murmured against his chest.

* * * *

Discarding her clothing one item at a time, his burning gaze raked over her flesh. Her breathing quickened as his arms wrapped around her, easing her down onto the bed.

A shiver of anticipation shot through her as he lowered himself. His mouth hovered closely until their lips brushed back and forth. The pressure of his lips increased shooting barbs of fire to her belly, snaking down to her thighs.

Her hands wrapped around his neck. She moved one moved through his silky dark hair and ran the other over the firm muscles in his back.

Propping himself with his elbows, he lowered himself onto her and the feeling of his chest overwhelmed any conscious thought she may have had. His fingers tickled and tantalized the sensitized buds of her breasts, at the same time he entered, filling her with hot passion.

Together they found their level—peaking with urgency until satisfaction exploded, reaching every vein of their tangled bodies, before their breathing slowed.

Chapter Ten

By the time Tegan arrived at the Apollo restaurant, she was late, very late.

There was no time to check her hair or anything for that matter. Across the large tiled foyer, Mathew chewed up his pace with impatient strides. He retraced his footsteps. Tegan thought he'd be verging on the edge of boiling point by now, as she put one unsteady step in front of the other, hoping her legs would sustain her during the short distance.

He briefly looked up only to return his gaze quickly. In an instant, he'd forgotten what he was diligently pondering. Now Tegan consumed his mind, the beauty before his eyes.

A long blue evening gown graced her curves, flowing seductively as she walked toward him. When he opened the doors, a soft oriental fragrance floated into his nostrils.

Her lips were full and sensual, hinting the color of bronze; her hair swept into a French roll with long strands spiraling down each side of her cheeks.

He put his hand out and smiled a welcoming smile that warmed Tegan to the core of her heart. He looked the picture of an all-charming prince in blue, a very wealthy prince in blue. When he linked his arm around hers, she tried to curb the hot jolts of electricity shooting up her arm, splintering through to her heart. *Breathe, breathe*, but it was impossible especially with the previous nights activities fresh in her mind.

When they arrived by the table, her gaze swept over strange faces.

A soft whisper hummed into her ears. "Stan said he'd give you a ring later. He wasn't up to coming." When his contact disconnected, Mathew slipped out a chair. She sat, unable to bear his touch much longer for fear of inducing another crazed love affair. Ideally, she liked it, but not here, not now. It wasn't the place to have such thoughts escalating through her mind.

Mathew positioned himself close by and took care of introductions.

"Rob is from Broadbeach. He wants to sell his company and heard King Enterprises gives a fair sum."

"Oh."

"Wine?" Mathew asked, as his smoldering gaze connected with hers.

By now she knew a glass of wine would be appreciated. She needed something to release the knot tightening in her stomach. "Um...no. Water would be nice, thank you." She wouldn't touch alcohol until the doctor confirmed if she were pregnant or not.

Her meal consisted of fresh, local fish and she enjoyed every mouth-watering taste. Then formalities took over for the rest of the meal. After dessert, the men began to leave, and within a short time, she found herself sitting alone with Mathew.

"You look beautiful tonight. You dress extremely well," he murmured, with a husky drawl.

"I wouldn't consider myself beautiful. It's amazing what a bit of makeup and clothing will do."

Mathew knew otherwise. He'd seen her deathly pale, strewn out on a couch with a debilitating sickness, and she still looked like a home coming queen.

"Don't tell me you didn't notice all eyes upon you when you walked in."

Tegan focused on his words. "I think you're going a bit over-board Mathew."

"I never go overboard when it comes to a beautiful woman." Well, he might have gone overboard and was now in the first stages of drowning but he didn't mind at all.

"Dance?"

"I...I don't dance."

"Don't tell me that. Is it the same with the wine—only when you feel like it?"

Tegan gazed at him. The truth was she didn't want to dance with him. The contact would be too shattering. It was becoming quite an ordeal and she was afraid she'd fail and fall into a heap all over him, in view of the public eye and make a fool of herself.

Before she had time to protest, he led her onto the dance floor. When his hand rested on her hip, her insides froze.

"You seem a little jittery. Just relax."

She rested her head on his shoulder as the constant fear that niggled for such a long time faded. Finally that thick, ice shell she'd woven around herself was shattering, an ice shell that only a bad relationship could build.

When the music stopped, she turned and walked to the table. Mathew followed.

"I should get going. It's getting late."

He glanced at his watch. "Before midnight and the lady turns into a pumpkin."

Tegan grinned. "No, I don't but I have a long way to drive."

"Sorry. I hadn't considered that. I'll escort you to your car."

They stepped out into the still night and the humidity swirled around them. Tegan looked toward the sky. Not one cloud obscured the moon or stars. She drew in a slow, steady breath.

He bent forward and, before she realized what was happening, his lips were over hers. She took the journey with him—slow, wet, and passionate until he moved back a little.

His hand ran around to the concave of her back, pulling her closer again. Heat radiated from his body. His pupils grew smaller with a raging, dark desire.

"It was a pleasure tonight, Tegan."

"Yes, it was nice." She cleared her throat. "I've got to go." It was but a whisper.

"Thank you, for a nice evening."

"See you tomorrow."

Glancing over her shoulder, she noticed for the first time the usually confident man stooped his shoulders. His hands were in his pockets, the look of desire and disillusion roamed in his eyes. In one instance, she thought she saw annoyance making a path over his blue spheres but she put it down to her highly imaginative mind. Besides, it was impossible to be sure of anything on this night.

Thankfully, a late night pharmacy was opened and she pulled in to purchase a pregnancy test kit before continuing her drive home.

* * * *

Saying good night to Clare and checking on Robert, Tegan went to the en-suite, showered, and undertook the test. After making a cup of coffee, she sipped it as she walked back into the ensuite. She glared at the strip shaking her head with uncertainty. Two stripes of blue sliced across the top half of the stick.

A baby...a baby...letting go of a deep breath she knew she'd have to see a doctor to have it confirmed.

* * * *

Tegan waited by the elevator the following morning.

"Good morning, Tegan."

The voice startled her. Turning sideways, Mathew's gaze drifted over the navy blue suit. He raised his eyebrows.

His voice was enough to dispatch her senses into orbit, let alone his eyes blasting her directly to Venus.

"Good morning." Struggling to maintain some professionalism against his intoxicating aura failed. After all, she didn't want the entire staff of Coleman and Associates knowing she was having an affair with the new boss.

People crowded around the lift, putting some distance between them.

"Morning, Tegan."

"Morning, Andrew." She nodded and slid sideways. Time slowed as she waited for the lift, or so she thought. It gave only temporary aid when it did arrive.

Stepping to one side, and letting it fill, she ducked in moments before the doors snapped shut.

She studied the digits highlighted on the panel. What was the matter with the damn thing? Why was it crawling as though making its last ride? It was working efficiently yesterday.

The lift grunted, and then let out a few groans. She stiffened and drew in a lungful of air, glaring at the red light resting on level one. Over half of the occupants stepped out before the doors slid shut.

Continuing to stare at the panel of lights, knowing Mathew was behind her, she felt the skin on her spine tingle as the little hairs on the back of her neck stood upright.

The lift groaned before jerking to a halt stopping at level two.

She watched as people moved out into the corridor. Under hooded lashes, a quick glance confirmed her suspicions—they were alone.

The doors smacked shut within seconds. Mathew took two steps before coming to a standstill beside her. Her body temperature upped a few degrees.

"How are you feeling this morning?"

"Good, but if I'm going to have an affair with you, I don't want the entire building to find out and start a gossip session."

His eyebrows shot up and a devilish grin slipped to his lips.

"Why not?"

"Mathew, you're my boss."

He chuckled. A gleam set in his eye. "An affair. Is that what you call it?"

Biting on her lip, she didn't know what else to brand a few short, hot, whimsical nights together other than an affair.

"What would you call it?"

His eyes brooded darkly. "An affair." A laugh jolted from his lips, his hands circled her waist.

"You're impossible. Someone will find out if you continue to put your hands all over me, especially in the building. I'd prefer it if you kept our private life, private." She sucked in another breath, a deep quick one that wasn't a good idea at all. His aftershave rammed into her senses, almost knocking her legless.

The lift grunted loudly. The grating sounds kept repeating until the lift squealed and ground to a bumpy stop.

"We haven't reached the next level." It rose as a splutter before a clamping device snapped around her throat. *Damn claustrophobia.*

A firm hand on her back prompted her gaze to lock with his only to be presented by a perilous depth of blue.

"It's all right. It'll start soon or someone will open it from the other side."

Sudden darkness filled the lift. With teeth firmly together, her lungs desperately tried to find oxygen.

"The emergency lights should come on at any moment."

As soon as he spoke, two dim lights bathed the lift.

Keep it together. There's still oxygen in here, she assured herself, glancing around at the small confined space with no...no windows...no escape route. She gulped.

The air grew warmer, heated...stifling. She fanned her face ,hoping to stir up some cooler air.

"Doesn't this thing have a damn phone in it?" She glanced around the lift, her breathing sporadic.

Mathew snatched his mobile from his pocket.

"Mike, it's Mister King. Tegan Ryan and I are stuck in one of the lifts. There must be something you can do...what? We'll do something." He flipped his mobile closed.

"They're doing all they can. We're stuck between floors."

"How long do they...do they expect us to stay here without any oxygen?"

"There's enough oxygen in here to last a few hours, Tegan."

"You could have fooled me."

"It'll give us time to talk, alone." His sexy voice purred, crippling what was left of her senses. She struggled against not one obstacle, but two.

"I don't think we have much to speak about at present except getting out of here."

He reached out; his fingers tripped lightly down the side of a soft cheek, stoking a fire deep within her belly. Desire stirred with urgency. His breath feathered her neck before kisses rained up her throat.

"Mathew, stop it."

"So, now you're telling me you don't like me kissing you." He grated on a whisper.

She stepped back but he quickly closed the space.

"I didn't say that. I merely...someone may see us."

He glanced around. "I don't think there's any one here to witness...what did you say...an affair," he playfully added.

When his lips caressed hers, she wondered about his ability to drown all thoughts within a space of a heartbeat. The kiss, soft, sensual, a temporary escape from reality was short-lived.

She drew back, lashes blinking rapidly as she gazed lazily into his eyes.

"Don't fight what we have Tegan. Don't deny yourself happiness when it's plain to see you do enjoy my company? You didn't seem to mind it in Port Macquarie."

She bit on her lip and pushed a stray piece of hair from her face. "I'm not fighting. It..."

His lips smothered any attempt to continue. The kiss, hot and stormy, filled with desire and want. She fell onto him as he deepened the kiss, his hands trailing over her body. Quivering helplessly, his tongue dived into her mouth until he broke free at the sound of his mobile echoing in the confined space.

While he answered his mobile, she managed to regain some control and straightened her suit, oddly embarrassed. They were stuck in a lift for heaven's sake, and here she was playing around with the boss.

Grabbing hold of the railing, reality crashed around her. She thought she'd conquered the claustrophobia but it rose again.

The Lift.

Trapped.

She panicked.

"No, oh no."

Folding to the floor, her hand fluttered in front of her, in a desperate attempt to cool the air. It was unsuccessful.

Mathew knelt beside her. She looked vulnerable and fragile,

giving rise to his protectiveness. It was something he'd never felt except for the brotherly kind he'd had for his brother when they were kids.

"Hey, it's all right. You'll be okay. We'll be okay." His hand moved over her back, rubbing in small circles, knowing it would be a while before they got out of there.

Trapped between two floors was a problem. The emergency system wasn't working and now they had to wait for the fire brigade. He knew what it all meant. However, explaining everything to Tegan wasn't a good idea.

"We have to wait a little while longer."

"Why? What's happening?"

The green in those eyes haunted him, twisted his gut in knots. It was then he remembered she suffered from claustrophobia and recalled the time they flew to Port Macquarie. Such a feeling wouldn't disappear overnight. He'd have to choose his words with care.

"We're a bit stuck between two floors. The fire brigade will get us out. They'll probably climb into the shaft of the lift and open the roof."

"You mean to say...we can't...oh, no..." She sobbed. He settled down, closely drawing her into his arms.

"Come on. Shush." His hand ran down the back of her hair, then up again, only to repeat. "You're not alone. I'm here, Tegan. I won't let anything happen to you."

He prompted her head to rest on his chest. The warming sensation was calming, as was the steady pump of his heart.

Voices yelled from the other side of the lift drawing them apart.

"You'll have to try to pry the doors open from the inside. The emergency system is not working. You're just short of the next floor."

Tegan pulled herself upright using the railing. *Trapped. Pry the doors open.* She swayed. Her knuckles grew white as she gripped the railing harder.

Mathew tugged on the doors. They didn't budge. He tried once again and slid them apart just a fraction.

Rubbing her lips together and holding them firmly in place was the only way to stop screams from escaping her throat. Realizing she couldn't move, her body folded to the floor once again.

Mathew turned. Her face looked as though it had a fine dusting of powder. It twisted his gut into a deep ache seeing her in such a state.

"Once I get the damn thing opened, we have to crawl out through the gap."

She nodded in a vague acknowledgement while biting on her bottom lip.

He tried again, tugging at the door until it slid open a few more inches, but not wide enough to climb through.

He ripped off his suit jacket, tossed it to the floor and rolled up his sleeves before trying again. Then it was like a miracle. The doors slid open far enough for them to climb through. A fireman bent down and peered through the opening.

"Are you both okay? You can climb out up here."

"Yeah mate, we're fine." Taking a step toward Tegan, Mathew put out his hand on her shoulder. She remained crouched on the floor like a wounded animal, too afraid to move a muscle.

He knelt. "Hey, it's all right now. There's lots of oxygen getting into the lift and plenty of room to get out now."

He took her hand. "Come on, up you get."

He swept her up into his arms. She remained quiet, huddled against his chest. For the life of him he wanted to kiss her again, kiss those sensual lips. But it wasn't the time or place. He glanced up at faces peering through the small gap.

It was only about one meter wide, but wide enough to climb through.

"Pass her up," called one of the firemen.

"Be careful, do you hear?"

The fireman laughed. "I've never dropped one yet mate."

Mathew hauled Tegan up as high as possible and the fireman reached down grabbing her arm pulling her upwards. Tegan was on automatic and followed instructions.

Fresh air caressed her face and she sank onto a bench opposite the lift. Mathew followed.

One of the staff offered a glass of water and Mathew took it. "Here drink this, then we'll call a doctor."

"No doctor. I'll be fine," she ground out.

He saw how much she trembled and held the glass to her lips as she sipped the water.

"It's okay now. You're safe."

She bit on her lip. "Thank you. I feel so silly."

"There is no need to feel that way. It's something that you can't help. Come on let's give you some privacy."

Sally rushed down the corridor. "Tegan, are you okay?"

"She's a little shaken Do you mind taking care of her until she's settled?"

"Yes, Mister King, sure will. Come on Teeg." She bent over, put an arm around Tegan's waist, and they walked down the corridor.

* * * *

Tegan returned after half an hour. Her nerves settled and she did feel a little better. Mathew stood and crossed the office toward her. "Feeling better?"

"Yes, thank...you." It was a broken whisper.

He took her in his arms and she fell against him before looking up leveling her gaze with his. "I'm always thanking you lately."

"I'm always saying there is no need for thanks."

"But thank you for helping me, Mathew. I really mean it."

"I know you do sweetheart."

"Has someone taken a look at the lift?"

"Yes, we have someone coming in later on today. It's so old, it's a wonder it lasted this long."

"I'm sure Stan had it serviced not long ago."

"It might run forever but I've organized to put a new one in. Next time it might not be as relenting."

When they broke from each other's embrace, she walked toward the desk realizing how comforting he really was. She realized how good she truly felt in his arms. Trying to concentrate on her work was arduous and managing for the next few hours was such a task.

Finally she slipped out and headed down toward the coffee machine.

When she returned he muttered, "I have an appointment at three."

He slipped on his suit jacket as she walked to the chair and sat down.

"I won't be back in the office for the rest of the day."

She admired him so much. He took care of her when she needed someone. He helped her when she needed help, comforted her so much.

* * * *

Saturday's relief was welcomed. Spending time with Robert was important, but the time apart from Mathew was agonizing. Robert hounded her to take him to the beach until she finally agreed to his pestering.

"Now stay on the edge, Robert." She watched him splash ankle deep in the cooling seawater. The waves were far too big to contemplate a swim today. They were dumpers right on the shoreline but further out it looked a little calmer, although ripples indicated there may be a rip. Nevertheless, she didn't want to take a chance. Sometimes the force of a wave could hold one under for minutes. At least there was a light southerly breeze which lessened the intense heat.

She settled on her stomach and watched Robert play on the sand. Turning away for a few short moments to rummage in a bag for some sunscreen only seemed like a minute since she'd taken her eyes off Robert.

No longer able to hear his squeals of delight she looked up.

He was no-where in sight.

Sudden alarm ripped through her.

Springing to her feet, she raced to the edge of the waves crashing onto the shore. A frantic gaze swept over the water then up and down the shoreline. There wasn't a soul in sight. Usually at this time of day there was someone around. Now, at the very time she needed help, there was no one.

Her gaze swept over the white water only to spot a small, dark head bobbing up and down well past the breakers. Her heart pounded as she quickly ran into the water, screaming for him to hang on.

She had to reach him. She had to reach her child, no matter what. Taking a dive through a huge wave that savagely released, forced her deeper under the water. She clawed against the pressure and struggled to the surface for air.

Tegan wasn't a strong swimmer but continued to swim through the waves. She didn't seem to be closing the distance between them. Her heart beat dangerously fast. Robert was floating on his back at this stage—something she taught him a long time ago if he ever got into difficulty. Tears welled. How was she going to reach him in time? The undercurrent had dragged him further out.

"Hang on Robert, mummy's coming," her voice a spluttering shriek as she continued to reach him.

Something swam past her. She opened her mouth to scream, but instead drew in a mouthful of seawater. Coughing numerous times, she tried to clear the gag in her throat.

The dark mass was confident in the strong, muscular strokes he took.

Mathew.

Hope rose. Keeping afloat by treading water, she watched as he reached Robert. He was safe! She closed her eyes momentarily.

A huge dumper pounded down with building pressure, pushing her under, further and further. Her body was pliable against the strength of one wave as it pushed and pulled her like a rag doll. Bubbles formed around her face. Her arms struggled against the overpowering force. Her legs kicked violently. The current dragged her deeper and deeper, draining all energy until her body went limp.

She was drowning.

Mathew finally got Robert to shore.

"Wait here and don't move a fraction," he demanded. Swinging around, he tried to spot Tegan. Alarm bells banged in his mind; his heart thudded harshly against his chest. He dived through large, frothy waves only to reappear swimming to the last place he'd seen her.

He'd failed his brother. He'd even failed him at his death. He wasn't about to fail the woman he loved. He was frantic as he took a third dive. Then he spotted a body, like a mermaid, dangling gracefully, sinking slowly as though hanging peacefully in space.

He darted to the surface dragging in a huge gulp of oxygen and then dived under again. Finally, as he closed in, he noticed her eyes closed, hair floating above like ribbons in the soft waves. His hand closed over a small wrist and he pulled her against his body, before swimming to the surface.

Oh, hell. Lord no, don't you dare take Tegan from me. Not now, not ever, please. Not when I've just found her, you can't, you just can't. Anguish ripped through his chest, through his heart. He laid her on her back, one hand securely around her neck while he rode a giant wave which almost took him to shore. The waves came in sets, seconds after each other. Trying to hold Tegan above the next wave, he held his breath as it pounded his body. He'd never let go, never give into the force of the ocean.

Finally getting her to shore he carried her to dry sand. His body trembled, almost weakening as he laid her on the sand.

She wasn't breathing.

He performed thirty compressions with two breaths. He repeated, hoping to evacuate her water-filled lungs. She started spluttering and he rolled her over to one side, his fingers settled on her wrist. Her pulse was weak, but hell, there was still a pulse.

"Robert, come and sit by your mother," he called, noticing he was still huddled in a ball, crying, where he'd left him.

"Hey matey, she's asleep now. She'll be okay. She's had a big swim, that's all."

Blood surged in his veins as he ran to where he'd left his belongings, searching for his mobile phone. Snatching it up, he rang for an ambulance then returned to Tegan.

Tegan gasped for oxygen, coughed, and spluttered. The sound of sirens and mutterings of voices were distant. What was happening?

"Robert," she moaned.

"Your little boy is fine," a strange voice said.

Those words were precious. *My little boy is fine.*

She passed out.

Chapter Eleven

Struggling to push her eyelids apart, Tegan glanced around at a sterile hospital room. Her bikini and T-shirt were missing, in their place, a white hospital gown.

"You're a worry woman."

Tilting her head to one side, she noticed Mathew was in the room. "Mathew." It was only a murmur.

He moved to sit on the edge of the bed.

"Where's Robert?"

"He's in the next room. He's fine, a little shaken by the whole ordeal but he'll be okay."

"Thank you, thank you," she croaked.

Mathew's brows drew together. "Shush, it's okay." He brushed a lock of hair from her face. "I'm pleased you're safe; pleased I came along just in time. You gave me the fright of my life."

"Are you okay?"

He grinned. "Don't worry about me, I'm fine. More important-ly, are you okay? You've been through a lot. You need to rest."

Her lips quivered. "Thank you." Her eyelids closed, as she fell asleep.

It wasn't until well after lunch she woke. It took some time to figure out what was happening.

Pushing upwards to a sitting position, she dangled her legs over the edge of the bed. Standing, she padded barefooted though the door and into the next room in search of Robert. Her emo-tions folded much too quickly. He was sitting up in bed chatting to Mathew.

Stepping forward she put her arms out around Robert. For long moments, he huddled against his mother. Silent moments slid by as she absorbed their embrace, and happy tears slid down her cheeks.

"Thank heavens you're safe." She uttered, still clutching the child she thought she might never seen again.

"Mathew saved me. He's my hero." Robert struggled from her embrace.

"Thank you." Uneasiness rose, until Mathew slipped an arm around her waist.

"The nurse said I could take you both home when you're ready. Are you feeling up to it?"

"Yes."

"I took the liberty of collecting some clothes for both of you. I hope you don't mind?"

"No...um, thank you." She gazed at the bags sitting on the chair.

Mathew waited until they showered and dressed before driving them home.

* * * *

Sitting in the passenger seat of his car, embarrassment wasn't the word to describe how she felt by the underwear he'd picked out. He'd chosen a lacy red bra and red knickers along with a pair of three quarter pants and white top. *Men! Don't they know one never wears a red bra under a white top? Heavens, you could see right through the top.* As for her knickers, she grinned. It wasn't something she would have chosen but he'd made sure they had fresh clothes to wear and she was thankful. When she left the hospital she had her arms crossed at her chest until they were in the car.

"Sorry about the selection. I know the coordination isn't spectacular." He smirked, taking a glance toward her breasts and noticing how distinct the outline of the red bra really was. "I didn't want to snoop any deeper into your drawers. They were the first ones I grabbed on top."

Her cheeks warmed.

"Nice car. Mum, why don't you buy one like this?"

Tegan laughed. "A little past my price range, darling."

Mathew shook his head and chuckled. When they pulled up in front of the house, Mathew walked around to open the door.

"Are you sure you're all right? The doctor said if you didn't feel well enough, you should return to the hospital."

"I'm feeling much better, believe me."

Tegan wondered what would have happen if he hadn't shown up. Maybe Robert as well as herself. *No, that isn't the case, we're both fine now.*

Mathew helped them inside. Tegan and Robert went upstairs. She gave Robert a big cuddle when they reached his room, then ruffled his hair.

"I love you, sweetheart," she said warmly.

"I love you too, Mum. Mathew saved both of us didn't he?"

"Yes, he did indeed."

"So, he's your hero too isn't he Mum?"

"Yes he is," she whispered and gave him another cuddle.

If it wasn't for Mathew, they might not be alive. He was her hero. She helped Robert change into his pajamas.

"You pop downstairs and keep Mathew company while I go and change."

"Put something pretty on Mum."

"Oh, you boys." She tousled his hair and tapped him on the backside as they walked toward the door.

"Off you go. I won't be long."

She walked into her room and sat on her bed as flashes of Robert's head bobbing up and down in the ocean painted pictures in her mind. Tears collected in the corners of her eyes.

A rap on the door made her realize it had been quite some time since she'd dressed Robert.

"Yes."

Mathew walked into the room. "Is everything all right?"

A soft purr circled her heart when she heard the warmth and tenderness in his voice. "I'll be down soon."

"I'd say you're still pretty weak and probably still suffering from the shock of it all. I was wondering if you need a hand."

"I'm okay." She shook her head and pursed her lips to prevent herself from smiling.

"I think I've seen it all before." He grinned wickedly.

"No thanks." She watched him walk from the room, unable to believe that the new boss of Coleman Enterprises had a heart, one full of genuine concern.

Moments later, Tegan arrived down stairs dressed in a pair of denim shorts and a red top. Her blonde hair fell loosely to her shoulders.

Mathew glanced up.

"Told you so." Robert grinned.

"What are you two up to?" she questioned, noticing they had Cheshire cat grins plastered over their face.

"Not much," Mathew stated. "Tea is ready."

Tegan was delighted when she set eyes on the neatly laid table. A red cloth covered the rectangle table, in the center two red candles burned on low flame.

"Robert helped, didn't you?"

"We found the candles...I showed him."

"Where did you get all the food?" She sat at the table,

contemplating the seafood.

"When I collected your clothes, I stopped off to re-stock your refrigerator."

Maybe he truly is my hero after all. She knew now he was so very different from Peter. But why did Peter strike her, drunk or not. Did he witness that type of abusive behavior when younger? If so, if Mathew was his brother, would he also repeat what he'd seen when he was a child? The thought terrified the hell out of her.

She tried not to let her concerns show and concentrated on eating. She popped a piece of bread into her mouth. Her imagination was entirely responsible as always. When they'd finished, Mathew insisted he clean up. After all, he'd made the mess, he explained.

Tegan relaxed on the sofa, flicking through a magazine, recalling the dramatic change from the last meal they'd shared. He'd been the one sitting on the couch while she'd cleaned up.

As they walked into the lounge, Robert disappeared in a rush and returned with a book in his hand. "Can you read me a story Mathew?" he pleaded.

"Robert..."

"All right. It's no trouble at all."

Here was the man who stated he had no time for children, yet he settled himself quite comfortably on the floor next to her son and read the story full of expression. Robert enjoyed it. Tegan shook her head.

After he'd finished reading, Tegan put Robert to bed. When she came back into the lounge, Mathew produced a glass of wine. Once again, she didn't drink it.

"He's a great kid." Mathew sat beside her.

"I want to thank you again, for..."

"I think once is enough. I'm pleased you're both safe. I'm more than pleased, Tegan. I happen to care for you."

She looked into his eyes and bit on her lip. They were full of sincerity and the blue in them had deepened to a deep, electric blue.

He moved closer, their lips a breath apart.

"You're my hero, my son's hero and..." Tears rolled down her cheeks. "I just..."

"Shush." He raised his right index finger and placed it softly over her lips.

Dropping his arm, he slid it around her waist. Her vision distorted, moments before a surge of warmth cascaded over her lips. She closed her eyes and tried to forget about the day and tried to enjoy his company, thinking heroes arrive in many disguises.

"Come," he whispered, as he broke from the kiss. He took her by the hand, and as he led her upstairs, he turned off the lights then closed the door behind them.

He guided her toward the bed and switched on the bedside lamp.

"Are you up to...well?"

"Yes, it's okay and I'm okay." She grinned.

His lips sought hers, passionate and compelling. Sensations curled in her belly. His right hand moved over her slender neck, bringing warmth. Shivers ran down her spine, slowly dissolving any weak objection that remained.

"Tegan," he murmured. His lips showered kisses over her face, tripping down her neck.

A hand slipped to the zipper on her shorts and they fell to the floor. He took hold of the soft, red material of her top and discarded it at once. He lowered her gently on the bed and propped himself on one elbow.

A trail of kisses started at the base of her neck, and moved downwards, nipping at all visible flesh before his fingers tripped caressing strokes upwards.

"You are mesmerizing." He moved her hair from her face. "Don't ever give me a fright like that again," he murmured.

Tegan could only manage a murmuring sound, her body lost in oblivion, in the tenderness of his touch, in the deep husky tones of his voice. She sank further and further into temptation, realizing this is what she wanted all along—him.

The very moment they joined, she thought she'd gone to a place that wasn't possible. Their urgency had them racing at peak level. Sensations heightened to a sharper level until they were both united. Delirious with passion, not wanting it to end, wanting to go on forever, until neither one of them could stop the explosion that rocked their world. Shattering with electric frissons, bathing each other with gratification, they lay silent—listening to the sound of the ocean nearby.

It wasn't until the early hours of the morning Tegan stirred. Opening her eyes, she noticed shadows over the walls from the bedside lamp, which she had forgotten to switch off. Dragging the sheet up, she clutched it to her chest—reminding herself to keep her arms down.

"You okay?" he whispered sleepily. The slightest movement woke him.

"Yes. Would you like a drink?"

"Hey, before you go." He dragged her toward him. His lips captured hers. Drawing back he said, "That's what I call a good morning kiss."

She smiled. "Would you like that coffee?"

"I'll help you make it."

He sprung from the bed and slipped on a pair of jeans. Tegan grabbed a robe. She turned and lifted one arm to slip it into the sleeve.

"What's that?" He hadn't seen them in the dim light before, but now the light from the lamp lit them up vividly especially when she lifted her arm.

She quickly finished slipping the other arm into the robe, then yanked the robe to the front and secured it at the waist with a belt.

Mathew walked over to the other side of the bed for a closer inspection, and eased her arm from the sleeve of the robe. His gut churned.

"They're nothing, um..." Her stomach shriveled with nervous tension.

"It's the scars Robert mentioned on the beach that day, aren't they?"

"As I said, it's nothing."

"Is that why you always wear clothing with sleeves? Is that why you covered up the day I arrived on the beach?" His fingers still clutching her arm he turned it around.

"Cigarette burns, hell, Tegan." Heat flared to his face as anger ripped through his body. "Sweetheart, are they cigarette burns? Who did this to you? Did your ex do this?"

"Yes...and yes they are cigarette burns," she whispered. Humiliation ripped at her insides. They were so ugly. "It's in the past Mathew. No one can do anything about it now." Dragging in an unsteady breath, she lowered her gaze.

"Hell, he wasn't a man—he was a monster."

He pulled her into his arms. His hand moved over silken hair. "What else did that monster do? What else?"

Their eyes leveled. "He tried..." She swallowed. "He tried to smother me." Shame for what she allowed to happen caught up to her.

"Hell." He cursed under his breath. "At least now I know why you don't like confined spaces, why you suffer horribly from claustrophobia."

"He told me it was my fault. Perhaps it was."

"Don't ever blame yourself. It wasn't you. If I'd known about this at the time, I would have beaten the man to a pulp. No one will ever lay a hand on you ever again, on you or Robert. This man needs to be reported. What was your address?"

"No," she pulled from his arms.

"I want you to be safe. I want to take care of you."

"He doesn't know where we live. For over six years I haven't heard from him. There's no need to worry."

He took hold of her other arm and eased it from the sleeve, then turned it around exposing the underarm. "Hell, there are four on each arm. I'm going to make it my business to see that the lunatic responsible for this will pay dearly for what he's done to you." His jaw clenched. His gut twisted with sickening concern. They were discreetly placed near each armpit running toward the outer edges.

"As I said it happened far too long ago to do anything about now." She moved from his touch and slipped the robe back in place before walking toward the door.

"Do you still want that coffee?" she called over her shoulder.

Mathew followed. Torment ripped at his heart. He couldn't believe someone would actually do such a thing.

Tegan put the jug on and turned into his arms.

"I want to help you. You have suffered so much."

"You are helping me. You're helping me by just being here with me. You helped me by saving my life, and Robert's. What more could a person ask for?"

She folded into the cocoon of his sincerity. They stayed like that for long moments. The overriding comfort was unbelievable. Finally she'd learned to put her trust in another man. A man who was honest, caring, and considerate. A smile tugged at her lips.

"What is it sweetheart?"

"Nothing, just looking."

He kissed her with such compassion and tenderness she knew she'd found a safe haven not only in his arms, but also with him. He drew back and Tegan swung around to make the coffee.

"I need to talk to you about something else."

"It's about Robert, isn't it?" Cupping a hand over her mouth was the only way to stop a shriek exploding.

"I know it's absurd but I think you know more than you're letting on."

Her heart missed a beat. She didn't answer, couldn't answer. Her throat was sticky, she was barely able to swallow. She'd dreaded this moment, although managing to avoid it for a time, now she still wasn't prepared.

"Well?" Her body took on robot mode as she forced herself toward the table with the coffees and sat.

Mathew pulled out a chair.

"You stated your ex and you lived in Port Macquarie. You left him a little over six years ago."

"Yes. What is it? What are you getting at?" Having an idea of what he was getting at, she didn't want their relationship to change—not now, not when she'd learned to trust again, to love a man after such a long time of wondering, of sadness, and loneliness.

"I have to go through a few steps. Please be patient." He moved forward on the chair, legs apart with his hands clasped together. "How long ago did you leave him?"

Raising her head their gaze linked. "Six years or so...I was almost three months pregnant with Robert when I left, so about six and a half years."

"How old was Peter Knight?"

"As I said, when I left he was just over thirty. Why?"

"My brother died at the age of thirty and a half. Could it be possible that my brother and your Peter were the same person?"

A threatening flood of tears surfaced. Iciness chilled her skin. His brother is dead, but Robert's father is alive.

"Don't tell me you haven't tried to put the pieces together." He ran a heavy hand through his hair, stood and begun to pace.

Tegan's gaze trailed after Mathew. "I can't lie. Yes. At first I did but..."

"Mum, I want a drink." Robert's voice made her jump and she swiped the tears from her cheeks.

"I have to get Robert a drink."

"You made my mummy cry. Why did you make Mum cry?" He rubbed sleepy eyes.

Mathew didn't answer as he watched Tegan pour Robert a glass of water and then accompany him back upstairs.

Mathew was pacing when she arrived back in the kitchen.

"I think you have it wrong."

"Will you just listen, please?"

"Yes, but remember my ex-husband's name was Knight not King."

"I have no explanation for the name at present. Have you noticed Robert's eyes? They're similar to mine but much more similar to my brother's." He yanked a chair out from under the table and plonked down.

"It's just eye color. A lot of people have blue eyes."

"What? Like Robert's and my brother's? I don't think so. It's a definite family characteristic. My brother had a darker blue hue around the outside of his eyes. Robert has the same hue. I have never seen it ever on anyone else."

Screaming at her heart to continue beating and willing herself to draw breath was difficult. Tegan hadn't seen the darker hue in anyone eyes either. But it could be a coincidence. She tried to reinforce her mind. "When...did you notice the similarity?"

"The very day I met Robert, I had a passing thought. It was only a passing thought, until a few days ago. You did tell me Robert's father's last name is Knight, not King...anyhow. What did your ex do for a living?"

"Well...he was in and out of jobs, he..."

"So was Pete."

Tegan's lashes blinked with incredulity. Her right hand grabbed hold of a chair and she took comfort by sliding onto its support.

"I think it's possible they're the same person. Dad and Pete had a fall out. Pete didn't want to contribute to King Enterprises; he only wanted to enjoy the profits. So, Dad wiped him out completely, hoping he would come to his senses. He didn't. He moved away and for years we couldn't find him. That was something we didn't expect to happen. He rang me on his mobile once when he was intoxicated. I then had his number.

"When Mum had a cancer scare, I rang him. I flew to Port Macquarie to pick him up and he returned with me to Sydney. He didn't say much about the women in his life or his life in general, but he did mention he'd met a woman. He said she'd left him about six months previously."

"Tegan, what date was Robert born?"

"You have it all wrong."

"Please listen."

"You mean to say Robert's father has died? How absurd? You mean to say...." Her body succumbed to a wavering motion as tears flooded her cheeks.

The first signs of hammering began to bash at her temples. Her fingers crawled over the intense dull ache—her past was about to explode. A dull blur hovered in her mind. Was her imagination so close to reality? Were her suspicions bordering truth? But Peter wasn't dead.

"It couldn't get any weirder than this...Peter...he was born on the...tenth of January."

Mathew's face grew paler. "My brother died on the tenth of June in an aircraft accident. An aircraft I was flying. I'm responsible for his death."

He sprung from his seat and walked through the doorway, out onto the veranda, gripping its railing with both hands. With outstretched arms, he dropped his head.

"Math...Mathew, wh...what is it?"

"Stay sitting," he demanded. "I hope I have this wrong." He swallowed against a ball of anxiety lodged in his throat, then swung around. "What time was Robert born?" His brows knitted, his forehead etched with lines.

"Two in the afternoon, June tenth."

"Peter King died at two in the aft...afternoon on June the tenth."

Tegan sat in shock. Her body vibrated from an internal explosion. One...life...taken...one given." She cringed. The very day Robert was born, his father died. Cloudiness distorted any means to think rational.

"Hang on. I think I have a photograph. I forgot about it." He dug through his wallet. "That's if it's still here...got it. Here. This is the last photo I have of him."

Staring at the upturned photograph, she reached out with a trembling hand.

"It was taken on one of his final trips to Sydney around five months before he died."

Tegan turned the photo upright. Panic swirled, rising like a slow tide, filling her throat with bile. She bit on her bottom lip ,drawing two small droplets of blood as a cold fist clawed her heart. It was as though that weird tug she'd experienced in the office dipped like a ghostly cobweb throughout the silence. Death tapped on her doorstep.

"It couldn't be true...Robert's father is dead. They're the same... person." That internal explosion busted through to the surface lacerating her heart on its way. "Robert's father, my ex. It couldn't be, it just couldn't be." She sobbed.

Mathew was horrified as he knelt beside her. His right hand rubbed comfort into her shoulder but her sobs grew louder. Standing, he paced. "So, your Peter Knight was actually my...my brother...Peter King."

"You're Robert's uncle! It means...Robert was born the very

minute his father died."

"You had your suspicions the day you dropped the photograph in my office."

"No. I had a passing thought the very first day I met you, in the downpour in Newcastle."

"You knew then. Why didn't you say something?"

"I tried to say something when I had that virus, flu whatever it was, but it wasn't confirmed Mathew. It was an idea, a passing thought. I thought it was a silly assumption, and as I stated, eye color does not belong specifically to one family. But the names, he must have changed his name. I didn't see any documentation that stated King, only Knight. We rented but it was only for a short time. He drank quite a bit."

"So, my little brother turned out to be that monster. He was the evil you crossed paths with." Heat flared in his face, anguish ripped at his gut.

The sound of sobbing drifted through the atmosphere. Pins, needles, daggers, and spears along with the first stages of shock set in. All her constant suspicions confirmed. Would Mathew's parents try to take Robert from her? Mathew had no children and he did say the bloodline of a family was important. Robert was that bloodline. Fear coiled with snake-like fingers around her heart.

Mathew drew closer. "It's not as bad as you think...try not to cry anymore."

"Oh, yes it is...I've slept with not only my boss but also my son's uncle." One who is responsible for Peter's death. Her heart almost stopped before it jump-started itself.

"What about the part when you told me your husband had died?"

"What else was I supposed to tell you? I had no idea Peter was dead. Hell Mathew, I'm your brother's ex. Robert is your nephew. How much worse can it get than that?" Her thoughts jumped hastily from one to the other in an arduous attempt to digest the facts.

"It means a part of my brother lives on—it's great news. My mother and father will be overwhelmed with happiness when they meet Robert.

Tegan sprung from the seat. The thought of his parents along with their bags of money sent her into a dilemma. Do grandparents have rights to their grandchildren? Ice fingers crawled up her spine.

"That won't happen."

"Meaning?"

"I have no intention of letting them meet Robert."

Scornful objection hung in his eyes. His brows knitted with hot anger, the muscles in his face tensed. "As I said, it would delight my parents. A part of them died when Pete died. This may be a turning point for them. This may make them feel alive again—happy."

"Turning point or not, the answer is no. I need time, Mathew. I really need some space here. I think it would be a good idea if we had a short break. I'm sorry but we have received some pretty powerful news. I'm...well...I really don't know how I feel at present. Shocked seems a lesser word. I'm numb all over but you...you seem overjoyed."

His gaze settled on her face as though searching for answers. She was on guard now, suited with her armor of words. The fear he recognized previously ruptured to the surface and split her open. It was then he wondered if this was the only fear she faced, besides her claustrophobia and flying. Something told him it wasn't.

"This is the fear I see clouding your eyes constantly. Is it the fear that someone may take Robert from you?"

She glared at him. Sucked in a breath. "No, no."

He is so close to the truth. A lump welled in her throat.

"Is there something else? Something else I should know."

"No."

"It's written in your eyes. Something else has happened to you. Something you're not telling me. Why don't you tell me? Hell! It's not as though I'm a complete stranger."

"There's nothing more...I guess...it's the shock of the news, that's all."

"Are you sure you'll be all right?" He needed a little space as well. His gut felt like the grounds for a current football match and he didn't want Tegan to notice, didn't want to upset her any more than necessary.

Nausea rose, bringing bile to his throat restricting his lungs. A pressure like no other settled in his chest.

"Yes," she whispered.

He moved and kissed her on the lips. A light brush that spoke so much. Although she didn't want him to go, trying to get around the new information would take some time.

"I'll give you a call in the morning."

"Thank you."

Through a waterfall of tears, she stared blankly as he walked away. The sound of his car vanished in the distance leaving her alone in silence.

For hours she remained seated, torn apart by her so-called myths. Having a highly active imagination was not responsible after all.

Mathew only mentioned his parent's joy but that joy could turn hostile. Grandparents may have rights. They have the money and money can do almost anything.

She wandered out onto the balcony. The distant sounds of crashing waves and the wind teasing the leaves broke the silence of the night. Her blank gaze rested on shadows as they waltzed over the trees.

The reason she couldn't contact Peter was because he'd...he'd... died. She sniffled back the remembrance of the time they'd had together, the time they had before he took to the alcohol.

She didn't wish death upon anyone.

Was that eerie tug in the office that night Peter? Was he trying to lead her to Mathew, his brother?

Don't be ridiculous. I don't believe in ghosts...or do I?

A chill worked its way up her spine. She couldn't comprehend that Robert was born on the tenth day of June, the same date and hour of his father's death.

She crossed her arms and sat on a deck chair as though trying to cocoon herself from pain. Cocooning herself from reality didn't help one bit. This was her reality.

A reality she had to face.

A reality laced with fear.

The fear of losing her son.

Chapter Twelve

Tegan turned to Mathew.

"I need to have some time off."

His angle of perception intensified. The muscles in his face flexed.

"You never had any time off when Stan was here."

"I know but this is important."

"Can I do anything to help?"

"No. Thank you but I need to finish at two this afternoon." She hated lying but couldn't up and say she'd applied for two positions and the interviews were that afternoon.

"Also, I have three weeks holiday owing. I'd like to take them. Robert needs a holiday and the break would be good."

"What's brought the sudden change?" Rising from the chair, he approached the desk.

Three weeks, hell. Three weeks without setting eyes on that gorgeous face, without inhaling her fragrance. He knew there was some adjustment time required. He also welcomed time to adjust to his little brother being a monster. Something that was difficult to digest.

There were plenty of temps around who could cover a job as secretary but he wasn't sure they'd be as efficient as Tegan.

With an outstretched hand, he pulled her upwards. "Are you sure you want that break?"

Trembling from his touch she spluttered, "Yes."

His hand slipped around her waist, his lips brushed softly over hers, and for long moments the kiss continued until he pulled back.

"I'm going to miss that."

"Yes, me too. I'm sorry it's something I have to do."

"I realize this...but don't make it too long."

By the time two o'clock arrived, Tegan fought a rising well of emotion. The office was unusually so quiet you could hear a pin drop. Tegan cleared the desk, she hadn't told anyone else about taking a holiday, or that she was looking for employment elsewhere.

"Looks like you're clearing out for good."

The passionate trap of his piercing gaze was a struggle to ignore, as she desperately tried not to let him witness how much she was suffering. But time apart, time...was something she needed.

"I need this break. I think you, too, should take some time off. It will do us both good."

"You have a point but I've got too much work at this stage to even think about taking a holiday."

She shook her head. "You can take time out whenever you want. It's not as though you have to work."

"I know but I promised Stan a lot of things and I'm not about to trip around the country side any time soon until a few things are settled." Lines etched into his forehead. His smoldering gaze remained as she picked up her bag and an armful of books.

"I'll keep in touch." It was only a whisper dragging from her throat.

He stood once more and closed the space between them.

"When would you like your holiday to start?"

"I...um. I know it's impossible but today would be good..." Full lashed eyes blinked quickly. "But I suppose as soon as possible. Next week perhaps?"

"A bit of short notice but I think we can arrange something. Today will be fine." His index finger cupped her chin and he leveled their gaze.

"You take it easy, okay? I'm at a bit of a loss that you want time off now...but considering what we've found out, I don't blame you."

"I'm sorry, Mathew I need this time." She didn't tell him she also had a doctor's appointment for later on that day.

"I know you do. Let me know when you get back from your holiday and I'll give you a call, perhaps come down."

"Yes...I will."

"Please be careful."

"I will."

His lips brushed hers before he drew back. His eyes midnight blue singed her blood.

"Thanks." Turning she walked out feeling oddly strange.

Tegan stopped by Sally's office to break the news.

"You what? So soon?"

"Listen Sal, give me a call or come down. I'll fill you in on the details. I know it's a shock, but I have to go."

* * * *

Tegan called around to her first interview, an accountancy firm, one that was highly respectable and was only four blocks from Coleman Enterprises. The interview went well and then she headed for the second one.

When she drove to Charlestown, a suburb of Newcastle, it was past four o'clock. The interview was at four fifteen and thankfully a park was free outside the solicitor's office.

It had been a grueling afternoon but both interviews went well. Although knowing a lot of people were looking for work, excitement flared in her belly. Perhaps she'd get lucky.

Five years working at Coleman Enterprises justified a good enough excuse for a change. All she had to do now was to tell her father.

Picking up her mobile, she hit Clare's name.

"Hi, Clare. Yes, could you stay an extra hour this afternoon? No. Nothings up, I've just got a little extra work to catch up on."

Clicking end, she stared at her mobile. Telling a number of white lies in the past few weeks had regret ripping at her stomach. What else could she tell Clare? Besides, they were only fibs. That thought made her feel better.

Walking into the doctor's office, her gaze circled the small room. Two people were waiting as she made her way to the reception hub.

"Miss Ryan."

"Yes."

"Please take a seat. Doctor Subia shouldn't be too long."

"Thank you." Turning to one side, she sat down on a nearby seat and picked up a magazine. All she managed was to stare at the pictures. Nothing sank in with her mind preoccupied. A brother or sister for Robert. Her lips drew a fine line.

"Miss Ryan."

"Yes." Tegan placed the magazine down and followed the doctor.

"How have you been?"

"I've been okay, thank you."

She sat in a small office. The doctor closed the door and turned.

"I haven't seen you in quite a while. How can I help you?"

She toyed with her bottom lip before answering, "I think I'm pregnant. I undertook a few of those home tests but I want to make sure."

"What did they show?"

"I did it twice and got two different readings. That's why I'm here."

"Okay. Here's a specimen jar. Do you remember where the toilet is?"

"Yes." Tegan took the jar and disappeared only to return within a few moments.

"All done."

She waited while Doctor Subia performed the test. Her hands knitted in her lap and every few seconds she crossed and uncrossed her legs.

Doctor Subia turned. "You're definitely pregnant."

Tegan felt warmth seep to her cheeks. "Oh."

"Is there a man in your life, Tegan? As I noticed you're still not wearing a wedding band."

Chewing on the side of her lip she answered, "Yes, I think so... what I mean to say...yes, there is."

"I do hope everything goes well. You know how much your son wants a father."

Tegan held her lips firmly closed and nodded. She recalled her last visit when she had trouble with Robert. He wouldn't ease up and pestered her about not having a dad.

After leaving the office, her mind was pre-occupied. Sitting in the car for what felt like ages, rubbing a hand in a circular motion over her stomach, the realization of having another child finally sunk in.

Mathew's baby.

Whatever happened, this baby was important and she'd let Mathew know when the time was right. Driving home, the huge, red sun dipped over the mountains but Tegan didn't notice. Her thoughts, her mind was consumed with the baby, with Mathew.

* * * *

As she tucked Robert into bed, the lions head clanged. After a kiss and cuddle she hurried downstairs to answer the door.

"Sally," she cried, after swinging the door open.

"All right fairy princess, you can't do the disappearing act on me now."

Tegan smiled. "Come in. Robert has just gone to bed. Want a coffee?"

"Thanks."

"What's this all about, running off and not telling anyone?"

Tegan explained that she was still married to Peter and by the time the explanation was finished Sally's mouth gaped.

"I never thought about Mathew being Robert's uncle. Wow! However, come to think of it, he does look very much like Robert. You could easily land him if you wanted." Sally grinned mischievously.

"I finally learned to trust someone and he turns out to be my husband's brother. I'm a little concerned that he, too, might turn out like Peter."

"I would be too. I guess it will take a bit of time for you to really get to know him."

"I think I know him quite well now...but I can't be too careful. I'm not rushing into anything. I do care for him Sal...he's treated me well. Oh, I forgot to tell you. I've applied for two positions this afternoon—one in Charlestown the other not too far from Coleman's."

"You what? Hell, oh Teeg, you know I'll be so sad to see you go. I'll miss you a hell of a lot."

"We'll still see each other. Don't let on to Mathew that I'm looking for work elsewhere. I took three weeks annual leave. If I succeed in getting one of these jobs, I'll call him and give notice."

"Are you sure this is what you want?"

"Yes, what other choice do I have? Mathew and I both need time out, and I just can't work with him. He's choking up all my oxygen, seeing him during the day, at night, weekends."

"What did your father say?"

"I haven't told him as yet."

Sally stayed well into the night. They watched a video, sat out on the veranda drinking coffee, and chatted.

After Sally left, a longing ache hung low in Tegan's stomach. An emptiness that wasn't possible. Even crawling into bed that night a sense of loss rose, especially after being so independant and living alone for many years.

Hanging in the recess of her mind she wondered if this would be the perfect opportunity for Mathew's parents to file for access or perhaps custody. What about Mathew? He told her children were imporant. She wondered where he stood in having access. Did he have any rights as an uncle? Unsure of what he really wanted didn't help matters—it only increased her worry.

* * * *

Sally called in the following week.

"A day off?"

"Yeah. I was going to ask for more time but considering you weren't working I thought better of it." She chuckled.

"You've lost a lot of weight Teeg, and your coloring...you're so pale. What's the matter?"

"Nothing, I'm just on edge."

"It's Mathew isn't it?"

"I find it hard adjusting. Mathew thinks I'm away taking a holiday. It'll be all right once I start work at the Solicitors in two weeks."

"Have you told Mathew?"

"No, but I will."

"You will! Here." Sally bent and retrieved the cordless phone and passed it to her. "It might be better if you have someone with you while you do it."

Tegan hesitated at first but then agreed. She punched the digits in on the telephone to connect with Coleman Enterprises.

"Bridget, Tegan Ryan. Is Mister King in please?"

"Tegan."

Her eyes watered the moment his seductive hum caressed her ears. She cleared her throat. "Mathew, it's Tegan...Yes...I miss you too...soon. This may come as a surprise, but well, relationships are much harder when a couple work together...um...and I have decided to give...one weeks' notice." She dragged in a nervous breath. The silence was nerve racking.

"Hell, are you sure? I wish you had discussed this with me first...we could've worked something out, come to some arrangement. Put you into another office...something."

"I think it's best if I work elsewhere. I've heard about office relationships. They just don't work...and well...I'm sorry."

"When you get back from holidays, I'll come and see you. Will you please ring me the moment you arrive home?"

She felt guilty not telling him that she was at home but answered, "Yes...I will."

"Look after yourself."

"I will...thank you." She clicked end.

"Well, all done."

"Wasn't there some other way?"

Tegan shook her head. "No...no other way."

* * * *

After ringing her father and informing him she was calling in, she drove through the heart of Newcastle to a small suburb nestled beside the ocean, Merewether.

Driving around the main part of the beach, she passed a large hotel before taking a left turn and spotted his house beside the ocean. A large spare block of green grass separated it from the cliff face below. She pulled her car into the driveway and saw her father standing on the balcony waving.

"Poppy," Robert called and waved with eagerness. It took a few moments before they let themselves in and walked up to the balcony.

"Dad, hello." She noticed him sitting in a comfortable deck chair.

"It's good to see you and Robert."

Robert ran up to him and kissed him on the cheek.

"Well, well, you've grown sonny. Hey, there might be a surprise next to the television."

"Wow." Robert's eyes lit up and he quickly disappeared.

"Would you like some iced tea?"

"No thanks, Stan."

"You don't have to call me Stan you know. Dad would be great. No one is around."

"I guess I get confused, especially after calling you Stan at the office. She smiled. "I'll try to remember. How are you anyhow?"

"Not bad. It's been a relief not having the entire responsibility of the business. Mathew is a Godsend." He gave her a peculiar gaze. "What's troubling you?"

"When you first met Mathew, did you notice anything about him?"

Stan glanced at her peculiarly. "What do you mean?"

"Well, Mathew's and Robert's eyes are the same color."

"Meaning?"

"Mathew is Robert's Uncle," she whispered, hoping Robert was out of earshot.

Stan sat forward. "Impossible...it couldn't be true."

"But it is."

"I had no idea. I noticed the eye color when Robert was born, eye color that was similar to Mathew's father, John. But hell, how many people have blue eyes?"

"Apparently it runs in the family. It's a family trait that has been passed down for generations. It's the depth of the deep blue. If you've ever looked closely at Robert's, you will see a fine outline in a much darker blue. They're quite unusual. Robert's father had it as well."

"That means Robert is related to one of the wealthiest men in Australia—actually to two of the wealthiest men: Mathew and John." He let out a chuckle.

"I don't care who he's related to. I'm worried that Mathew will turn out like Peter. I find it so hard to trust. I'm trying, Dad. Believe me, I'm trying.

"Mathew produced a photograph of Peter. Dad...he's dead. Robert's father is dead. He died."

"I'm sorry to hear that. It's such a shame Robert won't remember his father."

"He died six months after I left him. Mathew was flying the plane when it went down into the ocean."

Stan rubbed his chin. "That would be a hell of a thing to live with. How's he taking it now?"

"When I first met him, it bothered him a lot. I think he's finally learning to live with it and knows it wasn't his fault."

"Good...listen Tegan, you've got to let go of the past and start afresh. Think of Robert."

"I have...sort of. I'm seeing Mathew again soon...but what if he wants access and what about his parents? Do Grandparents have rights these days? I know some parts of the law have changed and I've heard something about the rights of Grandparents a while ago." She dragged in a worried breath. "It was on the television. Someone filed for custody of their grandchildren...that's it...and they won. They actually took the children away from the mother. Mathew said his parents would be delighted to know a part of their son lives on."

"Don't be ridiculous. You're charging ahead as if they would truly take Robert from you. Nonsense!"

"We don't really know them. We don't know how much they suffered when their son died. They could be really desperate."

"I know John a little more than on a business level and I don't think he'd do such a thing...but if they wanted to it'd be up to a court to decide. I can't see a judge ordering Robert away. You're a good mother. They'd have to prove you weren't looking after Robert properly, that you weren't sending him to school. Things like that."

A sickening wave of terror rose to her stomach. "What if they try to say I drank heavily like Peter did?"

Stan shook his head and ran a handkerchief over his brow.

"You're overreacting. John has never mentioned a son that died. I really think you're stretching the situation."

Tegan bit on her lip before plastering a fake smile to her lips. "It's always in the back of my mind. I can't ignore it."

"Why don't you let Mathew's parents meet Robert? Then you'll find out. It will ease some of the stress you're carrying around."

"No...no...I could never do that."

"Why not? Ask them to a barbeque or meet them at a restaurant. Let Mathew tell them beforehand so they can get used to the idea."

Tegan shrugged her shoulders. "Why didn't you tell me you were friends with Mathew's father?"

Stan cocked his head forward and stretched his spine. "I didn't think it was necessary. Are you sure I didn't tell you?"

"No, Dad. Mathew was the one who told me." She blew out a frustrated breath and leaned against the timber railing.

"I don't see it making much difference."

"I know. There are a few things you should have made sure I knew."

"You know what my mind is like lately. I forget things so readily. That's one of the reasons why I pursued a partner."

"There's nothing wrong with your mind, Dad." Her lips thinned. "It would have been nice if I'd known a little about Mathew before he arrived."

"The only problem I see is that picture on your face."

Tegan pulled a quirky face and shook her head.

"That picture tells me you are in love with him."

A high-pitched sound passed her lips.

"You're fighting something which won't go away. When a person falls in love, you can't switch it off just like that. The sparks that bounced off the walls when you two first met surprised me."

Tegan pushed a strand of hair from her eyes. "That's because we had a conflict of personalities."

"Conflict of personalities, my foot. I felt a romance in the making. Come off it Tegan. I saw the way you two looked at each other."

"I do care for him...but as I said, it's so difficult trying to learn to trust another male. I started to trust him...but when I found out about Peter, it shot me right back to the beginning of our relationship."

"Why don't you let go? Let Mathew take care of you and Robert."

"I'm doing fine for the time being."

He peered at her. "If you learn to love a little maybe it will take the edge off that hurt."

"How would Robert feel when he found out the truth? Would he blame Mathew for killing his father? I don't think I could endure more pain, more heartache."

Stan's eyes rounded. "More pain...tell Robert. Let him know now. Don't wait until he's older for him to find out. Let him grow with the truth."

"I...I don't know. I..."

"What made you put your notice in?" He moved his right hand to his chin and rubbed it in thought.

Tegan opened her mouth and drew in a large breath of salt-air. "Who told you?" she spluttered.

"Hey, nothing gets past an old man like me."

She shook her head.

"Mathew told me."

"I didn't want to work beside Mathew anymore. If we do get into a deeper relationship, it wouldn't work. Oh, I don't know...it was too intense."

"From what I hear the intensity was from both of you fighting the attraction. He's got good blood—very wealthy and could give you and Robert a wonderful life."

"Heavens! Peter was his brother and he didn't have good blood." She turned slightly and her gaze rested over the ocean. "I'm scared of another abusive relationship. I haven't told Mathew...I only said I needed a break, which is true."

"Abusive relationship? Not all men are abusive. I don't see Mathew being an abusive man. He's not that type."

She turned to face him, catching her hair as the breeze fanned it over her face before moving to sit in the deck chair beside him. "Why does it have to be so complicated? When you came in every day at work, my life was great."

"Was it? Or were you trying to fool yourself? I know what living alone can do to a person. Ever since your mother left us, I haven't been the same man. I've had a few female friends but nothing solid. Don't make the same mistake I made, thinking life gave you what it could. Hell, life can give you anything you want. Go to him. Tell him. Go after the man you love."

Knowing exactly what he meant by not being alone was something she didn't want. A husband, a family—yes, she wanted it all. She whooshed out a breath.

"By the looks of it I can see that you've worried yourself sick.

Look at you. I've never seen you so thin, you're skin on bone."

Tegan grinned. "It won't take long to come back when I settle in my new job."

"New job?"

"Yes, I applied for a position as a secretary at a solicitor's firm in Charlestown and got it. I start in less than two weeks."

"It seems like you have it all worked out."

"I wish I did."

Tegan left after lunch.

She missed Mathew each day. He had only shown care, consideration, and respect. He was truly concerned although he'd never said the words, 'I love you'.

It was as though half of her was missing and the love she held for Mathew was real. It couldn't be ignored much longer. She wanted him, needed him. So much was at stake. The ache of emptiness in her heart grew each day.

Chapter Thirteen

Mathew stared at the telephone on his desk as it rang and kept ringing. He'd shunned conversation and avoided meetings for the better part of a week.

His gut twisted with tension.

Nothing registered. The telephone continued to ring.

What was happening to him? What had Tegan done to make him lost, empty, and feeling like a real heel? He'd never experienced these feelings in his life.

He had no time for them.

Now, time dragged like the ticking of an old grandfather clock—each day slower and more painful than the last.

The ringing of the telephone persisted. With great effort he reached over and hit the button, putting it on speaker.

"Mathew King speaking." His voice firm and assertive.

"Hello."

All the blood slowed in his body, he was sure of it. He'd know that voice anywhere. His heart felt like it was squeezing through his rib cage.

"Tegan?" He let out on a breath.

"Yes. I...I want to speak with you."

"I thought you went away on a holiday."

"I...no. I decided not to take Robert out of school."

"Are you okay?"

"Yes." She cleared her throat. "I think so. You?"

"Coping. What can I do for you?"

A noticeable lapse of time passed before she answered.

"Would it be possible for you to take a drive down here? I really need to speak with you."

"If that is what you want. I was just finishing up here. I'll be down before dark."

"Thank you." She hung up, turned and walked out onto the balcony. The sound of his rich, smooth voice crept into the recess of her heart. How she loved that voice. But what was she going to say to him?

Crossing her arms tightly didn't relieve the unbearable ache in her heart. It wasn't like anything she'd ever suffered. Robert's

Uncle or not, her reality finally hit home. Her heart was full of love for Mathew, brimming over the top. Taking one more chance at happiness would be a giant leap. But she wanted the dream, wanted to reach out and nurture it for the rest of her life. Knowing how much of a risk it could be didn't matter, not anymore. If things turned sour, she could always pick up the pieces and start over again.

She drew in a deep breath, looking through the trees toward the ocean as it glistened under twilight. A twinge of excitement raced through her, before knotting with nervousness.

Soon she would set eyes on Mathew.

After she tucked Robert into bed, she went into the bedroom to make sure she was presentable. Dressing in a white, thin, strapped dress and popping a matching white bolero over it, she knew there wasn't much she could do about those red, swollen eyes. She brushed her hair and twisted it into a knot at the nape of her neck.

Loving Mathew more than anything else in this world truly mattered. After all, he only had her best interests at heart.

* * * *

Mathew was going to see Tegan the very moment she arrived back from her holiday. He'd had it planned. He shook his head. She was here, home in Catherine Hill Bay, and no one would stop him from seeing the one woman he couldn't live without.

The only woman he wanted to marry.

God he missed her.

Adrenaline pumped through his veins.

As soon as he reached the freeway, he jammed the accelerator to the floor, headlights blazed against the bitumen ahead. His heart beat dangerously fast. Slowing the car to a crawl, he approached the black wrought iron gates. They were closed as usual. He sprung from the car, raced to the gates, and yanked them open, then resumed the short drive up to the house.

The front light was on. His breathing quickened and he almost bashed the lion's head from its screws. Noticing all blinds were drawn, he knocked again and peered around.

Quiet. It was so damn quiet. He couldn't hear a sound. Reaching for the doorknob, he gave it a turn. Locked.

Tegan tilted her head to one side when the clang of the door-knocker repeated. She put the magazine down, one she'd been trying to read for the best part of an hour. When she opened the door, the rhythm of her heart accelerated. His aura suddenly filled the atmosphere like a gust of wind.

"Hello, Tegan."

A shiver of anticipation folded through her as precious memories came to mind. Steadying herself, she let the door fall the rest of the way open. He was dressed in a pair of denim jeans with a blue, polo shirt. Her breath hitched in her throat and their gaze locked.

She counted the heavy beats of her heart to ten before she spoke. "Hello. Come in." Plastering a nervous, tight grin on her face she turned and walked into the kitchen to boil the kettle.

"Would you...would you like a cup of coffee?" Her voice rose an octave.

"Thank you."

She felt his presence behind her and jumped when warm hands glided down her hips drawing her around to face him.

"I thought you went away. You told me you and Robert were going away on a holiday." His words were a husky drawl.

"Yes...but I changed my mind. I've been thinking...well, with our circumstances I thought it wouldn't work..."

"To hell with our circumstances! Why wouldn't we work? Why wouldn't we?" The muscles in his face twitched before the strong line of his jaw tightened.

"At first I thought about your relationship with Robert. You're his Uncle and responsible for his father's death. I know it was an accident but how do you think Robert will feel when he's older? When he finds out the truth?"

"I'll explain it to him. I'll tell him I'm his uncle. Or you can tell him—whatever you want."

"You also said your parents would be thrilled. What if they want him, want to take Robert away from me? I don't know anything about the rights of Grandparents."

Mathew was horrified when he heard those words. That panic-stricken look surfaced over her face, embedded in her eyes.

He shook his head. "I never...I never thought you'd think such things. Why didn't you say something earlier? My parents would never take a child from their mother. Do you think they are monsters? They wouldn't contemplate such a thing. They're not barbaric."

"But you said they'd be overjoyed, that it would be what they wanted."

"Yes...to have a part of their son. To know a part of him lives on. Robert is their grandchild. Why don't we meet them together? Just the two of us. In that way you will get to know what they're really like. They are nice people. My mother would love you."

"What about you? Don't think for one minute I'll ever let you take Robert away. I know you said you hadn't time for children, but I'm warning you—" she choked out.

Now he was appalled. He shook his head and took a step backwards.

"Tegan, something's missing. I know you love me the way I love you. You fight that love. I've witnessed it several times. I know you had a bad relationship but I swear I'm not at all like my brother. I have never loved any woman so deeply, so strongly, and I have never stopped loving you since the day I met you. I'd never hurt you or Robert in any way. Why do you hide the way you feel for me?"

Her eyes widened with disbelief. "You love me?" She blinked back rising tears. "You love me...but you never said—you only told me you cared as an employer to an employee."

He stepped closer and moved his right hand up under her chin, leveling their eyes.

"I want you, sweetheart. I've always wanted you," he murmured. He pulled her into his arms and closed his lips over hers.

She fell onto his strong support, feeling his hands caress her back, moving downwards, pulling her closer.

Breaking the kiss, he moved back a little. "I know I said I never thought about children and didn't have time. Remember when I told you about Peter breaking his arm, about being responsible for his death. I thought if I couldn't look after my brother, there wasn't a chance in hell that I'd be good at looking after my own child, to be a father."

"But you have. You've taken care of us, especially the day we almost drowned. You've been here for us. You've even spent time with Robert, fishing, reading a book. That's what a father does. And..." Choking on her words, she looked into his compassionate eyes.

"You made me realize what happened to Pete wasn't my fault. All these years I've carried a fear of knowing I couldn't be a good father. You've helped take away that fear."

Closing the gap between them, she stood on tiptoes and kissed him on the mouth before pulling back. "Shush. You'll make a great father. I know you will. As I said, I've witnessed just how good you are for us."

He drew back. "I want you as my wife. Do you hear me? I want you and Robert forever. Not because I'm his Uncle, not because my parents would adore him, because I love you both."

She gazed in astonishment.

"Even if you didn't have Robert, it wouldn't change the way I feel toward you. My love goes much deeper. He'll gradually know that I'm his Uncle if you like. Not when he's older—as he grows up. Whatever you decide is fine with me. I want you as my wife. I need you to give me an answer. I've had a long thought about our circumstances. Robert is my blood. You do want a family, don't you?"

Tegan rolled her bottom lip inward and held it firmly with her teeth, unable to believe what she was hearing.

"If you don't like that idea, we could...live together. Why don't you give us a chance?"

She raised a cupped hand and smothered his words. "I love you Mathew, with all my heart. And yes...I will marry you. Why do you think I rang your office? Why do you think I wanted to see you?" Joy bubbled in her heart. Her words barely audible, "And yes, I do want a family."

Their lips joined. She melted into his hypnotic embrace until she had to come up for a breath. "I have something else to tell you. Another reason I wanted to speak with you."

His body went rigid. "What else could there possibly be? My heart is thumping against metal. I think it's a miracle we found each other, and under difficult, and somewhat intriguing circumstances."

Taking hold of his hand, she led him to the lounge, and sat still clutching his hand. She turned sideways to face him.

"Mathew...I'm...well...are you ready to be a father?"

"Yes, sweetheart I've already told you I'm convinced that I'll make a good father." He jested.

"No...no...hell. Why do I find it's such a hard time lately with my words? They twist in my mouth before tripping over my tongue, coming out distorted."

"Steady down." He moved a lock of hair from her eyes; his fingers lingered over her temple.

"I'm going to have a...baby."

His spine stiffened. "You...a baby? What, our baby?"

"Yes."

"I couldn't have received better news." He took her in his arms, his lips roaming, warm and comforting before he drew back.

"It's another reason for us to be married." The jewel in his eyes sparkled.

"How long have you known?"

"Only a while...I'm three months pregnant."

"Looks like you have a wedding to plan, and soon, but don't ever expect me to wear a white suit. They're gay."

Tegan frowned. "I love a man in a white suit."

"Well, not this man. You'll just have to find something else about me to love," he joked.

"That might be hard." She grinned. She rubbed her lips in thought and then said, "There's something else I have to tell you."

"Hit me with it. If I can take all this, I can take anything." A low chuckle rumbled up his throat.

"Peter, your brother, was not a monster all the time. I was with him for two years. Most of that time was good until he began drinking heavily. Please don't let anyone know, not even your parents. Don't let them know he told me he had no relatives as well. It's best that people remember the good side of him. I want Robert to know what his father was like before he took to the drink."

"You're a remarkable woman, sweetheart. You're too kind after what he did to you."

"As I said, it's in the past and it was the alcohol that changed him."

"If that's what you want." He was amazed by her ability to see past the ugly truth but he knew she had such a caring nature. "I can assure you, I don't drink in excess."

She managed a wavering grin before rolling her lips together. Then she said, "Can you tell me how he died? I mean..."

"Are you sure you want to know?"

"Yes, just a little. Do you want that coffee first?"

"Yes. But I don't want to let you go. I want you in my arms, always."

She smiled and pulled from his grasp to make the coffee.

* * * *

Carrying the coffees, they sat at the dining room table.

"As I said, we were coming back from Sydney but I had to make a detour to one of the small islands off the coast to drop off a mate. It was late when we started to return, on dusk. Not long after, we took off the control column lost tension and went limp. Then I heard a snapping sound like a cable had broken followed by a rattling sound. It was the cable against the fuselage. It'd snapped for sure as I couldn't maintain altitude. We nose-dived."

"You don't have to...I'm sorry I should have known it would be painful."

"I'd like you to know. Yes, painful perhaps, nevertheless you need to know. I put in a mayday call before we went down."

Mathew pictured that tortuous day when every instinct told him they were headed for doomsday. "We nose-dived into the ocean. I got out, the aircraft vanished...I thought Pete got out as well but there wasn't a sign of him. I called to him through the darkness so many times but there wasn't an answer."

Goose bumps splintered her flesh. "I'm so sorry. Did you... were there any remains?"

"No. The aircraft dived and apparently kept diving. There's a shelf not far from the island and it drops off into a fathomless pit. The aircraft is too deep to retrieve."

"I'm so sorry, darling." Darkness filled his eyes. She walked around the table and sat on his lap. Wrapping her arms around him, she knew he was a lucky man to escape such a horrific accident.

"Having a memorial was good for Mum. She visits as often as she likes."

"Oh." Tegan shook her head, thinking of the pain his mother must have suffered losing a son.

"Are you ready to take on a family?"

"Yes, sweetheart."

He pulled her into his arms, raining kisses over her forehead. His lips connected with hers. He savored the moment, knowing she held the key to his heart.

He mumbled from under the kiss, "How many children would you like to have?"

"Four." Tears curtained happy eyes. "There's one more thing." She sniffled.

"You mean...something else? I don't think my heart can take anymore."

She let out a giggle. "Stan is my father."

"I know, sweetheart." The corners of his lips twitched.

"You knew? You mean to say you knew all along and didn't let on, didn't say a word?" She poked him in the shoulder.

"Yes, since the day I met him."

"But how?

"A promise is a promise and I'm not one for breaking promises," he whispered huskily. "Perhaps soon I will let you know but at present I can't."

"You didn't say anything. Why did you continue to let me believe you didn't know?"

"I knew you and your father wanted to keep it a secret so I played along."

Her lips drew a fine line. "My father...Dad told you." She let out a giggle.

"Now, how did you guess that one?" A devilish glint shone from his eyes.

Without warning, she playfully hit his shoulder. He grabbed her hand brought it to his lips, nipping her fingertips.

"You are so beautiful; do you know that? You're something my life has been missing for such a long time."

She grinned. "Sally knows Stan is my father as well."

"Sally?"

"Yes. We've become good friends over the years. She's given me a lot of support. She's a breath of fresh air."

He laughed. "You're the breath of fresh air."

"There's one more thing."

"Give it to me baby." He grinned. "I think my heart can handle anything after everything that has happened." He smiled, filling that empty void in her heart as each minute passed.

"I really need to know how King Enterprises operates."

"I thought you knew?"

"Yes. I do know a little of King Enterprises but I want to hear it from you."

"My father owns a multi-million dollar business. I have worked my way up from the bottom and bought into the business, as well as acquiring many of my own. We do buy businesses that are in the pitfalls of insolvency. However, we do it honestly and at a fair price. We save the employees' jobs. Once we buy the business, we set up managers and the like. Ninety-nine times out of a hundred those companies prosper. With Coleman Enterprises it was a one-off thing, as a favor to your father from my father."

"I feel so bad about leaving the business, especially leaving you up in the air."

"You didn't waste time but I managed. Am I right to say you were running from me?"

She bit on the corner of her lip. "I was thinking."

"Oh no, not again, this could become problematic," he teased.

"Peter...I knew him as Peter Knight although he had a Kings

blood and they say: once a Knight always a Knight. I wonder if a King will be any better?"

His wide lips slid into an easy grin. "Certainly, this King will take care of his Queen with the utmost care and respect." He held her closely and moved his lips over hers before breaking contact.

"I'll call my parents in the morning and organize a time for you to meet them, if that's okay with you?"

She pulled a quirky face with the thought of meeting them. "Yes, that's okay." She wondered what she'd say, how she'd cope.

"I've got a surprise," Mathew said.

"What is it?"

"Come on, let's sit in the lounge." Taking her hand, he led her toward the lounge before he dragged a little gold box from his suit pocket, just inside the right side of his jacket. He held it out, palm upwards.

Drawing in a deep breath, Tegan touched the gold box with the tip of her index finger.

"It won't bite." He placed it in her palm and flipped the lid open. A diamond the size of Uluru flashed at her. "Mathew...it's... it's so big."

The expression of delight quickly disappeared from his face. "What you don't like it?"

"Oh, yes...darling. I adore it. It must have cost a fortune."

"And worth every dollar, I can assure you." He took the ring from the box and slipped it on her wedding finger. "I thought it would match you." He smirked.

"When did you buy it?"

"That's a long story." He smiled one of those big smiles that melted her heart.

"Come on now...when did you get it?"

"I've had it in my pocket a few days after we arrived back from Port Macquarie."

"Way back then...what if I'd said 'no'? What if I didn't want to marry you?"

"It would be one ring that would never wrap around such a beautiful finger as yours. It'd never find an owner."

She shook her head. "I can't believe you wanted to marry me so long ago."

"I've wanted you for my wife the very first night we made love. I knew you were the one from the very moment I met you."

"That's impossible. How can you know someone is the right person without knowing anything about them?"

"Oh, I did. I knew what you were like at that very moment. I wanted to get to know you more." He laughed. "You even rejected my first offer for a coffee. But I wasn't going to let that stop me. I wasn't going to stop until you were mine."

She pulled a quizzical face. "The ring, it's beautiful...thank you." After staring at it for the space of ten or more heartbeats, she piped up, "I might get married in red."

Mathew's puzzled gaze was just the response she was looking for. "Well, if you have a choice of not wearing white, I do also." She chided.

"Many men get married in a dark blue suit."

She pulled a face. "Suit yourself." Then she gazed at the brilliance of one single diamond, princess cut. Falling into his embrace, she felt very lucky and very spoilt. His lips connected with hers before they took the flight of stairs up and into her bedroom.

"I have to leave early in the morning. So, if you wake up and I'm not here...I've got three meetings tomorrow that can't be cancelled."

"That's okay. I know what it's like. I only want you for the night," she jested.

"What? Only for one night?" His eyes were playful, mesmerizing.

"Well, perhaps many nights." She giggled. "Um...I need to shower...in fact I might pop in the spa, relieve some aching muscles."

Mathew watched her disappear into the ensuite. Fifteen minutes later he opened the door.

Tegan thought she heard a noise. Through the vapor filled ensuite she noticed the flicker of two candles and then the top light flicked off.

"I hope you don't mind."

Her heartbeat accelerated. "I knew you'd come," she croaked, before he climbed in front of her, into the bubble filled spa.

Mathew noticed her approval and smiled. "I thought you might need some help."

Her lips thinned trying to prevent a giggle. "Thank you."

Aware of his gaze over her breasts as they shimmered enticingly against the glow of the candlelight, she moved more bubbles over them in a teasing fashion.

His blue eyes glistened as they caressed her skin seductively. "Turn around."

Tegan turned, settling back into his arms, against a warm,

solid and inviting chest.

He lathered the soap and reached over to rub a single soapy hand over her abdomen.

"The soap will make all the bubbles vanish."

"What a shame. That means we'll have to start over and over."

He lathered the soap once more. His hand reached over her shoulder, down toward her tummy, and around her hips in soft circular motions.

She dissolved at his touch. A delightful shudder stroked her body the moment his thumb flicked over a tight nipple. His lips lingered near her ear before his tongue stroked lightly, sending a rush of warmth scooting to her abdomen. Drawing in a leisurely breath, knowing she was captive to his touch, she eased deeper into submission.

He lowered his head and kissed her on the corner of the mouth, enticing her to turn, pulling her weight over him. She felt the delicious, silky feeling of skin on skin and almost shed a tear as his magical touch continued to caress her, continued to wash away all thoughts, and all doubt.

Following his instruction she stood, placing her back against the tiles.

With one hand above him, palm flat against the white tiled wall, he steadied his balance, while the other tucked neatly around her bottom.

"Oh...Mathew...I...I."

His lips fused with hers, savagely, crushing any words she had to say or moan. His hand yanked one of her legs up and she wrapped it around him, as the shaft of his masculinity, hot and quick, penetrated.

With his free hand, his thumb caressed her nipples sending signals directly to the core of her femininity.

Urgency raced through his burning blue eyes, as she arched back joining his rhythm. He groaned. She drowned in a spa of ecstasy, his name on her breath, nails digging into his flesh, until momentum slowed and the tingle of his magical touch hummed through her body.

Breathless, mind-shattering, she hung limply in his arms until he lowered her into the warmth of the spa below. She snuggled against his chest, his arms entwined around her.

For long luxurious moments they didn't move, until he swooped her into his arms and stood stepping from the spa.

Grabbing a white towel, he patted gently at her wet skin, before wrapping another warm towel around her. With his right hand, he slung a towel around his midline, picked her up, and carried her toward the bed.

Freeing a hand, he tossed back the quilt, tugged the towel free and eased her down onto the bed. Discarding the towel from his hips, he climbed in and slipped an arm under her neck. As he did, she mumbled and stirred before he pulled the quilt over them and placed a soft kiss in the center of her forehead.

* * * *

For hours he watched her sleep, watched the way her cute nose turned slightly, the high cheek bones, the thick lashes now concealing eyes that he'd previously thought were colored by green contact lenses.

A tug curled his lips. Was it possible to love someone so deeply, to crave her as much as he did?

She slept peacefully in his arms before he drifted to sleep.

Chapter Fourteen

The thrumming of a car in the distance drew closer. Standing, Tegan walked around toward the front of the house. A dark blue sedan came to a standstill opposite the gates.

She squinted against the sun's reflection bouncing off the windscreen, making it impossible to recognize who was driving.

A tall, solid frame stepped from the car, dark hair, shiny against the sun's rays as he opened the gates before returning to the car.

As the car crawled toward the house, her piercing gaze zeroed in. Her heart charged with deep thuds. Its beat throbbed in her throat. Was her mind so off-track that a ghost had come to haunt her?

With an indrawn breath, eyes hawk-like, the familiar face drifted into view. Her legs gave way from beneath her, hands grappled for support, knuckles turned white, as the pounding of blood echoed in her ears. Suddenly she released the indrawn breath and rushed inside. Closing the door behind her and locking it securely, she peered through the window.

Peter.

My husband.

Peter.

He's dead.

Dead.

Dead.

Dead.

Cool chills exploded over her body, shattering her senseless. Shaking her head, trying to push the image as far away as possible failed. Her body filled with shock.

He's alive. He's alive.

Impossible.

What does he want?

What is he doing here?

The clang of the lion's head rattled non-stop, forcing Tegan to reel back in shock.

"I know you're in there. I saw you when I drove up," he said.

Holy hell, what will I do?

"If you don't open the door, I'll bash it down."

"I'll be there in a minute."

Walking to the door, her trembling body wavered with uncertainty but she didn't open it.

"What do you want? I thought you were dead."

A sinister roar shot a cold splinter of fear up her spine, forcing her to take a retreating step backwards.

"I fooled everyone, didn't I? Well, are you going to open the bloody door? You know, I can knock it down at any time."

Time slowed. She stilled. The beat of her heart knocked hard, her breathing quick and shallow. She couldn't answer.

"I'm warning you...open the bloody door."

"What for, Peter? What do you want?"

"Don't be a fool...open the door."

A nervous hand reached for the doorknob. Turning it slowly, she let it fall open.

He slammed his hand against the door. "My, my, six years has made a difference hasn't it? You've turned into quite a looker I see."

His hair, a crop of dark messy waves fell to his collar. A three perhaps four-day growth partly hid the pallor of his complexion.

Flinging a hand on her hip she blurted, "You were supposed to be de...I mean what do you want?"

A cunning grin sliced across his face. "So, my family has been telling you stories. I survived, don't worry. A fishing trawler picked me up after I'd swum for ages. It was dark and I decided to fake my death to get away from my sickening family for good. I've been hiding out in Queensland, plenty of sunshine and fresh air."

"Yeah, I bet. "You told me you didn't have any family at all...you told—what...do you want?"

"That'd be a statement. You know what I want and I'm not leaving without him."

Tegan's mouth formed a circle. Breath lodged in her throat. "I have no idea what you're talking about."

"You can't fool me again. You did a pretty good job of hiding when you took off over six years ago but you can't keep my son from me."

He stalked through the door and glanced around. "Where's my son?" He demanded. His face grew red with heat, his eyes blazed with a wild craziness.

The sickly smell of stale beer hung in the atmosphere, drowning out the fragrance of a frangipani growing closely beside the entrance door.

"If you won't tell me, I'll find him myself."

Tegan watched helplessly, as he pounded up the stairs. If she rang the police, they'd take at least forty minutes to arrive. Then, if they did book him or lock him up, he'd only return when he was released. What would happen then? What choice did she have?

A loud curse erupted through the house before he stormed back down the stairs. His black shirt hung loosely over faded denim jeans and there was a crazed look in his eyes. Nothing, resembled the man she'd left all those years ago.

"Come on, babe. I don't have all day. Where is he?"

"You won't take my son away. You will never take him from me."

"I'll just wait here until I see him. Then we'll be going."

He reached out but Tegan was much too quick and ducked from his attempt.

"Come on, babe. Remember the good times we had?"

"How did you find me?"

"How do you think? I've always kept in contact with Dave. Didn't you realize he's an old mate of mine? I found out you were in Newcastle. It didn't take long then. I've been following you for the last few weeks. You had some guy with you." He laughed. "You've got a new lover. Is that it? Did you tell him you're as cold as a fish?"

Did she tell Dave about having a son? What a stupid thing to do. She wasn't sure if she'd said son or not. Peter hadn't mentioned Robert's name and she wasn't going to tell him. What a mistake! How stupid of her.

"How...do you know? How...do you know if I had...a boy...or girl?"

"I saw him from a distance the other day. You were picking him up from school. So don't give me any trouble."

Tears threatened to cloud her eyes but she used all the strength she could muster not to let him witness how unnerving he made her feel. Instead, she propped both hands on her hips.

"He's on a holiday school camp." It was the first thought that popped to mind. Perhaps it would put him off, send him away.

"When's he coming back?"

"Three weeks," she spluttered.

"That's a pity. I'll be back. Don't you try to run again because when I return you had better be here and with my son. If not, I'll come looking for you and it won't be pretty."

"Don't forget to inform lover boy I'll be back. I saw his car leave early this morning. Fancy damn thing. I suppose you're after his money."

"How can you say such a thing when you don't really know me? You don't know who I am—not now."

His cool regard and his hardening face sent a shiver of fear through her body.

"Just get my kid ready for when I get back."

"You can't take him and leave. The law won't allow it."

"I'll file for custody."

He grabbed her around the waist, jerked her up against him, and crushed his lips over hers. As quickly as it happened, he let go, then he staggered before storming out.

Tegan's right hand moved to her lip, feeling a cold sensation trickle over her skin. She heard him call out.

"I'll be back in three weeks. You have him ready."

When the car was out of sight, she ran through the grass toward the gates and locked them. Returning indoors, she tried to stop the ridiculous trembling, and the quiver of her lips, before ringing the police to report the incident.

"What? Can't you do anything?"

"Not really. Has he threatened you?"

"He's threatened to take my son away. He's threatened to file for custody." A sickening wave knotted her stomach. As it heaved with nerves, she ran her right hand over the tender spot.

"You need to come in and fill out a report. If you like, you can take out an Apprehensive Violence Order against him. It's what they call an A.V.O. I can tell you, there isn't much we can do to stop him coming around. He's the child's father...unless he attempts to harm you or your child. But it's his right to file for custody or access."

"Access? My son doesn't even know him. I'll be in to sign whatever documents are necessary."

Before leaving the house, she checked her face in the mirror. Dried blood left a trail from lip to chin. Sucking in a nervous breath, she dabbed it with a tissue.

* * * *

Tegan answered the door, knowing it was Sally. Mathew was in Sydney for the day on business and wasn't due back until the following morning. She didn't want to be alone—not now, knowing

Peter could return at any time.

"I'm so glad you could come and stay for the night."

"That's fine…I don't mind really. You're trembling. Come on. Tell me what's happened."

They walked into the lounge room and Sally went to the kitchen to put on the jug.

Tegan sank onto the sofa. "I don't want to talk too loud. Robert is playing in his room."

Sally returned with the coffee and sat beside her.

"I took an A.V.O. out on Peter." A nervous laugh hitched in her throat.

"Oh gosh, Teeg." She smiled before giving Tegan a kiss on the cheek. "Drink your coffee; it'll make you feel better. What did the cops have to say?"

"Seeing I live so far out of town, it'd take them a while to get here even if he shows up again. They advised me to have someone stay with me for a while."

"You could always move."

"No…I couldn't do that."

"He might not turn up again. You know what he's like. You've told me he used to say one thing and then do the opposite."

"That's true…but I'm not letting Robert out of my sight. I told Peter he was at camp for three weeks. At the time I thought it would give me three weeks relief but he could turn up now. He said he's coming back. He'd been drinking. At times I wonder if he meant what he said."

"You can't take chances. So, don't believe he will wait three weeks. He probably said that to put you off-guard. Please be careful. You are going to tell, Mathew aren't you?"

"I have to…he thinks his brother is dead. His parents think he is dead as well. Everyone thought he died the day…well…about six years ago. Mathew and I figured out they are the same person. A photograph proved it. But he's alive…what a shock! I thought I was seeing a ghost when he pulled up." She let out a strained breath. "Not a word to Stan though. Not until I can explain things myself."

"Oh, and another thing." Tegan glanced at Sally.

"Gee Teeg, your life seems so happening—pretty full all ready."

"This will make it fuller believe me. I'm going to have Mathew's baby."

Sally jumped from her seat and swung her arms around Tegan. "Congratulations. Oh, wow. This is so exciting. How far are you?"

"I'm three months. I have to see the doctor again in a few weeks but there's something else."

"Oh, Teeg. What...I can't imagine what it'd be, as you've already gone through so much."

"It's good news." She moved her left hand out, palm down with splayed fingers only to bounce it up and down.

"Wow, what a ring. You're getting married. I couldn't be more happy for you."

"Thanks Sally...but there is a tad bit of a problem. You see, Peter is still my husband. I've never gotten a divorce. I'm still married to the man. What will Mathew think of me if I tell him?"

"Well, for starters...you thought he was dead so there was no need for a divorce. You have to tell him."

"I know but I'm pretty good at making a mess of things, aren't I?"

"No...don't say that. It's only circumstances. You didn't know he was alive, noone did."

* * * *

"Can I speak to Mathew King please? It's Tegan Ryan."

"Hi, Tegan, I'll put you through."

"Mathew King."

"Mathew, it's Tegan."

"I was just about to ring you."

"I need to speak to you."

"Yes. What is it?"

"No. I need to speak to you in person—in private."

"When?"

"I know there's a lot going on at work but you have to come down now, please."

"Is everything all right?"

"Not really."

"Is Robert okay?"

"Yes...please come down."

"I'll be down soon...as fast as I can get there. I'll leave now."

Mathew recognized the tightness of her words, the difficulty she had speaking.

* * * *

Jamming the accelerator to the floor, he headed south on the freeway. His mind was torn with worry, his heart in overkill.

The gates were opened and the car crawled up toward the house.

Tegan swung the door open when she spotted his car from the window.

"Mathew."

He stepped up and drew her into his arms.

"Your lip, what happened to your lip?"

Putting a hand to her lip, she said, "Come in." Breaking from his touch, she closed the door, and they walked into the lounge and sat down.

He traced his finger over her lip. "Who's done this to you? You're shaking, hell Tegan."

"P...Peter..."

"I thought you said the photograph was the Peter you married."

"It was." Drawing in a composing breath, she struggled against the shock determined to destroy her nervous system. Your brother...Pete...was here." Shaking her head she tried to wake up her senses, words grated from her throat. "Your brother...he...he...he's alive...he...he was here."

"What in the hell...what?" Mathew jerked forward.

"He was here looking for...Robert." Her bottom lip wouldn't stop quivering.

"Impossible."

"No...not impossible. I thought I was seeing a ghost...but it was Peter for sure. He said he was in hiding. He...he wanted everyone to know he was dead...apparently a fishing trawler picked him up. He's been living in Queensland."

Mathew raked a heavy hand through his hair. His muscles involuntarily contracted as disbelief hurtled through him. "Did he do this to you?"

"Yes, he grabbed me and tried to kiss me. I struggled before he let me go."

"Are you sure you're okay?"

"Yes, I will be."

"When, when was he here?"

"Yesterday...you were still in Sydney."

"Hell. You should have rang. I would have left. Hell, Tegan."

"I rang Sally. She stayed last night."

"It doesn't make any difference. You're my fiancée, for crying out loud."

"I'm s...sorry."

"He didn't hurt our baby did he?"

"No...no he didn't."

"He's a complete lunatic. I don't know what in the hell has gotten into him. I'm so sorry, sweetheart."

"Peter said...he said he's been following me. He said..." Trying to concentrate as she spoke felt impossible. "He said he's been... he's been...following me for a few weeks. Mathew...I'm...well, I'm still married to him...I didn't get a divorce."

"I can't believe he'd go to so much trouble to let everyone believe he was dead. All these years...all these years, thinking he was dead, thinking I'd failed him."

He paced to the doors at the back of the house and returned to sit beside her. "Married? Teeg...we were going to be married."

"Yes, I know...but as you said, we thought he was dead. I didn't have a reason to file for a divorce...and well, I never thought I'd fall in love and especially not get married again."

"I know, sweetheart."

His slipped his arm around her waist.

"That's not all, Mathew. He said he knew about you as he saw you leave but he didn't know it was his brother."

Mathew shook his head. "What did you say to him?"

"I didn't say anything about you. I told him Robert was on a school holiday camp for three weeks."

"I'm not letting you out of my sight. I'll stay here. Work from here. Husband or no husband, I won't allow him to get anywhere near you or Robert. I won't let him hurt you again or our child. It'll be over my dead body."

Mathew stood, paced, the heel of his hand rubbed hard against his forehead. He walked to the window and gazed toward the tall, black gates.

"The gates need to be locked." He glanced at his watch. What time do you pick Robert up?"

"In about half an hour."

"In half an hour, we will pick Robert up. Then we'll go to the motel where I'm staying to collect my things, then back here."

Knowing how persistent Peter used to be, especially when he was intoxicated...well, nothing would surprise her now—nothing at all. "I'll get ready." She pushed herself to stand but faltered only to drop back onto the cushions on the lounge.

"You're not all right. Look at you. You haven't stopped trembling."

"I'll be fine. Can you help me up?"

Mathew slipped an arm around her waist with one hand, the

other steadied her while resting on her hip.

"Thanks," she said on a breathless whisper. "I guess it's the shock of it all. I can't believe this is happening."

"That makes two of us. Don't worry, sweetheart. I won't let him get within an inch of you or Robert."

Knowing Mathew was in the house was a relief. She ran her hand along the stair railing and disappeared into the bedroom. Before returning downstairs, she locked every window and double-checked to make sure they were securely locked.

"Ready," he called.

"Yes."

"I've locked all the windows down here. I want you to bring your car out of the garage and park it out front when we return. With both cars here, surely he won't show again."

A little tug pulled at her lips. She nodded before they walked out, locking the door behind them.

* * * *

The following few days passed by without incident. Tegan loved having Mathew staying, and Robert thought Christmas wasn't that good after all.

"You know I rang my parents and explained I want them to meet you. They're coming up this weekend. I haven't as yet explained anything about Pete being alive."

"What if he never shows? Do you think it's a good idea if your parents know just now?"

Mathew shook his head. "Here, let me do that."

Tegan glanced up before handing him the knife. Cutting up onions wasn't her forte. She moved to the sink to wash her hands.

"I'm not sure about Mum. I don't think she could handle it at this stage. How about we wait and see what happens? What did the police advise?"

"Even though I took an A.V.O. out, it won't stop him from returning. They can't even find him to deliver it so he won't even know." Tegan's mind raced with possibilities, with questions and filled with mounting concern. "I'm not sure it's a good idea for your parents to come here. What if he turns up?"

"Surely he wouldn't try anything with a few strange cars around the house. I'll get Sean to bring his car down and leave it here. He can drive the limo for a time. Then I have my car...surely Pete wouldn't make a spectacle of himself in front of people."

Tegan was the only person who knew what Peter was really capable of, especially after witnessing his crazed mask of determination. Nothing and no one would stop him.

"Let's hope not," she replied vaguely.

Mathew bent and brushed his lips over hers.

"On the other hand, I'd like to see him, find out what he's been up to. He is my brother. I have so many unanswered questions."

"Perhaps the police will track him down soon. Then we can find out an address or something to lead you to him."

"I know it's hard for you to understand, sweetheart. I need to settle a few things with him. Knowing he is the monster we talked about is so damn hard to accept...but there are necessities one has to attend to."

Tegan's lips thinned. "I do understand. If he were my brother, I guess I'd have to see him—even if it's for the very last time."

Chapter Fifteen

"What time did you say they'd be here? I'm so nervous. I don't think I can do this."

Mathew planted a kiss on Tegan's forehead before taking her hands. "Yes, you can, sweetheart. We can. Remember we're in this together and we go through it together."

She drew in a breath, shaking her head in small, quick jerks.

"They've had one week to adjust to the news. It's not as though they found out yesterday."

"Are you sure you told them everything?"

"Stop worrying. I told them everything except Pete showing up here or that he's alive. I think it's a good idea to let my parents meet you and Robert first before we dump more on them. Let them get used to a few facts beforehand. Besides, Mum was thrilled. She kept saying, 'a little grandson', repeatedly. I think it's made her life complete."

Tegan tore a hand from his and ran it down the side of her dress, then adjusted one of the fine straps. "Perhaps I should change. I don't like this dress. It's too floral and casual. Does the bolero go with it? I need to wear it."

"Sweetheart, you look beautiful. There is no need for the jacket."

"I'd feel so embarrassed if anyone saw my scars, especially your parents. How would I explain them?"

He moved his hands and cupped her face. "Please stop stressing."

She pulled a quirky face, her lips drawing tight. "Did your parents say anything about me?"

"Mum said that it must have been hard on you to raise Robert alone. She asked why you left Peter. I just said you had a fall-out six months before he died."

Tegan broke contact and took comfort by sitting on a bench.

"She understands. Mum's not as old-fashioned as you may think. You'll like her." Mathew sat beside her.

Her stomach rolled with nausea. Taking a quick glance to where Robert was kicking his legs out from under the swing, she called, "Don't get those clothes dirty. Try to keep clean Robert.

Mathew's parents will be here soon."

"How do you think Robert will handle it? After all, they are strangers. I told him two nights ago that your parents were coming to visit. I also told him they are his father's parents. He understands you're his uncle but I'm so worried about him. He's quiet. He's not as bubbly as he usually is." Her voice was quiet, almost a whisper so Robert couldn't hear.

Mathew ran his right hand down over her hair, falling loosely around her shoulders. "We should have a talk to him, find out his concerns."

"Hey Robert. Come up here. Your mother and I want to have a talk with you."

Robert bounced off the swing and ran up the stairs toward them, planting himself next to his mother.

She slipped an arm around his waist.

"Are you all right?"

"Yes, Mum. If they are Mathew's mum and dad, and..." He peeked at Mathew. "He's my uncle, are his mum and dad my family?"

Tegan bit on her lip and rubbed her hand along the bare skin of his arm. "They're your grandparent's, sweetie—your real dad's mother and father."

"So, why did Dad go with the angels?"

"He had no choice, sweetie. We'll miss him and he knows you are happy with us, with Mathew, and now his parents."

"Mathew is your uncle. Remember I explained it a few nights ago?"

"So, if he marries you, can he still be my dad? I wanted him to be my dad. I really wanted him to be my dad."

Tegan ruffled his hair and kissed him on the temple.

"So, that's what's been worrying you. Of course he can be your dad when we get married."

She looked into his eyes and saw that beam growing, the one he had the very first time he and Mathew met.

"Don't worry too much, sweetie. Mummy won't let anything happen to you and Mathew certainly won't."

Mathew leaned over Tegan.

"I think the sooner we get married the better. I'd be proud to be your dad, Robert. I always wanted a son like you."

Robert's eyes beamed. "Really?"

"Yes, really."

"Let's announce the wedding after everyone settles in."

Robert swung his legs into the air and jumped to his feet. "I hope Grandfather John likes fishing?"

"I hope he does as well...off you go. You can go back to the swing but please try to stay clean."

Robert stopped beside Mathew and pulled a quirky face. "Does that mean you can read me bedtime stories every night?"

"It sure does."

He swung his arms around Mathew's neck before rushing back to the swing.

"You see, he understands more than you realize."

"Thank you. He seems enthralled to know you will become his father. He adores you."

"We've just got to get you divorced first," he whispered against her ear.

She let out a sigh. "Yes."

The peal of the lions head echoed from the front door, startling Tegan and making her jump.

"Hey, settle down." He stood. "I'll get it. I'll bring the drinks while I'm inside. You just relax."

Relax...hell...relax... How could she? She closed her eyes briefly. What do they think of a woman who was married to one son and now about to marry the other? Trapped in doubt with mounting fear, her stomach coiled into a knot of tension. She drew in a deep breath moments before Mathew's voice forced her to snap her eyes open.

A breeze caught her hair. She sprung to her feet and tucked a stray wisp behind one ear. Mathew's parents stood behind him.

His mother, a striking lady with short silver, hair, dressed in a teal, ankle-length dress, appeared as though she'd just stepped from a fashion magazine. His father had a thick crop of grey hair, and wore tan pants with a white short-sleeved shirt.

Talk about feeling embarrassed. Her nerves prickled up her spine, a shiver following, unable to believe Peter had parents. Unable to believe they stood in her home barely feet away.

Mathew's mother broke the silence. "Oh, there she is. How lovely." She walked over to Tegan and gave her a cuddle. "Mathew has told us all about you, love. I feel as though I know you already."

An overwhelming rush of blood coursed through Tegan's veins.

"Thank you," she managed to say, fighting back a rising swell of emotion. *Peter's parents, Mathew's parents.*

"Tegan, my mother, Valerie and father, John."

"Pleased to meet you."

John approached. He was about to shake her hand when he moved in giving her a peck on the cheek. "You are a surprise, my dear."

Tegan stared at him. A cool chill shot through her. His eyes were a deep dreamy blue—the color where the sky touches the ocean at twilight, outlined by a darker blue hue. Such a distinct quality, she could barely stop herself from staring.

Robert's eyes—eyes he'd inherited from his father. The likeness which plagued her from the very moment she set eyes on Mathew. A likeness which ran in the King family for generations.

"It's nice to meet you too." Her words sounded gruff.

Tegan heard Valerie's voice in the distance. She looked around and saw Robert giving her a cuddle. Overcome by what was happening, she almost fell into the chair behind her.

"Dad and I are going to get the meat. Everything's fine." Mathew left after he'd planted a brief kiss on her forehead, leaving her startled, green gaze, trailing after him. Then turning to check on Robert, to her amazement he held Valerie's hand as they walked up the steps.

"I feel like I've missed out on so much of our grandson's first six years."

"There's plenty of time to catch up." Tegan surprised herself. Here were two people, two lovely people who deserved to know their grandson. They deserved every amount of happiness. Losing a son was something she could never face and keep a sane mind. She knew Robert would play a very important role in their healing process.

Fighting back tears, knowing she had so many good people around her, people who were family, was such a blessing. A wavering grin slid to her face.

Mathew and John carried the drinks to the table.

The lion's head clamored.

"I wonder who that could be." A tremor sliced up her spine as she stood and walked through the kitchen toward the front door. Peering through the window, she smiled.

When she swung the door open, her arms went around Stan's neck. "Dad."

"Surprise."

"Come in. Everyone's out on the balcony."

"Mathew, look who's here."

Mathew approached. "I took the liberty of inviting Stan. I wanted us all to be together today."

Stan spoke to John and Valerie while Tegan stood in Mathew's arms, knowing how important family was. She looked up into his eyes and his lips fused with hers before struggling to disconnect.

"I feel a little guilty. We should let them know Peter is alive."

"Not yet sweetheart...I don't want your father or my parents ending up in hospital, suffering from a heart attack. They aren't as young as us. Let's give them a little time to adjust," he whispered.

"Okay...a few days." She smiled.

"Come on, I want to break the news." He took Tegan's hand and walked to where everyone was mingling around the table.

"I'd like to announce something, Mum, Dad. I've run it past Stan."

Tegan glanced at Mathew. *Why the hide of him!* A grin tugged at her lips. Did he honestly ask her father for permission to marry?

"Tegan has agreed to marry me."

Valerie started crying. "What wonderful news. We couldn't be any happier than this day." She moved and kissed Tegan. "Congratulations, love." She then turned to Mathew. "I was wondering how long it would take you to come to your senses."

The smile on Mathew's face warmed Tegan's heart. She held her breath as his hand tightened over hers.

Valerie swung around and planted herself on a seat, drawing out a handkerchief.

"Are you all right Mum?" Mathew knelt.

"I'm so overwhelmed. I'm sorry." She wiped away tears, then looked at her son. "You have both brought so much happiness to our hearts. We wondered if we'd done something wrong not to deserve grandchildren, especially after what happened to Peter."

"No Mum, you did nothing wrong."

"We have a little grandchild, how wonderful."

John sat beside her slipping an arm to her waist. "Come on now love, you said you weren't going to cry."

"Oh, John, you know by now what I say and do are two different things." She slapped him playfully.

"That's not all." Mathew piped up.

Valerie glanced up, her mouth concealed by a tissue. "I hope it's good news."

"Yes, Mum." His hand slipped around Tegan's waist. "Tegan is going to have our baby."

The happy wail permeating the backyard startled everyone.

"Come on Val. It's happy news, not sad." John tried to comfort his wife.

"I know...I know...I'm just so overwhelmed. It's good news. Two grandchildren, we are blessed after all."

* * * *

After tucking Robert into bed, Tegan walked down to where Mathew sat at the dining table going through a bunch of files.

"How's it going?"

"Almost finished."

She smiled and walked out onto the veranda at the back of the house.

Breathing in the warm night air, contentment swirled within. After so long, after trying so damn hard, finally her heart had healed. She knew the love she held for Mathew would be the ever-lasting kind of love.

Warm hands snaked around her waist from behind and turning into them, Mathew's lips met hers. Drawing back, he gazed into her eyes. "I saw you checking toward the house a number of times today. I guess in the back of my mind I thought Pete may show up as well." He drew in a breath. "It would be great to speak to him though, to sort out some of our issues. Perhaps help him to overcome his addition to alcohol."

"Yes, but I don't want him here. I don't want Robert suffering especially now I've told him his father is dead."

He ran a hand over the back of her hair, which fell to her shoulders. "Would you like a wine?"

"No, thanks...a coffee will do fine. Remember I'm thinking of another life here." *Oh boy, wine*...just what she needed to settle her nerves. But with the baby inside, she wouldn't take that risk.

"Yes, I'm sorry. I forgot you can't drink alcohol." Placing his hand over hers, they walked into the house. Tegan locked the back door and cast a gaze around the kitchen before locking the windows and closing the blinds.

Mathew made the coffee while Tegan sat on the lounge. Every so often, she'd flick her gaze toward the window beside the front door.

Mathew passed her the coffee before sitting. The light from the television flickered over them and soft music drifted throughout the room. Sliding an arm around Tegan's shoulders, he pulled her closer, turned his head to one side, and planted a kiss on her cheek.

"Did I ever tell you I love you?"

"Hmm...come to think of it, I don't think so." She smirked.

Releasing a huge grin he said, "I love you with all my heart. I feel whole with you. Something I never thought was missing." His lips met hers, soft, assuring, and loving.

The sound of the lions head cut through the comfortable ambience, echoing throughout the house. Tegan jumped.

"I know you're in there with my son. Open the bloody door."

For some moments she didn't move. She held onto an indrawn breath, trying to intensify her hearing. Heavy soled boots thumped on the veranda. Tegan bolted upright, her eyes glaring white against the soft light.

"He's back," she whispered.

Mathew stood and took her hand, putting his index finger over his mouth, signaling not to answer.

"Open the bloody door or I'll bash the stupid thing down."

The piercing sound of splitting timber cracked throughout the house moments before the door swung open, the lock weakened against the blow of a shiny axe.

Sucking in a tight breath, Tegan took sanctuary closer to Mathew.

Peter stumbled into the lounge room.

Mathew couldn't believe his brother stood before him. His gut twisted, the muscles in his face hardened. All those years of worry, of self-hatred for not saving his brother, of being a failure, crashed through his mind. He stared and continued to stare until reality tumbled over him. Peter stood before him and very much alive. A blow right between the eyes.

"Bloody hell...I never thought you'd shack up with my wife, bro." His gaze raked the room, his face a dark, crazed mask.

"Listen Pete, we have to talk. There's a lot of things to explain."

A sinister laugh shot from his lips. "Me? Talk? What's there to explain? I'm not the one sleeping with my brother's wife."

"We thought you were dead. Mum, Dad, me...we thought you'd gone."

Tegan cupped her mouth with a trembling hand.

Peter moved closer. Mathew closed the space, his frame shielded Tegan from Peter's path.

"Why did you lead us to believe you were dead?"

"You never got it into you...that I hate the King family, hate any type of connection. What would you do if you were me, if you were kicked out, disinherited? Everything you wanted Matt you got at the click of your fingers. Not me," His words slurred.

The movement of shiny metal swinging slowly in Peter's hand caught Mathew's attention. "Give me the axe, Pete."

The axe swung higher. "What for? No bloody way."

"For starters, do you want your son to walk down those stairs to see his father swinging a damn axe at his mother? Don't you think it'd be a trigger for nightmares for years to come? Do it for him, Pete. Do it for your son."

"I thought the bitch was lying when she said he wasn't here, gone off to school holiday camp. You didn't fool me."

"Please put down the axe," Mathew pleaded.

Taking a steady step forward, Mathew put out his hand. "Come on, you don't want this. You don't want to hurt anyone." He beckoned with his hand. "Please." Mathew reached out and grabbed the axe. Surprisingly Peter let go of his hold.

"Don't think you're going to be a father to my son. I want him now and I'm not leaving without him."

"It doesn't work that way. There are certain legal formalities to consider."

Peter grinned in defiance. "Easy for you to say. I can't believe you've shacked up with my wife."

"We haven't shacked up. I'm going to marry Tegan."

"You've bloody got to be kiddin'. She's already married dear brother and I'm not giving her a divorce."

Tegan took a few unsteady steps and stood in front of Mathew only to breathe in the strong odor of beer. Containing herself she spoke, "We've been separated for well over one year. Just because you won't sign the forms, a judge will order the marriage broken down, irretrievable."

"Get my son, then I'll be gone for good."

"You aren't taking my son from me. You will never take him away."

Peter reached out and grabbed Tegan around the arm. On instinct Mathew's hand grabbed hold of his shirt and bunched it into a tight ball.

"Let her go, damn you. Let her go."

Peter's hand remained over Tegan's wrist.

Mathew clenched the other fist, brought it upwards. "I can't hit you. Hell, you're my damn brother." He cursed under his breath several times before reining in his temper and jerked his fisted hand from his shirt.

At the same moment, Peter released a struggling Tegan, who fell to the floor.

A smirk twisted his face.

"Why can't we talk about this, Pete?"

"Talk." Another sinister laugh echoed through the house. "I did talk to you and the family long ago. I'm coming back to get my son...you or Tegan won't stop me. I'll get him if it's the last thing I do." Swinging around, he stumbled to the door.

Mathew turned, swept Tegan into his arms, and carried her to the sofa. After checking to be certain she wasn't injured, he abandoned her to chase after Peter.

Racing outdoors, he caught a glimpse of the number plate of a dark blue sedan as it reached the gates, before it disappeared at a dangerous speed down the track.

Upon returning, Tegan wasn't where he'd left her. He glanced through the dim light up the stairs and bolted up quickly, taking two steps at a time. Spotting a light on towards the end of the hallway and Robert's door ajar, he walked toward it before he came to a standstill. Tegan sat on the edge of Robert's bed.

Sensing his presence, she turned.

"Hey, are you okay?"

"Yes." She stood and took Mathew's hand.

He closed the door. "He's a great little sleeper."

* * * *

When they arrived in the lounge, Tegan sank into the seat with Mathew following. His arms slipped around the back of her neck. Trying to overcome what had happened, Tegan didn't speak for long moments. She snuggled closer into his cocoon, feeling his strength surround her. Knowing he was there settled her nerves.

"Are you okay?"

"Yes. There's nothing broken, no bruises."

"I'm sorry you had to witness Pete like that. But I gather you've seen that side before. He's certainly not the brother I remembered. Not the Pete that I was so concerned about for such a long time."

"It's only the drink. He's a victim, an alcoholic."

Mathew's brows rose. "You're the victim. He has no right barging in here and demanding anything, especially splitting the damn door from its lock." He sucked in a labored breath.

"I'm ringing the police then I'll make you a coffee."

He stood and ran a heavy hand through his hair before pacing to the wall phone. Snatching it off its hook, he punched in the digits.

"Yes. My brother, Peter King, but he's been using the name Knight. Yes. It was a dark blue Holden sedan, the number plate, QQA-772.

"What? Yes, I'm sure it was him. He's got an A.V.O. out on him. His wife, Tegan..." He covered the mouthpiece and glanced at Tegan. "Hell, I don't know what your legal name is."

"It's Ryan. I had it changed legally."

"Yes. It's Ryan. Well, he smashed the front door from its lock and invited himself in. You will...thanks."

He disconnected the call and slipped beside Tegan on the lounge. "Are you okay?" He pulled her into his embrace.

"Yes, I think so. I'm so pleased Robert didn't wake up. It's a wonder with all the noise. How will we explain the door to him?"

"Leave that up to me." Mathew glanced at the door, drew himself up and walked toward it. "The lock is damaged. Do you have a hammer and nails?"

Her eyes rounded. "Yes. In the laundry. There's quite a few bits and pieces in there, left over after the renovations."

"I'll make us a coffee and then fix the door."

Tegan stood. "No...I'll do the coffee."

He stepped closer. "Okay." Taking her in his arms, he kissed her softly. "Hell...I wouldn't have let Pete hurt you. I'm sorry he pushed you though. I wasn't fast enough."

"You didn't see it coming. I didn't either. I hope he stays away... but I can't see it happening."

"We have to be extremely careful...perhaps we should go away for a while. I could get Sean to stay here, keep an eye on the house. We could go to Sydney for a while."

"Yes...I think that's a good idea. I don't want Robert to witness such things. I'm pleased he sleeps soundly. A bomb wouldn't wake him."

Tegan put the jug on while Mathew searched in the laundry. He put down a drill, hammer, and pieces of timber beside the front door and walked back to her.

"Why don't you take your coffee upstairs and have a shower? I'll be up as soon as the door is secured."

He kissed her on the lips, soft and lovingly. She nodded, picked up her cup, and walked up the stairs.

Before going to her bedroom, she slowly opened Robert's door and crept in to check once again. He was still sound asleep under a soft quilt, unaware of what had taken place.

A dull ache ribboned through her heart. *Mathew and I will*

protect you sweetie. Peter won't get near you. I will never let anything bad happen to you, I promise.

* * * *

Tegan couldn't believe she'd slept so well—that is, after she heard Mathew fall into bed beside her. Knowing he was beside her provided the safety and comfort she needed, and craved. She gazed down at the heavy arm anchored over her stomach then glanced upwards to meet his wide, blue eyes. A grin tugged on her lips.

"Good morning, sleepy head."

"Morning." Turning into his arms, she rested her head on his shoulder.

"I recall you saying you'd fixed the door, but how?"

"You'll see when you go down." He chuckled.

"Okay, what's so funny?"

"You'll see."

Tegan couldn't wait. She slipped from the bed, tossed on a robe, tiptoed down the stairs and smiled.

Mathew had secured the door all right. He'd used all the timber, or so she thought and nailed it across the door, securing it firmly to the wall. Her fingers curled around a piece of timber. No way in, and certainly no way out.

Mathew's mobile echoed from upstairs and she wondered who could possibly be ringing at this time, especially so early on a Sunday morning. Padding into the kitchen, she put the jug on to make a coffee. She snapped the blind up to reveal the morning sun shimmering through the tall, gum trees.

Hearing a noise behind her, she turned to witness Mathew's face glazed with shock. He staggered to the table dressed in a pair of boxer shorts, and dropped onto a chair.

Her heart hitched in her throat. "Are you all right?"

"I just got a phone call."

"I heard your phone ring. Who was it?"

Running a heavy hand through his hair, he let out a groan. "Pete's in intensive care. The Mater Hospital."

Chapter Sixteen

"What?" She reached for a chair with an unsteady hand and slid onto it, seeking relief.

"He's been in a car accident."

"What...when?"

"Last night. The police found him about six hours ago."

"I'm so sorry. He's going to be all right, isn't he?" Tegan didn't think her heart could take much more. She drew in a labored breath and her gaze settled over Mathew's dismal expression.

"They only told me he's in a bad way. I don't know any more. They said all relatives to visit as soon as possible."

Cool chills worked their way up Tegan's spine. "I'll...ring Clare to see if she can keep an eye on Robert."

Drawing herself up, she stopped beside him, put an arm around his shoulder, and bent to kiss him on the cheek. He turned his head and their lips brushed softly in silence.

Twenty minutes later they were almost at the hospital.

"I rang Mum and Dad. They're on their way. It's lucky they were still here in Newcastle."

"How did they take it? I can imagine your poor mum."

"Not good. Shocked isn't the word, dumfounded more like it. It's going to be difficult for them."

And difficult for you as well. She felt like saying but didn't.

As they stepped from the lift, they approached a reception desk, and asked for directions to the intensive care unit. The distinct sterile odor of hospital wafted to Tegan's nostrils as they walked through the maze of corridors. Nurses clad in white rushed in all directions. Some acknowledging with a smile or a shake of their head as they passed by.

Arriving outside the reception hub directly opposite the intensive care section, Tegan noticed two police officers approaching.

"Mister Mathew King, Miss Ryan."

"Yes." Mathew answered.

"I'm Detective Simon Blake and this is Detective Aaron Calder."

"I'm pleased to meet you." Mathew exchanged handshakes. Tegan nodded.

"We'd like a few questions answered. There's a room to your

left, do you mind?"

Tegan glanced at Mathew.

"No. We don't mind, not at all. We also need to find out what happened. Don't we, sweetheart?"

They followed the police officers and sat in a small room on two metal chairs opposite a metal desk. The police officers sat.

"Well, it's tragic," Detective Blake said. "Mister King, did you see your brother before the accident?"

"Yes." Mathew leaned forward, hands clasped between his legs. "He paid us an unexpected visit at Tegan's house, where I'm currently staying."

"What transpired?"

Mathew explained while Tegan listened.

"He was intoxicated—well past the limit," Detective Calder said. "His car took the sweeping bend just up from Catherine Hill Bay much too fast and slammed into a tree. From what we gather, he was doing at least one hundred and seventy in a one hundred kilometer zone."

Tegan gasped.

"He has extensive injuries. Mainly internal and is not expected to live. The doctor will fill you in on the rest of the details. We wanted to hear your story. We wanted to make sure you knew how the accident happened. Speed, alcohol, and driving don't mix."

After exchanging handshakes, the two police officers left the room. Tegan's arms slipped around Mathew's waist and they stood. Holding each other, they stood in silence for long moments before walking from the room.

Mathew approached a nurse. "Hello. We would like to see Peter King, or perhaps he is registered under Knight."

"Are you family?"

"Yes. I'm his brother and the lady is his...is my fiancée."

Tegan glanced up when she heard him say 'fiancée,' and chewed on the inner side of her lip before gazing down at the sparkle on her finger.

The nurse glanced at Tegan. "Doctor Moorebank will be here shortly. I've just informed him you are waiting. He wanted to speak with Mister King's family."

Mathew nodded. "Thank you."

They took a seat in an empty waiting room.

"I can't believe this is happening. I...it's such a shock."

He took one of her hands. "Yes...I'm having a hard time accepting it as well. It's bloody hard to take. I don't know why Pete turned out this way. It's not as though we didn't love him. Hell." He ran a hand through his hair and straightened his spine.

"After the aircraft accident, Mum, Dad and I were pretty shaken up. It took some time for any of us to come to terms with his death...and now this."

"I know...it must have been a blow, and as you've said, now to find out he's alive only to be dying. When we found out Robert's father and your brother were the same person, I had a hard time getting a grip on it...but now..." her words faded. She shook her head; she couldn't go on.

An elderly man in his fifties, wearing a long white coat, walked into the room.

"Mister King, Miss Ryan."

Mathew and Tegan stood. After introductions took place they sat down. Doctor Moorebank pulled out a chair and sat opposite.

"I dislike breaking bad news to relatives but someone has to do it." His lips thinned. "Your brother has internal bleeding and has lost a lot of blood. His injuries are too extensive to be able to save him. We've done our best, mind you. We've tried to fix up his face...it's not pretty. He's also suffered severe lacerations to internal organs due to hitting the steering wheel with such great force. He wasn't wearing a seat belt. He also has neck and spinal injuries. I'm afraid we've done all that we can. It's only a matter of time. I'm terribly sorry."

Mathew stood at the same time as Doctor Moorebank and they exchanged a handshake.

"Thank you, Doctor, for all you've done."

"Is there any more family arriving?"

"Yes, my mother and father."

"I'll explain his condition to them as well. In the meantime, he is drifting in and out of consciousness. It's best if you get to see him."

"Thank you."

As they walked out a nurse scurried over.

"Mister King, Miss Ryan, this way please. They walked down the hall a few meters, and she opened a cream door with a window insert.

"He's the third bed on the right."

"Thank you," Mathew said before coming to a standstill at the end of a grey, metal hospital bed.

The sound of breathing apparatus was distinct as they moved closer. Wires, hooked up to him, led to various contraptions.

Tegan gasped and placed a hand over her mouth.

"Hey Pete. It's me, Matt."

His eyelids slipped open, but formed small slits, surrounded by a bruised and swollen face. If it wasn't for his hair, Tegan thought she wouldn't have recognized him. Stitches wove up his right cheek and across his forehead.

Moving his right hand upwards in slow motion, he removed the breathing device from his mouth.

"Hey Matt. Fancy seeing you here," he grated.

Mathew heard the struggle of his lungs and the gurgle in his throat. "What did you go and do this for? You know I love you... Mum and Dad love you. We have always loved you."

"I'm sorry...Matt, for disappointing everyone. They...told me I haven't long. It's probably better. I wasn't good enough for anyone, not even Tegan." He gasped for oxygen, a deep struggle that had Tegan blinking against threatening tears.

"Hey, you shouldn't be saying that."

"Not much else to say. Eh?" He groaned. His eyelids unable to remain opened.

Tegan moved closer, standing beside Mathew. Holding her lips steady to prevent them from quivering was impossible, as was trying to put a stop to the tears rolling down her cheeks. She drew in a steadying breath. How she hated hospitals, hated seeing anyone sick, or injured.

Feeling Mathew's hand tighten around hers helped a little but he suddenly let go and sat on the bed.

"It's all right everything will be fine," Tegan whispered.

"No, you've always said that." Peter's eyes fluttered as he forced them to open. "I remember you used to tell me everything will be fine. It never was, was it? You take care of our son...won't you?" He looked at Mathew. "You'll make a good dad, Matt, much better than I ever would have. No kid likes a drunk for a father."

Tegan's heart swelled. She felt the pressure on her chest, the thickening of her throat.

"Sorry about the door."

"We aren't worried about a door, Pete. A door can be replaced. You can't."

"I don't think anyone would want to replace me. I've...failed this life...perhaps another life might give me the chance I need. Please forgive me, Matt, Tegan?" he spluttered.

"I forgive you. I've always forgiven you. I do still care for you—you're my son's father," she blurted.

"What did you call him? I...I don't...know, I don't even know my son's name." He closed his eyes.

"His...name is...Robert."

"Robert. Eh. Robert King. Sounds like a good name."

Mathew's gut churned with a force more than he'd ever experienced. "I've always forgiven you. You're the only brother I've ever had."

Peter's eyes opened and closed as he spoke. "Remember...when we were kids, Matt? We had such fun as kids. Do you remember? We were so close. You used to look out for me."

"Yeah, we did...Pete."

Tegan heard the strain in Mathew's voice and glanced up. His eyes glazed with tears and he choked on his words.

Unable to bear the agony of seeing Peter in so much pain, or Mathew so distraught, she bent over and kissed Peter on the cheek. "I have to go to the ladies' room. I'll be back shortly."

With a quick glance at Mathew, she touched his shoulder, then stood on tiptoes and whispered, "I won't be long."

As she walked through the door of the intensive care unit the doctor was speaking with Valerie and John.

Valerie was sobbing. John held her elbow, trying to provide some support.

"Tegan." John called.

Tegan walked slowly toward them and was certain her legs would cave in and they'd be picking her up to find a bed.

John slipped an arm around her shoulder.

"How is he?"

"He's...he's not good."

"How are you holding up?"

"I'm not sure. It's a terrible shock."

"Yeah...especially thinking he died all those years ago...and now to have him alive only to die on us again. It doesn't seem right."

Tegan glanced at Val, her eyes were swollen and red. "I'm so sorry."

"There, there. Is Mathew with him?"

"Yes." She sank her top teeth into her bottom lip.

The doctor escorted them to the intensive care unit, while Tegan sat on a chair looking blankly at the shiny, sterile floor. She didn't wish death upon anyone.

It wasn't long before Mathew arrived and sat beside her. He ran his hand over her small, pregnant tummy.

"Are you okay?" His face twisted in anguish.

"Yes...but you don't look as though you are."

"I have to be. I've been through his death once, but going through it twice doesn't make any sense. Nothing makes sense."

She slipped into the comfort of his arms. Her right hand moved slowly over his back. "It's kinda weird thinking he was dead for so many years, and now this. I don't know what to say."

"I know, sweetheart. It must be hard for you as well."

"Yes...it is...there was a nice Peter and I got to know that man very well. He didn't have a bad bone in his body. It's the drink—it was always the drink."

Their eyes leveled.

"If I'd known he had family years ago I would have contacted you. I would have asked for Val and John's help, for your help. It's too late now. It's all too late. I should have done something to help him instead of taking off like a wounded animal, instead of crawling away in the middle of the night to hide."

Mathew reeled back. "Hey, don't blame yourself. What else could you have done? Hell, sweetheart, he beat you, put scars over you. No woman would have endured something like that and tried to help him. Don't blame yourself. Please, it's not your fault." He drew her into his embrace and held her closely.

"I'm happy you left him. Otherwise we may never have met," he whispered hoarsely, raining kisses down the side of her cheek.

Val and John walked from the intensive care unit.

John approached them and Mathew broke his contact with Tegan and stood.

"He's gone this time. Pete's gone for good now."

Father and son embraced for long moments. He looked up, taking a glance toward his mother. "Mum." Taking a few steps toward her, he gave her a cuddle. "Pete was a good guy . He was just a little confused."

Tears worked paths through Valerie's foundation, and she sniffled into a tissue. "I know. He was a good child, just like you."

Valerie looked at Tegan. "I think Tegan would be the most distressed. After all, she was married to Peter—knew him better than any of us."

Tegan managed a wavering grin and sniffled trying to hold back the floodgates.

"We'll make the necessary arrangements to have him transported to Sydney for a proper funeral. Is that all right with you, Tegan? After all, you are his ex-wife."

Tegan glanced at Mathew before acknowledging a 'yes.' Tears stung the back of her eyes. *They think I'm divorced.* She let go of a breath.

"Okay, Dad. We have to go. Can you give us a ring tomorrow?"

"Yes. I'll do that."

"Are you sure you're okay?"

"Yes. I think I've already been through this and the second time around doesn't seem as hard. As for your mother..." He looked at Valerie and took her hand. "It will take some time, won't it love?"

"Ring me Dad, if you need anything."

"Okay son."

Mathew turned, slipped an arm around Tegan's shoulder and they walked from the hospital.

"I'm glad we made some sort of closure...that I had a chance to speak to Pete." His words choked from his throat. "I need to say a final goodbye."

Chapter Seventeen

Pulling into the car park at Williamtown airport, Tegan climbed from the limousine and smoothed the wrinkles from her cream linen dress.

Mathew took her hand. "You look lovely," he said, before planting a kiss on a rosy cheek.

"Thank you."

"Are you sure you're okay about flying to Sydney to do the funeral thing?"

"Yes. I want to go to his funeral. I need closure as well. I need to say goodbye for the very last time and get on with my life. We both need this."

He shot her a disbelieving look. "Flying is not your forte, remember."

"I may surprise you." She laughed but wondered if she would possibly surprise herself.

Mathew spoke to Sean as he gathered their luggage. They crossed over the parking lot through to a small gate towards an aircraft. A young man dressed in overalls stood beside it.

"All set Mark?"

"Yes, Mister King. All checked thoroughly."

"Thanks."

Tegan turned to Mathew. "What happened to the other plane we used when flying to Port Macquarie?"

"That's gone. This is virtually the same. It's new. King Enterprises owns this one now."

Tegan pulled a quirky face before stepping into the aircraft. The newness of leather seeped in her nostrils. She ran a hand over the seats before arriving behind the cockpit. Mathew eased up behind her.

"Where are you sitting?"

"Right here." She tapped the back of the seat next to his.

"Are you sure?"

Without answering, she plonked herself down and waited.

Mathew shook his head. "I'll be back in a few minutes."

Tegan glanced around and smiled. She knew Mathew was a good pilot. He wouldn't let anything happen to her.

She gazed through the windscreen. Moments later, she heard the hatch click into lock. When she tuned, Mathew was closing the space between them.

"Seat belt on...is everything okay?" he asked, pausing beside her.

"Yes, I'm fine." She lied. Her stomach clenched.

The engines fired up and Tegan grabbed the headphones, settling them into position.

Mathew put in a call. "Willy tower, Alfa Bravo Charlie, a Cessna Caravan, departing to Bankstown request taxi and airways clearance."

"Alfa, Bravo, Charlie, Willy Tower cleared to taxi runway one, two, report when ready."

The aircraft moved forward taxing toward the runway before stopping. Tegan was once again awed at Mathew's flying ability.

"Willy tower Alfa, Bravo, Charlie, lined up and ready runway one, two."

"Alfa, Bravo, Charlie, Willy Tower cleared for takeoff. Climb to five thousand feet, track one hundred and ninety degrees and report overhead Newcastle."

"Willy tower Alfa, Bravo, Charlie, cleared for takeoff. Climb to five thousand feet, track one hundred and ninety degrees."

Mathew turned to Tegan. "There, piece of cake." He smiled sending her heart fluttering.

The aircraft lifted and Tegan stared through the window. Trees grew smaller as they ascended and veered toward the ocean.

"How high are we?"

"Climbing to five thousand feet...how are you doing?" He rested his right hand over her bare knee.

"You know I think I could get used to this."

"I do hope so. I'd like to think my future wife could fly with me...all the time." He raised his eyebrows then winked.

"I think I could manage that...but one thing...Robert. I told him we'd take him for a scenic flight when we return...that is if it's okay. He's never been up in a plane."

"Whatever you want my lovely...I'm sure he'd love it."

"Mathew...how long after the accident...I mean the one that went down in the Pacific Ocean...how long did it take before you flew again?"

He cleared his throat, the sides of his face flexed. "Well, I didn't. Not for years. I avoided flying like the plague. In the end it drove me crazy. So, one day I went up alone and just flew and kept flying. You're the first person I've taken up with me since. You seem to be doing pretty well this time."

"Yes, I am. Although I'd be lying if I didn't say my stomach was flipping occasionally. You have helped me so much in overcoming my fears. I feel safe with you. I never thought that I'd feel this way in a plane, ever."

"I'm glad of that, sweetheart." He smiled. "You've helped me in many ways as well. Don't forget that."

Tegan gazed through the window at the clear, blue sky. Letting out a sigh in appreciation, she relaxed into the seat.

The flight was relatively short. Mathew put in a radio call.

"Bankstown Tower, Alpha, Bravo, Charlie, a Cessna Caravan, approaching Prospect at one thousand five hundred feet. Received, Delta inbound."

"Alpha, Bravo, Charlie, Bankstown tower, join downwind runway two niner right."

"Acknowledge. Alpha, Bravo, Charlie, runway two niner right," Mathew stated clearly.

"Do you want to keep an eye-out for other aircraft with me?"

"Why do you have to look?"

He grinned. "It could prevent an accident."

"You mean to say we might crash."

"No. It's precautionary. Look over there to your right. Another inbound aircraft...there are quite a considerable number of aircraft taking off as well."

Tegan concentrated on the aircraft below, watching as they departed the airstrip.

"How do you know where to go? What if a plane is heading for us?"

"We get out of their way." He chuckled. "Don't worry. That's why we put in calls. We check and double-check everything."

Fifteen minutes later, Mathew put in another call.

"Bankstown tower, Alpha, Bravo, Charlie, downwind runway two niner right for full stop landing."

"Alpha, Bravo, Charlie, cleared to land."

"Alpha, Bravo, Charlie, cleared to land."

Although feeling safe with Mathew, that certain niggle dragged in her stomach. She held her breath as the aircraft touched down smoothly.

Turning to Mathew, a smile spread over her face.

"There, as I've said before, a piece of cake."

* * * *

The electric gates slid aside and the limousine glided up the driveway leading through a maze of pine trees, native shrubs and rose bushes.

Tegan studied the multi-colored garden, astonished that Mathew owned this property. Closing in on the house, her breath caught in her throat when a magnificent cream home moved into view.

"It is your house, isn't it?"

"Yes. Why do you ask?"

"It's so big, so extravagant."

"As you can see it's relatively new."

Her forehead scrunched. "How new?"

He grinned. "Very new."

As she stepped from the limousine, the sound of lorikeets filled the atmosphere.

Mathew slipped his hand around her waist. "You're not disappointed are you?"

"No...just astounded. It's so huge for one person."

"It wasn't built for one person."

She frowned before stepping up marble steps which led to large timber, glassed-in double doors.

Mathew tapped in the code to unlock the door and pressed the security system, turning off the alarms. "I usually have someone staying here to keep an eye on the place. But seeing we were coming for the night, we are alone."

Images of a large, black leather bed flashed in her mind. A tremor of anticipation filled her.

"The security system is very effective with an audio visual intercom at the gates as well."

"Oh."

Taking the few steps into the house, she noticed the high ceilings and glanced up to a mosaic of tiles covering half of the foyer ceiling.

"It has ducted cycled air, heated floors in the four bathrooms, as you will see." He opened the blinds. "Also it has motorized blinds and shutters."

However, Tegan wasn't interested in the mechanics at that time. As the shutters slipped silently open, revealing floor to ceiling glass sliders, a sun drenched mosaic tiled swimming pool, with a wet bar came into view.

"It's very impressive."

He took her hand. "So far I've got impressive, astounded, and oh...do you like it?"

"Of course I do. It's so large and expensive—it's stolen my breath."

He moved a lock of hair from her face and his hands slipped to her waist. His lips sought hers as his arms slinked behind her, his fingers trailed over her back.

Molding against him, she gave into his touch as waves of delight teased every inch of her being.

Breaking from the kiss, he patted her bottom, turned, and walked to the front door.

Tegan continued staring in awe over the magnificent Sydney Harbor, with views to the Harbor Bridge.

When Mathew returned he noticed she hadn't moved. "Are you sure you're okay?"

She grinned. "Yes...it's a lovely home."

"It's pretty low maintenance. Sean has taken your luggage up to the room. We have a few hours before the funeral. Would you like a drink?"

Turning to him, she smiled, "Yes, please."

"Wine, coffee?" Tegan watched as he stood behind a bar pouring a glass of wine.

"You know I can't drink alcohol."

"Just testing. I'll make you a coffee." He grinned.

"What did you mean by, 'not built for one person'?"

"I had it built the day we met. It was built for us."

He strolled back toward Tegan, across the large, cream tiles.

"The day we met? You've got to be kidding."

"Okay sorry, lie—perhaps it was the day after we met."

"Why?"

"Why not? It was built for us—for when we married."

Her mouth gaped. "I thought we'd live in my home, in Catherine Hill Bay."

"Really?"

"Yes...we can use this one for a holiday home and for business trips."

"What? A holiday home as costly as this?"

"Or we can live six months of the year here and six months in Catherine Hill Bay."

"That idea does appeal." She grinned. "You certainly had tickets on yourself. What if we'd never gone out? What if we'd never got together or even married?"

"Well, I'd have had to keep on trying or this house would be pretty damn empty, not having a family between its walls. I'll go and make you a coffee."

Tegan looked out over the harbor until he returned.

"Here you go."

She took the coffee from him and sipped. "Thanks. I was thinking about the funeral. I'm not looking forward to it. I don't particularly like them."

"That makes two of us. I've only been to two previously."

"I've only been to one and I couldn't stop crying."

"It'll be all right." He slipped an arm around her waist. "I'll be there holding you up."

Shooting him a dubious glance, she took a sip of coffee and wondered who would hold him up.

* * * *

Large, green iron gates were propped open, revealing a well-manicured cemetery. Surrounding gum trees shaded most of the fresh summer flowers dotting the grave sites. Almost three hundred people were taking shelter from the hot Australian sun under large, black umbrellas.

"I didn't think there'd be so many people."

"Our family is pretty well-known in the area."

Tegan spotted men hanging around the entrance gates with large cameras. "The press—you didn't say anything about reporters being here."

"You didn't ask. Don't stress so much, sweetheart."

The driver opened the car door while Mathew walked around the back of the limousine and took Tegan's hand.

As they approached the gates, a cameraman stepped forward. A sudden flash exploded in her face. She glanced up to see a reporter, no, five reporters walking toward her. She swallowed, feeling her throat tighten as more flashes from the cameras jolted her nerves.

"Is it true that Peter King hadn't been seen in years, that he disowned the family?"

"No comment," Mathew stated as he tried to direct Tegan through the crowd.

"I feel sick," she blurted.

"What? Are you okay?"

"What are they trying to do?"

"Reporters get hold of anything these days and go for it. Just ignore them."

Trying to keep her legs moving was a chore. Her steps were awkward and she was glad for Mathew's support. Arriving beside the empty, cold hole in the ground, Tegan shuddered.

Reality stung and for long moments she stared at the mahogany coffin with gold handles. Drawing in a heavy breath, she looked at Mathew.

His face was pale and grief stricken, his jaw squared.

"Come on, let's sit," she whispered.

"Hi Mum, Dad. Are you all right?"

"Yes, Son—as best as can be expected."

"Valerie, John." Tegan nodded before focusing directly in front of her.

"I know it's hard Mum," Mathew said, noticing tears streaming down his mother's face. "Dad..."

"Yeah, son. We're going through it again. Truthfully, I'll be pleased when we finally put Pete to rest, and say our final goodbye. It's been a terrible strain on your mother."

"I know Dad."

"And you, I might add. How are you holding up?"

"Good Dad, good."

In actual fact Mathew's stomach felt like an empty gravel pit. His stomach muscles tightened as he watched two men approach the grave site meters from them.

Sobbing drifted through the hushed silence and continued throughout the service.

Mathew shook his head. *Well, Pete. I guess this is final now, mate. I guess we'll meet one...day. Hell, I've missed you so much over the last years. You were my little brother...my only brother.* He swallowed, tight, restricting. *Why didn't you come to me, Pete? I would have done anything to help you, anything in this world. I guess it's all too late now, eh. You rest in peace little brother. I'm going to miss you all the days of my life.* Mathew tried to contain the surge of emotion. His eyes misted and he looked at Tegan.

Taking her hand, his grip tightened, and a drawn look spread over his face.

Tegan turned and noticed Valerie dab her eyes with a tissue.

Flashes from the cameras startled her and she bent her head, focusing downwards. Tears were close to the surface for the following half an hour and she was thankful for the dark sunglasses she wore. Refocusing in front was all she could do before reaching into her handbag for a tissue to wipe her escaping tears.

The coffin disappeared slowly into the dark, cold earth. Tegan closed her eyes.

I know things didn't work out right Peter, but I will all ways remember you. You're my son's father and I'm sorry it had to turn out this way. I should have stayed and helped you. I will never forgive myself for not seeking help for you. Instead I snuck away in the night. I'm sorry...but you didn't leave me a choice at the time. I do forgive you for everything you did. I know it was only the alcohol. After all, no one is perfect. Rest in peace, Peter.

She sniffed and opened her eyes when she heard Mathew stand. His hand extended.

Tegan placed her hand in his drawing herself upwards.

"Are you okay, sweetheart?"

"Yes." She sniffled.

After saying goodbye to Mathew's parents, promising to meet them later at their house, they spoke to a few other people before walking toward the gates.

Flashes of bright light stopped them in their path as at least six reporters with their cameras came from nowhere.

"Is it true you were still married to Peter King when you got engaged to Mathew King?" One of the reporters asked as flashes continued to explode in Tegan's face.

She put up her hand, blocking the light and trying to cover her face at the same time.

"No comment," Mathew ground out.

"You must like the Kings, Miss Ryan?" Another reporter fired before adding, "Jumping from one wealthy son's bed to the other."

"Leave us alone," Mathew raised his voice.

Tegan was horrified as she clutched to Mathew's hand, squeezing it hard.

As they approached the limousine, Sean had already opened the door and they scrambled in quickly. The camera flashes continued even after the door closed behind them.

"How did they know? How did they know I was married to Peter?" she wailed.

"Hey, it's okay. As I said, they have their ways. The press get hold of anything they can and fluff it up for a story. Don't worry."

"It's okay for you to say, 'don't worry'. Your past isn't being exploited. Your parents were behind us and heard every damn word." She sucked in a breath before slamming her back against the seat. "What's your mother going to think now? She thought I was divorced."

Mathew shook his head. "She won't think any less of you. I know that...but I guess we should have told them earlier."

Twilight draped over the mountains, sank over the tall trees as the limousine crawled toward Mathew's parents home.

"I feel so bad."

He took her hand. "Don't. Mum doesn't judge a person on their marital status."

Tegan settled a little by the time they drove up a long driveway and came to a halt. When she stepped from the limousine, she faced even more luxury. "I expected this."

"What?"

"Wealth runs in your families veins."

"I have to remind you my father gained his money from hard work and having a good business sense."

"I know...it's just a little hard to take. I mean...well."

"I know what you mean. It's all a little overwhelming. I sometimes think that money can't buy happiness."

"It can't."

"I know. I've had to step very careful since meeting you." He let out a husky, deep chuckle.

"Meaning?" She gave him an elfish look.

"With you, it was different...you weren't interested in wealth. I had to win you over using my charm."

"Oh, come on now, I wasn't that hard to win over," she whispered, spotting a couple walk by.

"I'm glad it's turned out how it has. Come on...Mum will wonder where we are."

Taking her hand, they walked up to the three story brick home and into a foyer meant for a king, before entering a room the size of a ballroom. Caterers walked around offering canapés and banquet tables were set to one side.

After introductions and chatting, she couldn't spot Mathew anywhere. Walking to the balcony she stopped dead in her tracks, her heart upped a few paces.

From behind she saw a tall redhead practically making love to Mathew. Long limbs curled around his neck, and one leg anchored around his. Tegan bit on her lip as she stared with disbelief. She couldn't match that, couldn't match the perfect model image.

Her fiancé had his arm around the woman. Not wanting to cause a scene, she slipped from the room into a bathroom just down the hallway.

He actually enjoyed that woman's touch. Bile rose to her throat. She swallowed it down as she rubbed both hands under warm water, before applying more lipstick.

Sitting for some time, she recalled Peter one night with his arms around a woman. Brothers are alike. That thought forced a wave of nausea to pass through her stomach. What if he is exactly like Peter? They say you don't know a man unless you live with him for a while. She wasn't going to risk a thing, not her life, not Robert's, and not the precious baby growing inside, nothing.

What a fool she'd been, thinking this was the fairy tale she'd been searching for. *Well, as far as Mathew is concerned he can stick his money and his girl.*

There were two options—face them or run. She'd run once before and sometimes wished she'd stayed. Rather than cause a scene, she stood and ran.

Spotting the driver outside talking to another driver, she quickly walked toward him.

"I have a headache and I want to go back to Mister King's house. Do you mind taking me?"

"Not at all Miss Ryan. Does Mister King know?"

"He's pretty busy. I don't want to disturb him."

"Busy my foot." The explosion from behind had Tegan swinging around.

Mathew stalked toward them.

"Give us a little privacy," he snapped at the driver."

"What are you doing?"

"I'm leaving."

"What's going on?"

"You tell me and then we'll both know. I don't happen to like my man's arms around another woman."

He jerked back. "You what? Come here."

"No."

He glared at her. "We have one little misunderstanding and you're ready to ditch our relationship. Is that how much I mean to you...not much? I thought you loved me." He cursed under his breath. "You're carrying our child. Don't do this. I can explain, please?"

"What is there to explain? That woman was all over you."

He ran an irritated hand through his dark hair. "Don't throw away all we have."

Feeling heat seep to her cheeks and noticing a few onlookers pass by, she didn't say a word.

Mathew grabbed her around the wrist. "Hey sweetheart...it was Helen. You remember Helen, don't you?"

"What's your ex-girlfriend doing here?"

"I don't know. She wormed her way in."

A voice calling from behind had Tegan on alert. The redhead was crossing the driveway toward them.

"Mathew. Darling."

Tegan's blood boiled. She swallowed before closing her fists, fingers curling tightly into her palms. She stepped forward.

"Listen, Helen."

"Who's this?" Helen did a brief intake of Tegan and looked directly at Mathew.

"This is Mathew's fiancée." Tegan stuck out her left hand, flashing her engagement ring. "He is the father of my baby."

"That ring is bigger than the one I got. Engagement! Baby!"

"Which brother's baby, or did you hop from one to the other whenever you felt like it?"

Shocked and unable to believe what she was accused of, Tegan's fingers curled tighter into her palms.

"Where on Earth did you find this Mathew—under a pumpkin?" She waved an aloof hand in the air.

"No, I found the most beautiful woman in the world."

"Beautiful."

"You heard me. She's beautiful. Actually the most beautiful woman I have ever laid eyes upon."

"You wait until I tell Daddy. He'll make you regret what you've done, especially when he finds out you were seeing someone else who is married to your brother and has his child. Oh Mathew darling, can't you see what type she is, or are you so blind that she's charmed you with her wicked deceit?"

"I beg your pardon. I'm so glad I came to my senses and broke it off. As for your father, he'll be quite interested to learn that I'm marrying soon and getting on with my life."

"You've got to be joking."

"It isn't a joke Miss Haughty Toughty." Tegan propped her hands on her hips.

"Helen leave. I'll see to it you're escorted off the premises, never to set foot in any King residence again."

Mathew waved his hand, and one of the security guards strutted toward them. "Yes, Mister King."

"Can you escort this lady off the premises, please?"

"Yes, Mister King."

The security guard cupped a hand around Helen's elbow and they walked away with Helen babbling pitiful excuses.

Tegan looked at Mathew, her lips thinned.

"Come on ,sweetheart. Let's go and see Mum and Dad."

Tegan pressed her lips together. "No, not just yet. Let's walk. I need to settle."

She cupped her arm in Mathew's and headed down a little pathway leading to a bench seat in the garden. Round circular globes lit up the high shrubs and trees.

Tegan eased herself onto the bench. Mathew sat beside her.

"I want...I want you to know that I'm nothing like Helen said."

"Hey, you don't have to explain to me."

"I want to say something. Please listen. I didn't have a relationship with any man until I met you. Over six and a half years alone, by myself..." she choked on her words.

Moving his hand, he hooked his fingers under her chin and leveled their eyes before his lips roamed over hers. Soft, delicious and inviting—that was until he drew back.

"I know, sweetheart. I know what type of woman you are. We are going to be married, have a big family, and live happily ever after."

Her lips trembled. "Did you mean what you said to Helen, about me?"

"Yes. You are beautiful. You just don't realize how much beauty you hold, inside and out."

He stood and drew her into his arms, before turning and making their way toward the house.

Chapter Eighteen

A funeral, a wedding and a baby—what more did Tegan have to face, especially consecutively?

The funeral was over. Now all she had to do was get past the next few hours without being an emotional mess. She stood and glanced through the window at all the cars parked inside and outside the gates, as well as, lining up on the grass in front of the house.

What good is a romance if there isn't a wedding? She wanted that happy-ever-after and, by damn, she was going to get it.

"Almost time," Sally piped up.

Tegan turned and smiled.

"You look adorable."

Tegan wore a white one-piece, A-line gown with an inner lace-up closure. Splashes of intricate beading electrified the georgette chiffon gown with a fluted side drape and a cutaway feature accenting the train.

"Thank you. I do hope Mathew will have the same opinion. You also make a beautiful bridesmaid."

Sally smoothed her hands over the light pink, georgette, chiffon gown. "This probably cost you a fortune."

Tegan laughed. "Just book it to King Enterprises."

"It's almost time," Sally said.

Cool shivers raced up Tegan's spine. "I'm so nervous. Make sure I don't cry, please."

"You'll be fine. Everything is ready downstairs. The caterers make a wedding look so easy to organize. Even the decorations from Wedding Blitz are remarkable. It's so perfect, Teeg."

"You know it's really the first wedding I've had. Peter and I got married in a registry office in our day clothes. It didn't feel like a wedding but I suppose it was a marriage for a time."

"Well, this time you're doing it in style. Limo's the lot. Make the most of it and go for it girl. You deserve it all; you deserve Mathew King."

Tegan rubbed her lips together before walking down the steps with Sally. Stan stood at the bottom of the stairs.

"Well, well. I was looking for Tegan. You don't know where she is, do you?"

"Oh Dad, stop it." She smiled.

"My baby looks like a princess."

Tegan glanced out through the back French doors toward the garden. People sat facing east with the view of the ocean between the tall trees.

Pink and white roses in full bloom decorated tables. They splashed color on either side of a white runner as it lead toward the back of the yard. An archway decorated in pink and white adorned the end of the runner.

"It's beautiful," Tegan whispered to Sally. "Thank you for organizing so much."

"Hopefully you'll return the favor one day—like in the next one hundred years or so." She giggled.

Tegan nervously scanned the area looking for Mathew but she couldn't see him. "Where's Mathew?"

"He's here."

"Mum." Robert raced toward Tegan. He swung his arms around her but stepped back quickly. "That's yuck." He brushed his face.

"Robert, you're mother looks beautiful."

He stared at his mother.

"Come on stand here next to me." Sally said, as the music started humming in the background.

"It was Mathew's idea to choose this song, not mine," Tegan said.

Sally started mouthing the words, 'you're once twice, three times a lady, and I love you...' "It suits the occasion."

Sally did the last touch up, straightening Tegan's headpiece so that it covered her face. "There, you look lovely. Okay, this is it. Come on Robert."

Robert walked beside Sally, dressed in a little white suit with a sapphire tie and carrying a pink cushion. Sitting in the center of that cushion was one, small white box.

It was then Tegan spotted Mathew and she smiled so wide she thought her mouth would split. He was dressed in white with a sapphire tie. He'd repeatedly said he'd never dress in a white suit.

She'd always dreamed of a prince in white. *Come on now, this is so stupid. Hang on, it's no dream. This is happening for real. Get a grip. Isn't this the life you wanted, the life you longed for?*

Linking her arm in her father's, she put an awkward, gold strapless sandle-clad foot in front of the other and walked slowly passed sixty smiling guests.

Arriving beside Mathew, she was thankful when he extended a hand. After kissing her father on the cheek and acknowledging a ;thank you', she stepped beside Mathew.

Rose petals covered the ground underfoot and the rich fragrance of roses filled the still, warm air. After the introduction, and vows, Mathew lifted the fine lace and cupped her face with both hands, before easing his lips over hers. Clapping and cheering echoed around them.

Drawing back he said, "Welcome to my world, Mrs. Tegan King."

"I love you."

"I love you too," he whispered and took her hand.

Before they turned to mingle with the guests, Mathew said, I've done the white suit thing but don't ever expect me to charge up on a damn horse and draw my sword."

Tegan frowned and pulled a sulky face. "No darling. I would never expect you to do such a thing." Secretly she wished.

Epilogue

Three Years Later

A cooling sea breeze dispersed the heat of the day. Tegan walked outside, down the few steps into the backyard, dressed in a pair of denim shorts and a bulky pink T-shirt. Her hair, twisted into a knot at the nape of her neck.

Passing a plate to Mathew, he planted a kiss on her cheek. "You smell exotic," he whispered, his breath feathering her ear only to draw back, shooting a sexy wink her way.

"Robert, come on. Lunch is ready. Don't forget to bring your sister with you," she called. Robert and Amy tumbled from the sand pit, brushing sand from their clothes.

"Coming Mum," Robert said, taking his sister's hand. "Grandma, Grandpa, are you coming out?" he screeched at the top of his lungs.

"Robert, mind your manners. They'll be out soon."

Tegan turned back to Mathew, watching as he put the meat on the barbeque.

He looked at her heavily pregnant stomach before moving his hand gently over the sexy swell. "I hope this one's a prince, but don't get me wrong, little princesses are just as good."

"I want a brother this time Mum. Amy always wants me to play dolls. I hate dolls."

Laughter erupted behind them. Tegan watched Robert move into the arms of his grandparents.

Stan walked into the backyard.

"Hey, Poppy." Robert raced over to Stan, almost bowling him over.

"Robert, will you quiet down a little?"

Stan laughed.

"Just like you Mathew. He's just like you were," John remarked.

"Tegan." Valerie moved over to stand beside her. "You're an extraordinary woman. I can't begin to thank you enough for bringing a part of Peter into our lives. Tell me dear, what was he like before he died? After all, you're the only one who truly knew him."

Mathew slipped an arm around Tegan's waist.

"He was a nice person, Val. Always caring."

"Oh...how sweet. Did you hear that John? I don't understand why he kept hiding. You know he never contacted us once. I'm so sorry things didn't work out between you two. It must have been difficult for you to raise Robert alone. If only we'd known. We would have helped you in any way possible."

Tegan smiled. "Thank you, Val. Just by being here now, you are helping me, as well as Robert."

Valerie moved back to her husband's side.

"You don't have to put yourself through that," Mathew whispered, out of earshot of his mother.

"Shush. I will if I want to. If good memories are necessary to make your parents happy, then I'll deliver good memories."

He shook his head

"I have something I have to do before we eat. It won't take long—five minutes max."

"But Mathew, the..." He raced up the back steps before Tegan had time to finish what she was about to say.

"What is Mathew up to now?" John asked, as everyone looked around wondering why he'd disappeared right before eating lunch.

Tegan glanced at the barbeque. Mathew had turned it down to low and covered the meat with foil.

"By the looks of it, I think he's gone for more than five minutes."

They chatted for ten minutes. Tegan, kept looking back at the house, wondering what was so important.

Five minutes later, music reverberated from the house. Tegan spun around and shook her head only to see a white horse charge from around the side of the house.

Goose bumps rose on her flesh. It was Mathew dressed in a suit of armor. The horse stopped beside them. Mathew drew a sword from his hip and yelled, "I have come to rescue a damsel in distress."

Laughter filled the backyard.

"But Mathew, I'm not in distress."

"Well, I have come to announce my love to my wife and take her captive for the rest of her life." He held the sword high in the air.

Tegan shook her head and giggled.

"Where did you get the horse from? Can I have a ride?" Robert asked.

Mathew dismounted. "After we eat."

Placing his helmet and sword down, he tied the horse to a fence post and walked over to Tegan.

"You're completely mad." She giggled, before kissing him on the cheek. Mathew returned the kiss and tapped her on the bottom.

"I'm not mad. You're the mad one, for wanting a knight to charge up on his horse and draw his sword. I was only doing what the lady fantasized." He shot her a sexy wink.

She bit on her lip. "Fantasized..." Pressing her lips together to prevent an escape of laughter didn't help. "Oh, by the way, you make one hell of a sexy knight in shining armor."

"Well, don't expect me to fling you over my horse and carry you away. Well, not just now." He said looking at her belly with a huge grin plastered on his face.

"I might keep you to that one." She rolled her lips together waiting for an answer, but there was none.

"Would you like to know something, Mrs. King?"

She poked her chin in the air. "What is that my husband?" A grin eased to her lips.

"I love you very much. You have not only brought my family closer, you've given me so much happiness I didn't think I'd ever find."

It was then Tegan knew she could overcome anything, fear of claustrophobia, fear of flying, and especially the fear of not trusting. With Mathew by her side, anything was possible.

Blinking against a cascade of tears, Tegan knew she was blessed. She knew it was the eyes of a stranger which had brought them together.

What else could it have been?

About the Author:

From the east coast of Australia with its pristine beaches and dramatic coastlines to glamorous cities and the intriguing, red outback, Suzanne has lived and experienced these worlds bringing them to life in her contemporary romance, and romantic suspense novels.

Suzanne currently resides on the Mid-North coast of New South Wales, the East coast of Australia.

You can find Suzanne at:
http://www.suzannebrandyn.com

Other titles by Suzanne Brandyn:
Heat in the Outback
Forgotten Memories

Also by Suzanne Brandyn:

Heat in the Outback
by Suzanne Brandyn

eBook ISBN: 9781615721016
Print ISBN: 9781615721023

Romance Contemporary
Short Novel of 52,000 words

The soaring temperature in the Outback is not the only heat Sarah Munro faces when she returns home for her father's funeral. She wants to settle his affairs, sell the family's homestead, Munro Cattle Station, and return to Sydney, and her fiancé, as quickly as possible. Sarah doesn't want anyone to find out what she'd done in the past. She wants to close this chapter of her life for good. Then there will never be a reason to return to this dusty one horse town. She is wrong!

Ethan Wade, her first love is at the homestead. Ethan claims he owns half of Munro Station. Sarah wants him out! As they try to settle their differences, a raging attraction ignites.

Will Sarah and Ethan find each other again as their past explodes before them?

Also from Eternal Press:

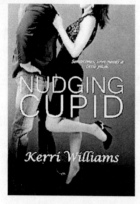

Nudging Cupid
by Kerri Williams

eBook ISBN: 9781615725021
Print ISBN: 9781615725038

Romance Contemporary
Novel of 59,642 words

It's lights, camera and love on the set of Nudging Cupid—Australia's new television show and Ivy Mason has big plans. Unfortunately, when it comes to love, nothing goes to plan.

Nudging Cupid was to be Ivy's first production, the ladder to her success. All she had to do was get three sexy as sin bachelors to find love in a mansion of twelve beautiful woman and capture it all on film for Australia to watch. How hard could that be?

But all Ivy's plans go awry when she comes into contact with the dark haired, blue eyed, Owen Radcliff. Somehow, against all her best judgment, Ivy falls for one of her bachelors.

Owen Radcliff's wasn't looking for love—he was looking for revenge. Infiltrating the latest Australian reality tv show was his only way to do it. But when he saves the life of the show's producer, Owen is suddenly torn between the vow of revenge for his sister and the need to protect Ivy—even from himself.